THE PATH TO WALKER'S BLUFF

FOLLOW ME THROUGH THE EVENTS OF MY LIFE AND
HOW I FOUND MAGIC, POWER, AND GREATNESS IN
THE WORD, LOVE. TOUCH YOUR LIPS ON MY
BUTTERFLY'S WINGS. THERE IS NOTHING SO SOFT.
LIGHTLY, THE DUST FROM THE WINDS WILL PAINT A
SMILE UPON YOUR FACE. LISTEN TO THE WORDS OF
MY SONG. FASCINATION WILL CAUSE YOUR SOUL TO
FLY AWAY. YOUR HEART WILL KNOW THE SHEER
JOY OF DESIRES. AT LAST, YOU WILL GAIN THE GIFT
OF LOVE AS IT CHANTS THE MYSTERIES OF
TOMORROW AND THE MEMORIES OF THE PAST. YOU
HAVE NOW GIVEN YOUR HEART AND SOUL TO ME.
TODAY YOU FOUND THE PATH TO THE SWEET
SILENT THRILL OF LOVE.

THE PATH TO WALKER'S B LUFF

FINAL EDITION

CHARLOTTE G WHALEY

A NOVEL

ACKNOWLEDGMENTS

To my late husband Alvin Whaley, I want to thank him for all the wonderful years we shared together. I think wherever he is, he has my heart and soul with him. When he was here, I had the whole world, now it is gone.

"This is the opening of my story. The greatest part of my life was when I learned to love and use courage, which both gave me control. This is a celebration of my accomplishments, going above and beyond deafness, and living a devoted and wonderful life. And how I followed an unbelievable and incredible pathway that led me from the beginning to close to the end of Walker's Bluff. "

Chapter 1

In my dreams

I remembered what my dear friend told me about courage and self-control: "We must not allow trouble in our life; we should forget and forgive problems and enjoy everyday life as it falls. This life is only borrowed, and no one has a guarantee for how long. Nothing is certain, not even today. We must live with faith in our heart and forgiveness for our mistakes. We are all living on this strange object that someone called Earth.

Today may be the ever-lasting mile. We must live this day only.

Life is like the mystery of the waves flowing over the deep blue sea. They will always blow away, but they will return.

When we are outdoors and the sky drops dew upon our face, we smile and know our God is up there. We must trust and obey while we live on His Earth. We hope we have been good sensible creatures. I have thought many times how many people have been here before us and how many will come after we are gone. We are like a small twig on the maple tree, it will dry and fade away.

We must pray that someday we will be with Him in the heavens above and we will find the loved ones that have gone on before us. Amen

Dreams are always with me, and the mysteries of the unanswered illusions remain in my imagination every day of my life. Some dreams seemed to be sincere and true, but some have left me under the mystery of doubt, there I find myself tangled in an isolated web of ghostly wonders.

Many, many years ago when I started losing my hearing, I dreamt I was living on a strange *soundless dark* planet, nothing like our own earth. I walked alone, and I had strange feelings of unfairness as low clouds captured me and created an odd shocking sound rushing through my mind. As I slowly moved forward, I could hardly see in this unusual color of darkness. Suddenly there were multicolored lines floating with glooming lights that seemed to be slowly approaching me. I stopped for just seconds, but I felt like something was moving me forward. I moved further down this strange pathway that I was suddenly on and there was an intense haze of lights hitting my face. But wait, at the end of these strange lights there was a beautiful gleaming rainbow, and I was standing underneath these gleaming beautiful lights that were my life. Instantly I knew the dreams were a challenge to help free me from the darkened life of deafness and not allow this offal confusion of deafness to keep hanging over my mind nor beat me in any way. In these dreams, I moved on a few feet, and I could see a gigantic beautiful green forest with deep rays of golden sunshine sifting over a flourishing canopy of trees. It was so beautiful. As I walked on, there was an abrupt, loud echo that produced an enormous vibration inside my confused mind, and the roaring sounds awakened me. In a few seconds, I could hear the sounds of life, through deafness, I had won and beat deafness. I was living in a new world. My world.

The good news was my IQ was way above the normal system. That would help me make it through the days of darkened deafness.

I needed to realize I should stop trying to cover the problems of not hearing and try to learn to live in a silent world. But slowly my music was being taken away, I loved music so much- it had helped save this wicked old world and me, and I was even losing the sound of the birds singing. I wished everyone would have to stop hearing for an entire day.

Hearing is more than a major part of one's life, it is existence.

<u>Deafness is an unseen handicap.</u>

I did beat the system in deafness. I learned the higher one goes to the top, the harder the winds will blow, but again I fought the high winds, and learned perfect hearing was not always the answer to success. I discovered that the most brilliant hearing minds did not always win first prize. In fact, those who could outperform others where always the winners. Therefore, I lived under my own power and performance.

I believe in God, and Angels—I have sensed air from my Angel's wings upon my face. I am aware of their magical results in the Holy Spirit. Every day, I request strength and shelter over my magnificent soul.

I am an Architect. I have built many properties over numerous years in Denton, Dallas, and New Mexico.

I had many honors, but the most amazing was that I became the first woman to be President of a HAB division. HAB has divisions all over this world.

I became quite wealthy, However in the mid-eighties, things changed, the interest rates went sky high and I lost several million dollars when money cost too much to borrow, it overpowered the use of building supplies and labor. Many builders lost a lot of dough.

Being a woman builder was not easy, in many ways. However, I completed numerous large projects and had many wonderful years. More than most women would care to accomplish.

Me and my husband created a grand life; mine, in the building business and later in writing books. His, as A High School Football Coach and later a High School Principial.

Let's say, most of us lived somewhere alone the way inside our secret life; it was also in a beautiful hidden box covered with love. All human beings have their secrets and memories which will stay in our soul until death do us part. Yes there is always a story to tell.

My lifetime friend wrote, (he called me Toy)

To My dear Toy, here are some memories for you. Once, when we talked, you told me as you got older, you took a deep helping of memories every day. My dear Toy, here are some things I love to remember about you.

You have accomplished so much in your wonderful life: you have a beautiful family, you are an Architect, you have built many beautiful homes, apartments and condominiums, and duplexes in many locations. You have remodeled a huge and wonderful office building. And my dear friend, you were the first woman to be President of a HAB Division. Which is enormously important for home builders.

You've owned racehorses; spending a lot of fun time in the Ruidoso, New Mexico racetracks. How do you really feel about your accomplishments? You and your husband have traveled the world over, on this good Earth, (eight countries and eight islands) and, yes, I was shocked as to how many countries you guys have been to. And you were almost deaf, a lot of that time, but you did not allow an ending to your glorious life.

Darling, you made it happen, your way. And finally, you had that strange cochlear implant hooked to the brain, so you could hear. To me, it was dangerous, but you said it was worth it a thousand times more. You said it saved your life.

Last week I had a beautiful painting done, it's of you and me. I will call you soon and give it to you. I plan to be in the US soon. You told me yesterday, when I talked with you that you had been down and out, lately. I told you; I have no mercy for you, my Toy. Don't you ever feel sorry for yourself, 'you are a legend in your time. 'Anyway, I will always love you, however you feel. I know I'm not supposed to. But I have been there with you, and I felt your feelings. You are astonishing in some ways, and that is what makes this old, wicked world turn.

As I told you I am living in the South of France. It is heaven on earth. Come, you will fit in well here; your French people are your own breed, and you always do everything your way. Toy would fit perfectly here. I remember after we had our first, shall we say attempt to have sex. We were only teenagers, and you would not. It took me some time to prove to you we would get married, and it was all right to have sex. I liked a few days being nineteen and you were seventeen. Yes, we were young, beautiful and pure. Nevertheless, what happened later was that you ran away from me and married someone else. Though, many times, lately, I still have thought of us; yes, touching and loving. I wished I could have put that little sex jewel of yours in my pocket to touch and keep for me only. Sinner, yes, I am, this is not fair to keep telling you all this, but we are getting old my sweetheart.

*   I wish you were here with me every day, but I try to understand. You told me you did love your husband. You liked your life. However, remember there are two sides to every love story. If you change your mind please let me know, anytime any moment of day or night. Please, keep me in your heart forever. I remember one of the songs I sang to you, 'I can't help it if I am still in love with you,' I think you still*

love me. You said once up on our time we can keep
all things for ever. Love,
      Carlos

Chapter 2

Fascination will make it so

This is how it all started. One week before my seventeenth birthday, I met the man of my dreams. Indeed, it was him. I fell in love with him the moment we touched not only our hands but our hearts. Once he was mine, I did not want him out of my sight. This is labeled under first affection, filled with fascination, and perhaps hot passion. Nevertheless, it is called one's first love. I learned later in life that all love feelings were not connected inside the heart and many only scattered high spirits, causing a hot sensation around the sex organs. Still, I knew it was some kind of love.

At that time in my young life, I was especially happy—I seemed to have it all. I did not think my life could have been more delightful. I loved every day and night, and yes, they were all mine. My grades had improved because I had a wonderful teacher, named Ms. Sidney Richardson. She was highly intelligent. She placed me under her soft wings to help me overcome some of my attention problems, and hearing problems. I could not always hear the spoken words. This hurt my heart and stepped on parts of my soul, causing me to be highly emotional. When I did not grasp what the speaker was saying, I would lose interest, and move into my own novel thoughts. It made me tense. I did admit a lot of people bored me. Yes, why were some women trying to beat someone up under simple practical ways of life? Oh well, not all of them, some were happy with their lives and let you have yours. I noticed that ninety percent of men were not worried about each other.

One thing that helped, I would study deeply into a person's face. It's surprising how much the face will show and tell.

All right, go back to seventeen. Several of my friends and I were at the football field practicing our cheerleading yells. We were trying out for cheerleader to hail the high school athletes. I had been a ninth-grade cheerleader, and I loved it. We had on our new blue and white uniforms. They were so cool, but my dad said they were too short and nasty, and showed our panties. I told him they were just tights, and we liked the way they looked, and how people looked at us when we had them on.

My group was getting ready for an end-of-school party next weekend, so we decided to stop our cheerleading practices today and work on the party arrangements.

I reached for a towel to dry the wetness around my face, and the rays from the setting sun hit me in the eyes. I turned away quickly. I could now see up toward the bleachers, this new guy, who had moved from California, was sitting there smoking and watching me. First, he was not allowed to smoke on the school grounds. Second, what was he doing up there? Whoa, he was good to look at. Anyway, I had a great boyfriend, Wendell Gray, who was also good looking and captain of the football team.

I heard the new guy was a bad dude. He was on probation, so Sally Rae Turnbow said--but she of course was an adulteress—and a gossiper. I wonder every time I saw her if she was still having immoral sex with the banker. (Later in story.) Anyway, she said this guy's dad moved him to Winters, Texas, that he called "Hooterville." The father was from here and the new guy was born here. He thought a small place might help to cool the kid down, since he was in trouble with the law.

The new guy's face stayed on my mischievous mind all evening. I tried to forget him, but I could see him puffing his cig and blowing the smoke out, so damn cool. He kept smiling at me; he waved, and I was shocked, but I nodded back. He looked interesting just sitting there.

When we left the gym to go home, he had already left. However, I knew I should "ease away from these thoughts," as my moral friend Anna said. "Let this type of thinking fade into the sunset."

But I might have desired to be near his sunset, am I crazy or just a person? I laughed to myself.

That night my family had plans to go to a summer party. For many years, we had been going to this grand supper and dance party in Rowena, Texas, a German community south of Winters. It was held at the Catholic Church. My dad was a great violinist and he and a group of his friends had formed a marvelous band. Their music was something between classic and western. He enjoyed his music and could play just about any instrument he picked up. He was really a genius in the music field, and he was told it was a gift from heaven. He told me he had learned every note he played, by sound which meant it was a gift. At some of these parties, my dad's group played into the morning hours. The kids would get a little wild, stay up, and praise the Lord for free time. They did not know what we were doing, and I do not think they cared. Back then, the younger kids slept in the car or anywhere they could find to rest their tired heads, while the older ones, like me, raised a little hell. As one guy said, *"Here we unite under the cords of thy music in the Lord's House, as we lay down and take in our music with* pleasure. *We fall into the spirit of the Lord, under the stars of His heaven.*

Morality is no longer successful in this century, so we lived and celebrated in our sins."
Amen

The parties were always great fun, and the food was German-made and delightful. I have never known anyone who could get more from everything than the Germans.

My family is mostly French; we were more party people and style people than the laboring society. The Germans even made their own beer and dad knew we would have a bit of it, but he said, no smoking. So, we took both. I had one beer and several smokes.

That night, there was no one at the party that I really wanted to visit with. Wendell had other plans and I was glad, so I slipped away and disappeared behind the beautiful Catholic Church with my beer in one hand and a cig in the other. I took a deep breath of delight in the fresh air as it tangled with my cig smoke. I was dressed in a beautiful yellow silk dress that my aunt Vi had given me for my seventeenth birthday. My hair looked stylish. I had let it grow longer each year; it had slowly turned a deep shade of darker brown. My eyes had finally decided to stay on the dark shades of green with a trace of strange brown. Okay, I was told I was remarkably pretty, and I adored any admiration, it gave me self-confidence. Nevertheless, like most young women, I was never satisfied with how I looked. As most ladies say, we covered our face with colored creams and dressed our bodies to kill. Yes, we all loved beautiful garments. They made us feel electrified.

As I crunched down and sat on the ground with my beer and smoke, in my sky, I could see the Big Romantic Dipper shining brightly, like a gift

23

filled with miracles, dropping wishes on one's head. It seemed to be hanging over the magnificent cross at the top of the church. I wanted to say, "Kind creator of divinity, allow me a big scoop of romance from this beautiful piece of magic." I loved it right here, in my own little world. I looked up above me at the long-arched trellis with many beautiful red climbing roses hanging irregularly all over the trellis. The moonlight was shining just over my left shoulder, when suddenly I saw a tall shadow coming towards me. I could hear light footsteps drawing near. I was trying to stomp out the cig when a voice with a very charming accent, said, "Hi."

The light around me was rather shadowy, but as he grew closer, I could see that it was, in fact, the new guy from California. He looked so classy.

"I am the new guy, as everyone is calling me."

Oh Hi, I said"

Wham! I thought he had unusually neat clothes: the jeans were very tight and drooped a little low from the waist; no belt; all I could see was perfect. His black, curly hair was in a wavy ducktail. Every detail of this guy was enough to make me forget about living on the other side of Heaven's Eden. As the light appeared over his face, he bowed. "Hi, I'm Carlos." He waited a second for me to answer.

I was still in this silly squat down and had pulled my dress way up to keep it off the grass. I was so embarrassed. Not a bit of sound came out of my mouth, it was soundproof. He laughed a bit.

"Get up, quiet, little girl, with pretty dimples on her cheeks. No one will see you but me."

He held out his hand and pulled me up. "I'm—"

"Do not worry. I know your name, 'Rooster'," he said. "By the way, how did you get that name? It is quite refreshing and amazingly special. It is just about the coolest name I have

25

heard, hung on such a beautiful, young lady. I know your real name is Tory, and that means 'thief.'" He chuckled.

"How did you get these names?"

"Came on the ticket," I said, quickly, without a speck of confidence. He chuckled and said, "Is that true? The ticket? I adore the way you talk. Does that mean you were bought?"

"Maybe," I chuckled, "I was told, I just kind of dropped off the clouds from somewhere and they decided to keep me. I never thought seriously of my names. My grandad named me Rooster because I would go out to the hen house with him to get the eggs, and I would mock the roosters; crow with them, from a young age." I held the cig low. "And the truth is, I am a thief. I stole these cigs from my mom's cafe and you kind of caught me smoking and you frightened me."

"Whoa, I like those reasons, my dear, and you were so cool, sitting here in *sin*, smoking and drinking at the back of a Lord's Church–– maybe in sins but I think it's pure luxurious."

"Well, mister, I, and this church, use life in a different meaning for how one uses their soul with sins."

"Really?" he said. "What is a sin? Are they only allowed tonight?" He moistened his thin lips. They seemed to be made for kissing and–– God, I wanted to touch them.

"Well, tonight is a celebration, and I'm just having my kind of fun; no sins, yet." I tightened my forehead and turned my head toward the white stone church. "At this moment, I'm not waiting for my soul to be taken out of harm's way," I said with a chuckle.

"Let me say this, about mankind's so-called soul or sins. It is all on the verge of some surprising problems and a lot of people do not have much faith in either side of faith anymore. Therefore, I do not think I have, or care to have a soul for sins," he chuckled. "What is it? We have only been told we have one, but still no real answers. I have only a puzzling desire to hold on to this strange human stuff called *a soul and taking it or leaving it here* after existence."

I frowned, "Does that mean you don't want Christ to take you home when you die, and do you believe in a spirit?

"Yeah, I guess, that is almost right, in my mind," he said. "And you said take me home. Is there another home place?"

"I think there must be. There must be something or all this stuff we are doing on Earth would be wasted. I am afraid not to believe, because if we do get up there at the Golden Gate, and you did not believe they might not keep you." We laughed.

"Your mind must choose something and hope you will go to Heaven after death, " I said.

" You think your soul flails around in your body until some day it walks away." said Carlos.

"Well, yes, I have chosen to believe in God, and I am a Christian in some ways. Are you not a Christian?"

"You are talking about a lot of stuff I never think of, but your mind does make the character," he chuckled. "I do believe in a God, but no, I am not under the Christian's belief," he answered and frowned a bit. "My people were raised in Greece. We are Jews. No, we are not under the Christian belief. Who wrote the Bible, my mom said the Jews? And some of my best friends are Jews and they do not believe in your Bible either."

"So, well-- anyway, you are Greek?"

"Yes, mostly, but we have a bit of English on my mom's side. I understand you are French. I know they are the sexiest people on Earth."

"Well, maybe, and on my Dad's side our ancestors were French, but on my Mom's side we have a mix of French and Irish."

I answered. "We are proud of our nationality."

"Yes, and we always have good thoughts about our own kind," he chuckled.

"Yes, true," I said. "How did we get so deep on this subject?"

"Because we are here under your ancestor's church," he chuckled. I nodded while watching his eyes, the movement of his body, oh dear God! Why do women love the strength, and the firmness, and even the vigorousness of a man. And this guy has what it takes, and its all over him...

We both transferred our positions. He touched my arm gently as I tried to move. I remember the preacher saying, people like touching, it heals the feeling. We all love bodily touch.

He didn't say, "I loved touching you, it joins desire and urges passion."

'Oh yes,' I said to myself as I kept staring at him. Oh, dear Lord, I wondered what was next.

The shadows cast over the red roses seemed to stand remarkably still and maybe they were staring down at us. Then, a simple rose bud fell to the ground at my feet. I trembled a bit. I could hear a slight bit of music in the background. It was "Amazing Grace." Indeed, it is true—really amazing. Maybe it was caused from the good German beer, which always made me happy, but something else was burning little stars on the east side of my now alerted heart.

I liked the way he said *our kind*, and I wanted to say, 'Don't make me wonder anymore about *your kind*, show me.' Truth is, I was experiencing a deep vision of desires about this guy, equally mixed together with now and ever.

"I watched you cheerleading today, and really, I have to confess I wanted to find you tonight and be near you," he boldly claimed, "even though I knew this visit might be different or difficult." He kept smiling and winking as the light caught his eyes--brown? No, brown, green. I am not sure what color. He just kept looking at me in this strange, wonderful way. Whoa, I think we both had this grand sensation ripping through our bodies—suspicious desires. It was like—a deep warning of want and need, how can it happen so fast? As one says it was there and found in the eyes of the beholder.

"I'll have a smoke, too," he said.

"May I offer one of mine?" he asked.

"I have my own," I chuckled.

Then, he took a pack of cigarettes and a gold lighter from his white, tight, knit shirt, out of his pocket. The shirt was exceptionally low cut—yes, the nice sizable chest was showing—and he placed a cig between those smooth thin lips. His hands were small compared to his nice-sized body. As the clouds seemed to move away and the night seemed very bright and was rolling over us. I could see his skin was very dark and smooth and his face exposed a perfect complexion. I did not like the gold earring; not sure if I liked the ducktails in his hair, but it was deep black full of waves that had been carefully smoothed down. This all came with remarkably interesting muscles under his swank clothing. He lit his cig —his gaze never strayed from me as he flipped his lighter off and, on a few times, then put it back into his pocket. He was smiling, showing he also had deep dimples in his cheeks. What an amazing grace. He lowered his head, studied his cig, and took a long drag. Puffed out a cloud of smoke while moving closer to me and then our eyes sincerely met. This scene was all it took. Baby, he took me and I, him. It is written on the first page of the instructions of dreams, called feelings of femininity. We talked about why we should not be smoking, about how he enjoyed watching me at the football field that day, and how he found out where I would be tonight. He said he had seen me at school when he came to sign up for classes a few weeks ago, and that I was with my boyfriend. He said we looked happy, and he let the feeling go, at first, but said that he later saw me at the City Drug Store. He decided not to ignore his feelings--and that is how it all started. I told him I remembered seeing him at the drugstore too. We talked about school and how glad he was that it was out. He told me about a boy who hated Texas and wanted to go home--home to California. I asked him what was so great in his California. He began telling me about some of the wonderful things he had done, and it was all so fascinating. He asked me to tell him about my life here. I told him we do pretty much as we please around here and I do enjoy my life. But I told him I would not want to get too deep and bore him and mess up our beautiful evening. We laughed, and he touched me gently again on the shoulder as we looked at each other, a bit demanding. I liked just being near him. And he said lady, I love being close to you. Suddenly, there was a soft breeze and the sound from the music seemed to drift into our mood. The music was "*Save Me; I am Falling in Love with You.*" He took my hand, and we walked down to a little bench and sat down under the arbor. He told me he would be right back, and he slipped off over to the beer kegs to get us more beer. We sipped our home-made beer, and we had a smoke. Then he moved closer to me. Under the shadow of the Lord, he said, "I think I'm going to kiss you. I fell for you today just watching you and I think it will last forever. You decided we have no sin to do so, because *your Lord* is looking over us here at this Holy Catholic Church," he said this while taking my hand into his and bringing me closer. The warmth of his body touched mine and our eyes softly had a wish covering the shadows of sensation. Amusing, how sweet it is, he kept touching my body, kind of moving his hands over me. Our romantic urges came under the lights of the heavenly stars.

Therefore, I saw no reason not to kiss this boy–I mean, man. Damn. So, I got my lips ready, closed my purple-green eyes and the dampness of our lips touched; a thousand violins began to play. Under the light of the silvery moon, we started to press our lips harder and as his arms tightened around my body and the whole, hot, wonderful, man-made, pure, purple affection under the vines of worship—except with terrible timing. Dad came swinging around the holly bushes.

"Tory!"

"Jesus, help," I whispered, and pushed quickly away from him.

Carlos whispered, "I knew *he* was near––he saw me getting the beer and he knew who I was, and that we would be getting too close to each other ––" We both dropped our tight handhold, but we did not take our eyes off each other. I could still feel the warmth of his body and affection of his lips on mine. He smiled and expressed feelings as he whispered something as he turned away.

"I'm right here, Dad," I said, as we got to our feet.

Dad held out his hand to greet Carlos, but he hardly took his scolding eyes from me. "Hi, Carlos. It is so good to see you. Your granddad told me you were moving back here." dad said, then quickly turning his gaze away from me.

"Yes, sir, but against my wishes," he balked. My father glanced back at me and said, "Tory, get to the car. Your mom has been looking for you."

Dad turned his steely, dark brown eyes to my new acquaintance, and with blunt insincerity snarled, "Nice to meet you, sir."

"Nice to meet you and your pretty daughter," he said, boldly. He stood very still and watched us leave. I turned and waved, while Dad walked faster. We were out of there fast. Soon we were on the other side of the church building and trotting down the long walk, bordered by beautiful purple irises. I wanted to fall in on them and roll around while I sealed the kiss that was still on my mind, and I also kept the smile on his face. Its torture. Damn, what a difference a few minutes can make.

We got into the car where my mom and Cody were waiting. They did not look like they had been anywhere else but there all night. I laughed to myself. Nasty frowns came on me, so let them stare.

I thought, so this is what people mean when they say, it is on the good Earth, you will know when you find it. Oh, yes, I found it. Dear Lord, on this good Earth, yes, it has been found. I could feel the simulation on my hand, and thought, why is harmless on the wrong side of the river? I closed my eyes and crossed over to my side of the bridge.

We drove a good distance before anyone said anything. Cody was asleep or pretending to be. My mom looked at me with a strong, solid glare, as she always did when she had a question. She always suspected the worst of me. Why didn't she ever give me a chance just to have fun, even if I was slightly rebellious? I did not do things like she wanted me to. Dear heart, Yes, I had been different, and she always had questions—why and what-- but that is what made everything tick faster for me. They treated me like I was eleven or twelve. Damn, I wanted to be away from them, and it was time to try to decide what to do.

Then, Dad said, hatefully, breaking the silence, "I don't want you around that boy."

"Dad, why would you say that? I am a senior in high school. Seventeen years old, and you make it sound like I am twelve." I spoke.

"It has nothing to do with age. He is in trouble and his dad sent him here for his granddad to see him for this summer and the next school year. I think his parents may move here, too. Your mom and I met his parents several years ago. They moved to California when Carlos was about five. I had not heard of them since then."

"You mean he will be here for the next school year?"

They nodded yes. *I will be there, too, you wicked, fascinating human thing. I will be seeing you every day in paradise. That night I knew the difference between a soul inspiration and a sole devotion.* I did not say anything back to any of them the rest of the way home. That night in my bed, I fell asleep thinking about him.

39

What a wonderful life is out there now for me. I can pick it up and carry it to all my pleasures.

The next morning, bright and early, I went directly to Sara Poppy's house because I knew she lived behind the target of my attention.

"Sara, get real, he is the most of the most. I fell for him last night. Baby, he has– what it takes." She laughed, "Hold on there, dear friend. He has been dating Jane Gotham." My warm heart dropped to a deep, subzero freeze.

"Well," I said more casually. "I met him last night at the Rowena and—"

"Did you have a date or what?" she interrupted.

"Well, no, but we talked for a wonderful hour--and he kissed me," I replied.

"Really? That is amusing. Jane is seeing him, tonight. Besides, she said he was going back to California."

"So," I smiled and spoke.

"And that's not what he told me," I muttered.

I was instantly shocked, and Sara was not helping with my new feelings, but that was fine. So, if he had a girlfriend, why did he follow me around all the time and last night, it was heaven outside of heavens Church?

"I must run. See you later," I said briskly. I left quickly and decided that I would keep my distance and wait and see if he really cared for me. There was a swimming party at Four Mile Crossing tonight. It was a beautiful river with miles of clean blue spring water that seemed romantic — the boys said it was famous for skinny-dipping because it was so clear. I keep thinking and wondering about the new guy. He really seemed too good to be true. He put me in a great fun feeling or happy mood, but really people like me put too much into their moods. There were a lot of hidden lyrics in this song, and I thought, but they are all mine.

Later that afternoon, my mom told me, my boyfriend—and she repeated *"boyfriend,"* Wendell, had called and was coming over to pick me up early, so I would need to hurry and get my things together. She said the food for the party was in the basket on the dining table. "Gee, great," I thanked her because I usually had to fix it myself. *What is up?* I wondered. She was encouraging my relationship with Wendell since she and my dad did not care for Carlos.

Wendell--I had almost forgotten about him. I liked Wendell, and he was cool, but not nearly as cool as the new guy. When he picked me up, he bent over close and barely kissed me on the cheek, but not the usual warm hug and deep, charming kiss. He seemed annoyed. All the way driving to the river, we were both silent. He knew something about the night before. I forgot; this is a small, inquisitive town. Finally, after a silent drive to the creek, we got out of the car, and I took out the food basket and carried it over to the table. Everyone was gathered around a beer bar, in which we were not supposed to be. But one of the guy's fathers owned a liquor store near Winters and he always got us hush, sweet, kids' beer. At this party we did not have a sponsor or parent. This was all our own celebration of school being out. Among the guys standing near the table was Carlos. He was standing there smiling and examining me. My eyes bugged out. I thought I had never seen such a perfect everything, the body, the face. He seemed to be stacked flawlessly: the dark skin, the little black swimsuit, and the golden earring in one ear was swaying. This was all set in a carving of a god-made, perfect human man, and it was guiding me straight down the path to delight with the need of touch. I have nothing more to add there, darling. As I set my basket on the table, Carlos had a beer in his hand, and he tipped it at me and walked slowly toward me. He whispered something, but I could not understand him, he shook his head and smiled and held out his hand. I took his hand and he kind of bowed and moved close and kissed me on each cheek. I could feel the warmth from his lips before they touched my skin.

"You look sexy and beautiful in that bathing suite," he whispered, softly. He whispered, 'I'm in love with you.'

"Thank you," I answered. I asked him what he had said at first. He whispered you do not need to know; it was too sweet. At that moment, I could feel people watching us. Was my swimsuit exposing too much of my body? It was called a bikini, my first one. Was his black suit too small? Did they see this beautiful thing called humans and the love from our eyes?

"Rooster," he whispered, "we need to talk. Let us move out of here, go further down the river."

"All right," I said.

I did not even look to see if Wendell or anyone else was watching me. I just kind of jumped on the wind and followed the physical shadow of this man.

I know it was rude, but, damn, I could not help myself. I imagined everyone was thinking what was going on. He reached over to the bar area and poured us some wine. We took our glasses and moved on. The guys saying, 'she is a bitch,' and the girls saying, 'make it happen,' with that dear Gallant man.

Once more, I loved this new world of mine. I just kind of froze again. My body was leveled by the waves of feelings.

He nodded and motioned for me to follow him; we walked briskly down a beautiful path under the pleasant shades of the summer trees. When we were out of sight, he took my hand. The beautiful live oak trees seemed to enclose us. The birds were chanting, and so was my heart—it was obvious, indeed, I would follow him wherever he led me. "There are some problems, and I must go back to California. Can you get away for two days? I want to spend every moment with you, night and day," he declared.

The bright sunlight was suddenly guarded by shadows of doubt. I needed to remember the shine of gold is only on a stone.

I was too shocked to think, but I finally said, "Alright."

When we returned to the picnic area, I could see that Wendell was angry and he took off from the party with other friends. I decided to let it be and have a wonderful time and live in offense. I did not leave Carlos's side. We had a nice swim down the river from the party, and he went back and got our towels. We are lying on the wonderful muddy grounds kissing and touching and talking about the good things in life. Damn, what a great change has come to me in just a few days. When it was time for us to go back to the picnic, he pulled me up and hugged me tightly, holding my hand and he said, "I am falling crazy in love with you." I thought, love. Yes, something in our life was more than amazing. I enjoyed just holding his hand as we walked along the river pathway. I kept looking at his face and the sparkling earring and thinking about how delightful this day with him had been. He told me I was exceptionally beautiful, and he loved Texas now for giving him, me.

Everyone was whispering because all the girls wanted him, and all the guys did not like him around. Later, when Wendell came back, as we were all leaving, I tried to tell him I was sorry.

He just looked at me for a moment and then said, "Why? What's that about? That you are, or will be, his whore? He is bad news."

"What!" I asked, "How could you say that? I know you are mad at me, and you have every right to be mad at me in some ways, but I am not ashamed. It just happened with Carlos and me."

"What happened?" He whispered something nasty as he walked away.

I grabbed my food basket and my bathing suit cover-up, tucked my tail, and rushed away to meet Carlos. I rode home with him, but I told him to let me get out of the car further on down the street and I would walk on to my house. He said do not start hiding our feelings, we do not need to be ashamed. But for now, I knew I had to.

That night when I got home, I told my parents I was going to San Angelo for the weekend to stay with my friend Gayle Waite, who had just moved there from Winters. I had called Gayle to cover for me, and she laughed and said I owed her one. My mom said it was fine since she was going with my dad to Sweetwater. His band was playing at a wedding, and they were staying the weekend. I was seventeen years old, and I did not think I was a kid that needed to ask, but I did still live at home. Say no more.

There was an old Ford car I shared with Cody, and she had plans which was good. I got all my stuff together and asked her to drop me off at the bus station since I did not think Carlos and I should drive over there together. I had not ridden on a bus in so long and I remember it was kind of fun. It was only an hour or so away and Carlos was there to pick me up at the San Angelo station. He was so happy to see me, and he was smiling from ear to ear. He hugged me as I got off the bus, holding my hands and looking at me, saying he was the happiest guy on this good Earth. "Hello Texas," he whispered, "you got what it takes." He took me to a charming hotel on the river walk, which was where we stayed for the entire weekend. Divinity—I did not know this life was so physical and so delightful until then. We had dinner at a small café on the river walk, but I could hardly eat. Later, when we went back to the room, I was scared to death when we climbed into the bed. It looked so big, so white, so starched, and dangerous--and perhaps two yards from getting up on the Devil's path. That might be a part of the other side of the bluff, north of Eden. At first, I had not taken all my clothes off. He closed his eyes like he would give me time. He pulled the sheet over and wrapped it about me. Finally, I stripped down all the way. I had never felt this sinful, but happy and so naked, in all my life. He eased over to the bed, and I lay still as a wet piece of fresh dust. I wanted to change my mind and run, but I did not know how to jump up and run, and really, I did not want to either--

Easing closer to me, he gently touched my body and kissed me tenderly. Then came the real kiss: I had not yet known about the open lip kissing, like with the full open mouth and a bit of tongue rubbing around in it. I remember how he smiled so beautifully when he first kissed me and then he showed me how it was done. I laughed at this kind of kissing. I thought it was too much, but as time went by, I liked it and that it was an important part of this deep loving connection. I knew I wanted to go on with the play. The feeling came, and all the things happening were not dreams. It was wonderful, yes, and now I understand why some things in our lives lead to wonders of amazement. I questioned if I was living against the rules or if I was in offender's paradise. However it should be, I decided it was purely delightful. When he was, shall I say, upon me, I have never felt anything so wonderful.... And the hurt and pain of pure enjoyment. I laughed to myself and thought, *I shall allow the devil to take today and worry about tomorrow.*

Later we walked in the park, we went skinny-dipping in the river, and laughed, kissed, and talked. I found out everything that sweet seventeen had to offer. I would never care to know more. That last night we were together he said, "You know, we may be just about seven miles from *your* 'heaven.' You are making me have this Christian feeling." He eyed me deeply and pulled the covers over me. He whispered, "Were you afraid at first?"

I breathed deeply and said, "No, yes, maybe. Our sex was out of this world, yes baby all the way out... it is good to go where you are afraid. How many times, let us not count the ways..."

Then it was the last day, and we were getting ready to go home. He began to sing, '*Life Without Autumn leaves*,' '*Wild for Loving You*' and

'Just One *Place On Earth For Me Is Loving With You,'* I was astonished; his voice was delightful. I sang, *'Amazing Grace,'* for him and he liked it. I told him I wished he would sing with Daddy's band. He said, "No, I sing only for me and you."

We were standing by the bus. And he said, "Miss Toy (he called me his Toy), you are the most beautiful person that I have ever cared for." He stepped back a bit, just looking at me, and then drew me close. He said, "Yes, a perfect work of art. I know it is hard to believe, but I needed someone, and you just happened along––like a gift and a promise. I have had lots of problems lately and you just kind of help cover it all up. I want to thank you for being with me. I think at this point, I will need and want you by my side forever."

I thought, *so this is called love.*

"Thank you," I said, "I have never felt true happiness, until I found you. I have enjoyed being with you, touching you, holding you, and I will carry every moment with me forever. Amen."

He smiled and stepped on the steps of the bus with me. The driver nodded at us and the people on the bus were watching us. He finally let go of my hand and stepped off the bus. I waved from the window. He threw kisses, and a group of people on the bus applauded. I closed my eyes to be alone. I had happy tears falling from my rosy cheeks, the cheeks that knew the kisses of happiness. All the way home, I did not know if my tears were because I was scared or if they were because I was so content, happy, and charmed. I truly adored this wonderful time, and the man, because of the way most of us were raised in this day and time--I was like the preacher and the bear: one of us had sinned, and did the good Lord see me? I thought, *yes, let the angels kiss my heart and let the devil stay away from this magical part of my private life, until* the end of time.

A week later, Mom found out what I had done with the new guy, so I was put under "deadbolt" for one month, but I did not care. Really,

I did not do as she said, which was true, and again I was the bad kid, so what the hell is a good kid? I needed that time with Carlos and to go out to have real fun and now I can sit here and dream of our time together, from real personal experience. I close my eyes and walk around in the paradise of yesterday––which was better than living in my so-called old, boring, world, or Hooterville as Carlos called my town. Our chef at Mom's café, C.C., also called it Hooterville. I was nailed down in it. At this moment Carlos's presence seemed to be touching me and I prayed for help, but not forgiveness. I was very depressed and one night I crawled out of my window onto the roof. I had not been out in a while. I called it my escape hatch. Now I was lying there, looking up at my beautiful sky and the stars seemed to twinkle down on me. Yes, and light clouds in the south were hanging over a gorgeous rainbow. The colors where more than just yellow and orange, there were blues and even green colors, and that

THE PATH TO WALKERS BLUFF

was when I felt the Angel of Mercy breathing life upon my lonely face.

I did not see Carlos for the rest of the summer. Finally, two days after school started, he came walking into the school lunchroom. I was sitting with some friends. "Damn," one of my friends said,   "look at that, he is so-so damn handsome, and sexy. Yes and he is dressed to kill." He looked wonderful, but something was wrong with the look on his face. He came directly to me and asked me to go out into the hall. I stood; everyone was watching us. I followed him, but as soon as I almost got out of the door, he grabbed me and kissed me. The kids all cheered. I was sure one of the teachers saw us, but she looked away. He kept patting my hand and rolling his eyes.

"Whoa! I missed you so damn much, my sweet Toy Rooster, I am so in love," he said.

"I know. I missed you, too." I had a tear. My heart was pumping real scarlet blood. "What happened?" I asked with deep wonder.

With a very distressed look on his face, he told me that he was in bad trouble. I thought I should have known that from the start.

He said, "there was more to this matter than I really wanted you to know, but I'm afraid to tell. "

I stiffened my body. I knew he was very alarmed. I then remembered Sally saying she had heard he killed someone, but I did not believe that—anyway most of us believe what we want to.

He shook his head and looked down. I told him to follow me. We went to an older part of the gym where no one ever went. It was kind of hidden behind the locker rooms. He told me that he had some problems with the police-- not tickets but other things. He had been put on trial, and he said he had many problems, for which there was a misunderstanding at the trial, and they had put him on probation.

"Trial?" I asked.

"Yes, I will explain later," he said.

I found out at that moment that he had been in real trouble--but he said we would make this new life of ours work someday. However, right now all things had fallen to the wrong system. He kept holding my hands and frowning. Yes, this was real, he said, just give me time and we will make plans for the rest of our lives. . . together.

He kept saying, "You are staring at me. I have missed those eyes and I have never known eyes like yours. They dance, they watch, and they demand me to obey, and they say, you must *trust and obey and me there forever.*" He would be on probation for eight months until his next trial.

We had a wonderful eight-month courtship. Yes, dear heart, it was a hell of a lot more than courtship.. I would tell my parents I was staying with friends while he and I hid from humankind at one of his grandparent's old, abandoned houses. It was dusty and messy. He cleaned and cleaned, and he got blankets, and towels and we made a bed out of an old sofa. We both loved those moments together, yes, in our heaven on Earth. He threw me down on the old sofa and, yes, wonderful sex. Baby, that's what it's all about. The dust was soon settled, and he kept bringing in roses. We went there and made hot love when we should have been at school, but he was a straight-A student, so he had no problems. Me, damn, I was only a good C.

But my dear teacher said don't worry you have what it will take all the way and a high IQ.

Carlos had told me my sex was double A plus. But it is us together because, yes, it takes two to tango....

The school offered an IQ test and mine was much higher than his or Cody's. It was 142. Deep down I needed to hear this. I knew my hearing was starting to get worse. I remember the doctor telling us many years ago, that after I had the bad virus, and took the medication. It would cause me to slowly lose my hearing. You don't believe what you hear if it is not what you want to hear.

Carlos and I let all of our time with others go and we were together, alone, most of the time. I did not try out for cheerleader that year, but I pretended to go there, to get more time with him. He withdrew from all sports. He said as soon as we finished school, and after the trial, we would move to California and get married. For some reason, the words *"get married"* still scared the hell out of me. For one, I did not want to move to California, and I also worried about the trouble he was in. Did I love and care for him with all my heart?

Then, like I thought, things went wrong. Just one week before graduation, he came into my class and asked the teacher if he could speak with me. He charmed even the teacher, I thought. She agreed, and we walked out to the schoolyard and sat down on the swings. He told me the courts in California had decided to charge him and he had to go back to spend some time in prison on manslaughter charges. He would still get his diploma – but he had to go right away. Until that moment, I knew actually, truly, little about what had really happened. He said, "I will tell you all of what happened just once, and then ask me everything you want to know about this bad predicament I am in, and then let me go."

I asked him why he had a gold band when I first met him. I was too afraid to ask before. He said it was a wedding ring and I almost dropped dead. My face turned red, then icy white. My heart stopped when the sun went down and darkened the whole wicked Earth. He had cut my heart from my soul. He then told me the complete story and heartbreaking report. He said he met a very wealthy girl when he was seventeen named Sarahi. She told him that if he had the time, she had the money and that whatever she wanted; 'her daddy' would get it. We started having sex, yes, many times, nasty. But honey, we guys will get it anytime it's given away free.

Again, I hated him for a moment. He said she was three years older than him and almost one month after the affair, she told him she was pregnant. Her rich father had put a bunch of money on the table for him to marry her, and he did, but he was miserable with her. He promised her he would wear the ring for a while after the baby, then, he would file for a divorce. He started worrying about the baby, was it his?

"Do not ask me why... but I did what she asked of me. She wanted me once more, how did I get it hard and lay it out, again ninety percent of us boys would do it," he said.

"Anyway, I found out she was not pregnant and told her I had run short of time and wanted a divorce. She asked me for one more night and I agreed because I felt guilty--It was so ridiculous. A group of our friends went out partying and got drunk on the way home or wherever we were going, and she was killed in this terrible car accident."

I gazed deeply at him. He said, "I hated myself."

"You mean this had all just happened when you came here? You sold your heart to me along dust from the old house where we shared our sex every day. Was I on this Earth with where you were just out receiving or hunting another free piece?" "No, No, my darling Toy. That is not at all how it was, please. I am sorry. But yes, it happened just a few months later. I love you so," he lamented, "I was in bad shape until I met you. You helped me so much. My dear precious mate, why do these kind of things happen when things have been so wonderful? Our life together, in moments, has just turned out to be so heart breaking. I tried to pick up the pieces, but everything just kept falling apart."

"Breakable is often the conclusion of events like ours," I said in a low tone.

"Yes, so true—but my darling we must not let it happen. We are all weak in many ways when things go wrong; when we start to lose, it all breaks loose from our soul and life begins to drift away," he said, "but, it is part of living that has no meaning. Please, let us not allow this love of ours to end. I will be back for you. I promise"

I nodded in wonder, and I asked, "What happened with the wreck?"

"I had not been driving. My friend, Richard, was and we were all very drunk. He hit a deep embankment and was thrown from the car. I thought he was still alive, lying somewhere on the ground. I was pinned in on the passenger side and tried to crawl my way out through the driver's side when I passed out. The police officers find me there and that is how I got in all the legal trouble," he said. We looked intently at each other.

He told me that he woke up three days later when his mom told him that his wife and friend were dead. Richard was in the Navy and so his legal matters were complicated when the Feds took his case.

My mind was going around and around, hitting one wall of my skull after another every few minutes. *What? Why?* I kept criticizing myself. *What was I thinking--falling for this guy?*

He kept studying me to see if he could read my feelings. He shook his head and looked away, and I could see he had tears. I had tears. He said, "I am so sorry that I did not tell you all of this before. I was afraid too. That is why I did not tell you all that had happen."

He reached into his pocket and pulled out a gold chain with a cross dangling from it. He handed it to me.

I stood silently as my emotional tears hung in my mixed-up mind. "Thank you. Why now?" I asked as he dropped his head down low. He muttered, "I think I have changed––or did we change each other?"

"Change," I said in a sigh. "My heart is not understanding, and I am gone. . . hiding behind my soul, and I am in deep and concern wondering where I go from here?"

He whispered, "Yes, I know, you are thinking too deeply here and, yes, you are right, and my Toy cat, please forgive me. I tried so hard to not let you see or know what I was hiding."

He took my hands and we stood for a moment looking at each other before we started walking back over to the car where his dad sat.

We stopped, and he said, "I want you to know I care so much for you, and I will always love you. Some way this problem will pass." He kissed me again and I pulled away.

"How could you have used me like a toy? Why didn't you tell me not to care so much for you? Maybe I should never have cherished every moment of our time together. I do love you," I said with pain in the words.

We walked over to the car, and he got in, holding his head down. He turned and looked at me with tears and said, "Please I cannot do this... not now. I must go. Please do not stop loving me."

His dad looked away and as he pulled slowly away from the curb to go to San Angelo airport. He did not look back a second time. He appeared to be in emotional agony and defeat. It was like a shameless dream. I looked up into the sky—there were copper-colored low clouds floating all over the bitter Earth. I tried to seal my feelings. I could remember the music from "Amazing Grace." I wondered if this was to tell me the end of this strange and promised story was over. I moved slowly away holding the cross to my heart; this could be the last place we ever stand, the last time we ever touch each other.

Weeks later, Carlos's mom, Leah, came by to see me. She said the trial was very unfair and that she and her husband had come back to pack. They were moving back to California as Carlos would be going to jail there on manslaughter charges. She said she would keep us posted from time to time. Again, I tried to understand what I was doing in all this. But, once again, I was lonely and lost. I started worrying about and thinking of my reactions when he left. Was I too unkind? Did I make him feel ashamed? I could still hear him asking me if I believed him. I could not answer him. Truthfully, he was like a dream that I needed to awaken from, and yet in some ways he was like a present I had wished for all my life.

However, when I opened this gift, perhaps, I had wished for the wrong thing? Can it be returned, or could there be a refund from the sender to restore my empty heart? The shadows over the clouds laid darkness to rest upon my sad soul.

I heard from him a few months later when he phoned my house.

It was a cold morning. I could hear the thumping of big, hard raindrops upon my windowpanes as I gripped the receiver of the phone. I could see the reflection of a sad face in the window glass, and I wanted to look away from the entire deal. When he talked to me about his many problems, his words merged with my own soul-suffering and anger. Everything he said seemed to be too complicated for me to understand. It was like being all alone and trying to examine something in deep, dangerous darkness, and then never finding the purpose or the reason. He told me to go on with my life and that I did not need him. He was not in the clear and that maybe I should not wait for him. He said he was a damn loser. Then he said, in kind of a whisper, "Do you even want me to call if I do get a second chance? My lawyer has challenged the last ruling, and it is looking a little better." He said he should know something by the end of summer. I did not know what to say. I needed to think. Finally, I am not sure what possessed me, I told him I had moved on, and we were moving to Odessa. He said that was great and he understood. He asked me again if I wanted him to call. I waited a second to answer—I really did not have an answer at that moment. I started to speak when I heard this hard click. He had hung up. I just stood there for a moment holding the phone. I finally hung up and walked over to the window and blocked the conversation, not allowing the sweet reminiscence of the wonderful times we had shared together. I said to myself that the truth would come, but I had said many times that the *truth* will not always set one free. I wondered if a miserable heart could be sold. I remember reading something about how you could not sell the heart, but you could exchange it for something better. I thought of many years ago—of my friend Willie, the cotton patch, and the smoke from the cotton gin and my mom's café. The first time I knew about sex, which was as far back as I needed to go. I wanted time to rest my heart and soul and have faith again and I kept telling myself, '*this too will pass..*

I have but one life to live. No amount of money or time or even fame can pay for a person to have a perfect life or love. I also know this man I just spoke with, is a masterpiece and few will ever be found on this wicked Earth.

The obligations for me to understand, is like watching the shining stars as they soothe and heal the lonely heart, but never touch my aching soul.

Chapter 3

Life, years ago

It was an extremely hot late summer evening when all my visions of an unadulterated human were taken off the so-called kid track. I had just turned thirteen and I was wide-eyed and bushy-tailed, dreaming of a long and wonderful future in the building business. The thought of being a teenager crossed my big, pink heart and called my attention to my unrealistic brain many times.

I took two deep breaths and three smells of the air as the smoky mist from the cotton gins started whirling into my hot lungs. No help wanted. That mess of smell only added to the uncertainty in my concentration. I could scarcely explain how I really felt after the view from the treetop I sat on.

Here is how it all began:

It was by complete accident that I saw the whole thing. Darling, that is a bit of a trivial lie, but let us move on. My best friend Ken Roberts told me he had seen this amazing event several times. He said it was always on a Thursday evening at Richard Turnbow home, when

Richard was off to West Texas on oil business. Ken could not take his weekly viewing on the extremely high and concealed pecan treetop, with a view of the master bedroom of Turnbow's. He told me to go to his place today, to watch this show. I walked barefoot down the shaded path, thinking what a fine evening it was just before night. The fresh flower scent from the dampness of the August showers had helped take away the smoke from the gin, and it was a pleasant day to look at Ken's find. I pussyfooted up on the tall, unsafe mulberry tree with lots of slick stuff, the messy stinking fruit berries that always came to visit on the first days of spring and stayed there decaying for the rest of the long, hot summer. I had to swat a few flies away from my face and butt. I eased out on the edge of a large overhanging limb. I dropped over a rotting fence and jumped to land just behind Elm Street, to Oxford Street. This area was just past the main road from downtown and one block south of the two-story, red brick building that held the Winters Drugstore. The place where I pocketed a bit of pink bubblegum and whatever else I could get my hefty firsthand. I was not a thief every day of the week, but some days, I needed things, so it happened. Most of my stuff came from my mom's place—she owned and operated the Cozy Café. There I got Camel cigs, more than anything else, that I took for free. Of course, she did not know. I sold the CIGS at school, two for a nickel; I made money for my own needs.   She was always working, and Dad was always--I do not know where.

Now back to the house on Oxford Street. I was in the tree holding back some of the leaves to camouflage myself when all of a sudden: Yes! I could see it all-right before my purple-green, innocent eyes. I closed them tightly and opened them, bug-eyed wide, to be sure they were seeing what I thought they were. 'Noel of God,' I lay as still as I possibly could, but I almost wet my pants, and I nearly fell from the tree twice before I got my bangs pushed back and trusted this amazing illustration.

My kindly neighbor, pretty Mrs. Sally Rae Turnbow, with her long blond hair and blue eyes was marching around in her ugly pink bedroom completely in the nude--save the spiky red heels on her feet. She had nice, proportioned thighs. She twirled around the big white bed whose covers had been thrown off onto the floor.   Mr. Fred Bangs, who was not her husband, looked like his eyes were going to pop right out of his wicked head. Our honorable banker was thought to be handsome by most of the women in our town, but he was very displeasing to my eye.

Fred stood to the left of her, wriggling his nude body like a worm dangling on a slick stick, and his *certain spot* was really dangling. They appeared to talk something over and then he flung a sack away and he jumped onto the bed where Mrs. Sally Rae was twisting and writhing like a DDT-sprayed spider. He sprang about on the bed atop her and then they began hitting one another's bodies. Suddenly, as if forgetting something important, Sally Rae jumped up and pulled down the window shades, maybe it was because there had been a light that had flashed from somewhere down on the street. *Why is this stuff a sin if they were getting such happiness from normal bodily pleasures? But deep down in my heart, I knew it was an immoral scene. I also knew that kids must see this for the first time, or wonder until it happened to them---later in this story. . .*

I did a good job of sliding down from the tree. Guess I was smarter now. I took the shortcut towards our house and walked directly through Mrs. Sally Rae's yard like I owned it. *So, let her catch me with her naked tits hanging out.*

"I took longer, faster steps, wishing I had on sandals. The night would soon grow spooky and ghostly, *dam-num-abs-que*, I said in my father's French, as I stepped on the hot concrete. I did not like being alone or too far from home in the dark. It was one thing I did not feel so brave about.

Finally, I was home and the first thing I did upon walking through the front door was check on Mom. She was home from her café. She turned her head to me and told me to go wash up for dinner. She came home from her café' only on Thursday nights to make dinner and be with the family. Why was it tonight?

I moved quickly over to the sink, hung my head under the faucet, dashed a tad bit of water on my face, and washed my hands, took a big sip to cool stuff to help cool my lips and mind. Mom did not look over at me, as I grabbed a big spoon from the counter that had cake mix on it. Really, I was getting too old to lick the batter off spoons. Cody, my sister, told me not to lick uncooked substances, its poison. Really, I did not believe her. I flew up the stairs and strutted into my sister' room. She was older than me. Cody was dressed like an old lady. Her full circled skirt was too long and spread out like a flag on her bed and her blouse was too silky for day wear. Extreme clothing made her feel older. Her sudden, dismissive glance turned into a wide-eyed glare when she saw what I was carrying.

My sister and I liked our rooms at the top of the squeaking wooden stairs that led into a long loft that my dad had built—two bedrooms for us and a small bathroom. The ceiling was high because the roof had a 10/12 pitch, and my dad had covered the rafters with rough-looking planks painted ice cream white. At the end of my bedroom was a large window. I could crawl out and lie on the cold wooden shingles, look at the sky, and watch Mars. I had always wondered if those people up there were looking at me, too.

"What do you want?" she asked.

"Cody, listen to all of this, you're going to want to know every speck of it," I shouted. I proceeded to detail the recent events I had just seen, not leaving out a single detail, to thoroughly disgust this perfect and proper sister. She gazed at me for a long time, trying to get a good visualization of the sin I had just dropped into her

75

pure white mind. She wore thick, round glasses, and one eye did not track very well with the other. But she was happy with her little book reading and living in a lonely world.

"Look, dear sister––," I continued.

"Shut up, Rooster. I am thinking," she snapped.

Cody was smart, but it took her too long to picture things sometimes. The perplexed look on her face made me realize just how mentally disorganized she was. Sometimes she could not remember the simplest things, but it might have been because she was lazy and just did not want to.

She put down her book, moved off her bed, and called me a "filthy, little mess."

"Well, is that all you've got to say?" I pried.

"Now, listen to me," she said. "I have told you to stop being so nosey, it only causes trouble. You need not be near your so-called friend Ken; I bet he is at the bottom of this. You two are mean and dangerous."

"Yes." I lied.

She turned away, then she slowly turned back to me and whispered, "Rooster, Sally Rae and Fred Bangs were having *illegal sex*." What a sin!"

"Do you think I committed a sin for viewing this crime?"

"No, that unquestionably comes from the men's side, they are the immoral abnormal ones, not women. I know this from listening to my older girlfriends. Men are all nasty about sex." she said.

"Really, Why?" I declared.

She threw her hands up in the air, disgusted, and continued: "No reason, they are born that way. I have been told many nasty stories about those two. Gunnel told me." Gunnel Brown was two-and-a-half years older than Cody and she was well informed about the matters of manhood and womanhood, and the BS.

"God bless America." I said, then, "there are flocks like that all around us like them, Cody?"

"Good, God, Yes, Rooster!" she scolded. "Do not go tell anyone else, this nasty stuff. Cross your heart."

"No," I answered, "not crossing my heart." I patted my chest as she looked away.

She frowned and shook her wiry curls around for a minute. I walked over to the window and looked out at the early moon. It even looked suspicious and different tonight.

"Rooster, stop these silly slip-ups, or mix-ups." she declared.

"I do not have any mix-ups. I pitch them out on their butt two days after I inspect them. You just sit and have more time than me to think about mix-ups," I said.

"Really. And with me sitting I find out more than most people," she laughed.

"Okay, you find it out, but I see it–– you just rest contented with what you find in your daily little reading results. You will grow up old and lonely," I said.

"Well, aren't we smart, today," she said.

"Yeah, I walked on the moon last night," and I walked out of her room.

Later that night, at dinner

"Rooster," Dad said, "answer me at once! What happened this afternoon? What did you see and what did you tell Cody about Sally Rae?"

Damn it, I thought, *Cody said*. I was madder than the red devil at her.

"Rooster, damn it, answer me!" he demanded.

"Dad, I have not sinned." I did not tell him what I was watching was a sin.

Mom leaned over toward him, brushing her beautiful auburn hair from her blue eyes, and whispering something, as she flipped the ties of her green and purple robe to one side while tactfully planting her direct, almost fat, hips.

"Tory! Go to your room." I knew when he called me by my proper name and not my nickname that I was in much more trouble than I had anticipated.

I did not even look back at them. I quickly turned and went down the hall, but just before I ran up the squeaky green carpeted stairs to my room, I swayed off and dashed down the six wood steps at the back of the house. I stepped carefully over my lazy dog, Candy, and headed past the weeded vegetable garden (that my dad did not tend to very well). I went toward the flower garden and snatched a hand full of purple lilacs, I loved these flowers and thought their beauty and scent might relax my sensitive and anxious mood. The dusty lilac fell to the ground where I'm lying and only the wind can know the smell today... I sniffed the flowers deeply and paused—that did help slightly. The scent is great for a moment, but like so many things, the scent blows away in the winds and is soon forgotten. As I reached my room, I took a long, relieved breath and remembered that I must kneel and thank the Lord of spirits for my gifts of the day. I then asked for forgiveness for watching and being where I should not have been. The praying did not help much. I was not exactly admitting to the old sky man that I was there on my own accord--that it was premeditated--and mostly because I did not feel like it was really a sin. Why would I ask forgiveness for a "sin" when I was not ashamed? I ended the prayer by saying, "--and thanks for the beautiful day."

I looked out my big window at the sky and I wondered what was going on in space—there had to be something important or it was sure a lot of wasted galaxy. It is all those people who have already died and are living and hanging around up there invisibly. I am sure because they say you leave your body down here and have only a spirit to take with you. In one of my history books at school, the scientists found skeletons that were thousands and thousands of years old. Now what happened to all those people? So, there must be a reason, and a reason for all that space stuff hanging above us. Therefore, I trust and obey our God. It keeps me from worrying all the time about hell, because if there is no heaven, then there should not be hell. Amen, and pass the members of the aristocracy.

Later, I talked to Ken about what I had seen. I knew he knew what it was all about. I wondered if he had done it. He is older than me. I was ashamed to look at him straight into his face. I could feel things in my pants when I looked at his private pants. I did ask him, what the "F" word was, and he said it meant "fuck." I was humiliated and uncomfortable around him after that look we gave each other. I was building most of my tree house and cave properties alone until I got old enough to have him help me.

Everyone was back to normal in a few weeks, but I loathed that word, *normal.* It does not match up with anything, it just kind of swings around waiting for an available place to fit in. Anyway, I was trying to be faithful to myself while doing my daily duties as I approached the development of my powers. My neighbor said children are all after powers. They are like a flower--they remain open to the softly falling dew but shut down in the violent downfalls of the stormy rains.

81

A few weeks later, I was still on autopilot. I needed to make some money to buy some more building studs, most were two by fours, to finish my tree house. My mom would not give me money for *objects* or *items* for that type of thing because she did not like me building. I am not sure if she really liked anything I did. She should be glad. It really kept me out of trouble-- well--on the border, like two days out of seven. Tomorrow was Friday, and Ken and I were going to the lake to fish--if he could get his bike back to functioning. Kids wandered all over the place many years ago; it was safe then.

Today I had on new white shorts and a red-and-white-striped body-hugging shirt that belonged to my sister. I think she had never worn it because it showed off her tits. I took a good look at myself in the mirror one more time, wearing my best leather sandals and I was happy with how I looked and set out to do some selling. I started at Briggs' house, because he was a retired banker, but I heard he was a part time wine-o, so he might need a resting place soon. When I knocked at the door, Mr. Briggs came and held the door half open. We talked for a while. Soon he said, "No thanks, Tory,

THE PATH TO WALKERS BLUFF

not this time. We have a plot in the Wingate area where my parents were laid to rest. But thanks, Tory." He closed the door. I pretended to march on, but I slipped by their open window and hunched down to listen to what the old man was telling his wife, Janie Sue. "What was Tory selling?" Mrs. Janie Briggs asked.

"Well, she wanted to sell us some of the space around her papa's grave site. She said she heard her father say there was a lot of wasted space and there was room for at least two more dead people," chuckled Mr. Briggs. "That kid would try to sell the devil an icebox,"

"Oh, dear, yes, I think she could," answered his wife.

I grinned all over my happy face and looked up at the big beautiful yellow and orange sky and said, "thank you for the light of each of these days."

Chapter 4

Moving on after Carlos

As soon as the oil boom began in West Texas, my dad wanted to move there. Finally, he decided it was time to go. He and three other guys were going to build houses in Odessa. Cody had already moved there several months ago and took a position at Wallace Savings and Loans. Dad moved three months before me and Mom. He was incredibly happy for the first time in many years. He and his partners began building small VA and FHA houses. He said they sold faster than they could get them up. I was incredibly happy and knew I could learn a lot watching him build. And I would be good a ways from my last settings. I did miss Carlos, but right now, he was still in prison.

My Mom sold and closed the deal on her café very quickly and she seemed happy. I was surprised she could be content without her work—she had lived there day after day for many years.

At last, we were on our way to Odessa. On the day we were leaving, when the mover's truck was loaded, the guys told my mom they would see us in Odessa.

I was throwing my last load in my car. I looked down and on each side of the sidewalk there were beautiful yellow flowers in full bloom, and around the corner, I could see my favorite lilac bush staring at me. Though the flowers are made sweeter-- by the sunshine and dew, what happens when there is no dew? I smiled and walked on, looking up at the Burkett Pecan trees. They seemed to be towering gracefully above the house, the house I had lived in all my life, and a few tears dropped. I knew there were few flowers or anything green in the deserts of West Texas. The vegetation was scant—only oceans of sand, and there were few trees unless they had been planted. So, I would miss the trees and flowers, but as my dad said, if you want trees and flowers then plant them. He said forget this place and go where the money is, and right now it is where the oil business is. My granddad said the farming business was almost over: the farmers were crawling off their tractors and going to West Texas to get rich. Both of my grandads had oil wells on their land that were tremendously productive, so they were blessed in money. As I pulled away from the curb, Mom pulled behind me in her car and she waved to me. I thought about how this house gave me countless memories of happiness. But it was time to go. I thought of Carlos, he said happiness depends upon the capacity of love continuously. He was way ahead of his time for his age.

Chapter 5

How I lost my hearing many years ago.

It was my birthday it was hot that August day, like always, but to me it was a beautiful summer morning. My sister and I were dressed in our best clothes because on the first day of school we wanted to look our best. I kissed my dog, Candy, goodbye, and we walked briskly down Mulberry Street toward town. We had to start school early because the cotton crops would need to be out of the fields between mid-September and early-October. School would be out for a month. There was a shortage in manpower to get the cotton out of the fields. So, some help came from the students. We knew we would be "picking cotton." It was the hardest labor people have ever been cursed with. It was backbreaking and filthy. When we did help, our fingers would get all cut up from the hulls over the cotton, and you sweat out a whole well of water. I hated it and was not satisfied with the outcome of money against the work, so I knew right away I would do other things to make my living. I started building tree houses at the young age of six. I was really thinking of building a big house someday. I wished we could move from here and go to a big city like Dallas, or Los Angles where they made movies.

I rubbed my forehead as a slight breeze whipped at my sticky, red face. I had been feeling ill for two days, but decided it was just nerves. I moved along, trying to be happy. It was important to be at school on my first day. I pulled back my sister's arm because she walked too fast. We crossed the newly paved street, which smelled bad and looked like black melted grease as we walked over to the south side of the square, along the Queen Theater area, where we went every Saturday to watch movies, eat popcorn. In the summer, we had red popsicles. Everyone from the country came and stayed in town all day on Saturdays because no one really knew what else to do. I do not know how they sat in cars and talked and gossiped in the heat or cold, but they did. The finest building on the square was the beautiful First State Bank building covered in a cream rock with lots of glass windows and the doors were beautiful thick glass with some kind of foggy-looking stuff stuck to them. It was one of the fine establishments cooled by refrigerated air.

The Freon industry was steadily growing in the North and South as a lot of businesses were getting this kind of cooling. A ways down the street was the Church of Christ building. It was nice and the only authorized church on Earth, according to my grandmother, that you must belong to if you wanted to go to see the Lord—in heaven. Now really, I did not think that was all true.

My grandmother's sister, Wilma Buffet, was in bad health, and she had willed her money to the preacher of the church. I never understood who was getting the money, and the preacher was supposed to add air conditioning with her money when she died. My dad was cursing the preacher. He said he was messing around with some old gal, but he would still get her money. (Her husband, Uncle Ross Buffet was a very wealthy man and had passed away only a few weeks before). Dad cursed like a mad sailor in his strange tongue of French all the time, anyway, so we closed our ears to him in more ways than one. But I was learning to curse in French. His dad told him that it was because he was a multi-layered Frenchman and they just had salty tongues. My good friend Ken had heard him curse and he said cursing was a poor excuse for not knowing how to use big words. I did a little cursing using my own big words for him that day.

I think everyone at church was secretly hoping Wilma would hurry up and make her exit to her Lord because we had just about burned up at the last service. We had hand fans waving like crazy and were sipping water, too. I was praying for the preacher to get it done and let us go home. If she passed on, she could be with Uncle Ross and then they could look down and be happy, knowing we were all cool from the air conditioner next Sunday.

Cody and I stood for a moment in front of the bank, as we always did, waiting for the cool breeze to move over us when someone opened the big glass door. My eyes met a well-dressed man in a fine gray pinstripe suit with a clean-shaved face. Mr. Howard Smith was the town's most respected man, and he was the president of the bank. My aunt said he was always dressed to kill in his beautiful, tailored suits. He fanned the door toward us as we inched closer in relief.

"Good morning, ladies. First day of school?"

"Yes, sir," I said.

"Go in," he coaxed. "Go inside and cool off for a bit."

My sister chimed in, "No, thank you, sir, we haven't the time today." She pulled me on.

He nodded, stepped aside, and moved quickly toward Bayle's Bakery. The bakery was owned and run by Germans and 70% of the people who lived in this town were German. Some German-Jews. My granddad always mulled over the odds and the fact that we were the only French people living in this area.

Mr. Smith had been going to Bayle's for what seemed like forever to eat the not-so-sweet cranberry sweet rolls and have a weak cup of coffee with two sugars. I remember having one of those bittersweet rolls—it did not meet my taste. They were practically sugarless, and they called them sweet rolls!

A lot of the townsmen went there to tell all they knew and make sure everyone else knew what they knew. Today, they would start with Sam Sanguine dying, leaving a mess with his money and his uncultivated cotton fields and the lady he visited in San Angelo, without his wife with him. Then, they would end with Sally Rae's yellow and pink panties hanging on the clothesline. People also picked up baked goods from the German bakery because they did not know how good food was until they ate at our place. Our food at the Cozy Café was the greatest food in this town.

Yes, it was my mom's café. The marble machine was my favorite thing to do. It was set to the left of the entrance beside a big window, and people liked it there because they could see the whole wide town while enjoying themselves. We made money on that thing as someone was playing it or the nickel-music-machine all the time. We also had a wonderful juke box with all kinds of records. We made money from it too. On the other side was a long white marble-topped counter with red leather and chrome stools anchored to the floor in front of it. Then, there were nice wood tables along the side wall with strong cane-bottom chairs that had brown pillows on the seats and matching back pads tied up tightly. If I had been fixing that place up, I would have never used those ugly red stools, but they came with the deal. There was a great seating area at the back with a long table and chairs for big families.

Our best help at the café was our evening cook, or chef, named C.C. Arnold. He was a pleasant man who was drunk by night but cooked delightful food by day. He cooked stuff we did not buy too often because of the price and the ability to get it down to Winters, Texas. He had to order most of it from the meat guy from Dallas and he came once a week. C.C. cooked these fancy foods like shrimp, lobster, and other things we did not know much about. C.C. would say this dish is beautiful, but as far as I was concerned at my age, nothing in a kitchen was beautiful. Come to think of it, a kitchen has never excited me in any way. On Friday nights we were busy because everyone came to eat and see what he had stirred up for dinner. We would turn the lights low and burn candles.

C.C. told Cody and me that he had been a chef in one of New York City's most famous restaurants. Later, he moved here to what so many city people called "Hooterville" for "rest." We had about 5,000 people living here. He laughed at the size of our town and at our lifestyles, and he called all of us hicks from the sticks, but so what? We were wonderful hicks. However, he was a nice man. C.C. moved in with his widowed sister, Wallace Marie, so he could use his money for drinking and have a free roof over his head. He said that old age was running in on him and he liked to be drunk so that he did not have to watch it. I asked him how it was to be drunk. He stopped for a moment and ran his shaking hands with the *too* long nails through his curly, gray hair. He had big, wrinkled lips and nice white teeth. His light gray eyes were frosted with circles of red rings around them, and his skin was too white, and his face was scarred from acne. I doubt he had ever been a good-looking man, but he had been married several times, so someone liked his looks or his cooking––or something else.   A waiter came and gave him an order at the window where we stood. He nodded to the waiter and turned back to us. "Anyway, about drunk," he said. "Well, it feels like you're floating up in dreamland for a while and then when you wake up and fall out of there, you're in pure agony." He thought for a moment and said, "When you're cooling or getting sober, it's like you've gotten down in the ground someplace pretty close to hell." He laughed, reached over, and started flipping some hamburgers. Oh, the trade market was booming! "It isn't a good way to be, because once you start it, it's hard to stop" he mumbled. I thought that it was fun to know this kind of stuff and in some ways, was great for our mom to have a café. We were never bored, but sometimes lonely at home. We raised ourselves a little bit.

My dad said C.C. was a "creature." My mom liked him and thought he was quite charming, but she would not know because Dad said she thought most men were charming if they told her she was pretty-- and most of them did. She always dressed classy, but sometimes on Fridays she wore a white uniform because that was the only time she waited tables. Our *rush time* was Friday nights. Cody and I always waited tables when we had time—we liked our tips. Lately, C.C. has been drinking more. I saw him go to the storage room and take a few sips of the stuff he concealed in his locker. Most of the time, he could hold out until we closed at 9:30. Usually, he made it to work the next day.

My sister pulled me on. I was just about dead by the time we got to school. I was so damn sick. I had no energy and had to work to hold my head up to keep from falling dead on the newly waxed ugly wood floors. So, I had to be here, but I was getting worse.

I could tell my fever was climbing from the warmth of my forehead. My eyes were burning and blurry and my lips were swelling and on fire. My mom should have touched my forehead when she was there. Now, I needed to go to the bathroom and throw up my eggs and toast. I would have bet my five-dollar bill that I was running a temperature of 106

My school was seven-and-a-half blocks from my house. If we did not go by town, I would have to cross the railroad tracks and I had to be extremely careful because the train was busy in this season. The cotton gin was just two blocks from the school and four-and-a-half blocks from our house. It smelled of burning cotton hulls from early fall to late summer. The owner of the gin, C.L. Ren's Mill, was a distant cousin of my dad's, but I did not like him. He let the smokestacks stay wide open and the whole town was covered in clouds of hard-to-breathe smoke. My Aunt Ethel was a nurse and she said it was dangerous to breathe it all the time, but it was what kept the town going. We breathed it, plus the gin roared day and night and the noise kept us awake at night. I will always wonder if that was what made me sick.

The school building was spread out over three city blocks, with lots of sidewalks, surrounded by acres of dirt and rocky grounds, no grass. The first thing anyone saw was the huge, wide front doors made of wood, metal, and safety glass. They were so ugly and heavy they growled like an animal when you touched them. The building was strongly built, but not an interesting shape. It was just a long, stacked up one-story with a flat roof. The building elevation was a little plain, but the white and cream-colored Austin stones were nice and made the walls very thick. There were lots of long narrow windows on the front and back of the building. I always wondered why they used ugly gray cement to seal the cracks around the light-colored stones. Most other kids, I am sure, would not even notice.

Finally, when we had all drifted around for a while and found our classrooms, we sat down at the wood and metal desks with new, funny-looking vinyl tops. I opened the drawer and put my stuff in it and sat for a few moments waiting for the teacher. I was burning up and knew my face was getting red as fire. I was at the front of the room and the teacher looked at me, walked over, touched my head and she intuitively knew. That look she gave me made me worry about whether I was to die soon. My burning eyes met hers. She shook her head and quickly called my mother, who came from work and picked me up. Since doctors made house calls back then, Dr. Ray Jennings came over and practically declared me dead. He said I had a dangerous case of double pneumonia—high fever and that it might cause me to lose convulsions. I had convulsions—I can remember that.

He came again on the third day, and I lay down without knowing what was going on. They could not get my fever down. His voice trembled when he told my mom he had done all he could and that I needed this new drug that was on the market, and only the government had it for soldiers. It was called sulfadiazine.

Fortunately, my Aunt Ethel was an army nurse at Dyess Air Force Base in Abilene, Texas, and she was able to get this medicine for infection from the base. They did not know exactly how much to give me, so they gave me half of the regular dose. It was too much for my body weight and I was sent into a convulsion, falling into a light coma. I was told my life was spared because of a Black woman named Emma. She was married to Will, a Black man who worked for my granddad on his farm, and she was a well-respected midwife. She came to see me after my grandfather told her how sick I was. She brought her younger son, Willie. He was my age, and he was quiet, obedient, and observant as his mother tended to me. People said she was a doctor without the licenses.

"The lungs are too full," she said. "The medicine is extraordinarily strong for this child, but it will help in time. She warned my mother that it could give me problems in the future. Mom did not understand or tell me until many years later. Emma stared at me for a long time and checked me as well as she could. She told my mom to get her some clean white rags and she cut out a little shirt and sewed it together. The parties acknowledge that Women's Wellness, Inc. has invested substantially in the same with a flour sack, making this shirt bigger than the first. She sewed all but the bottom edges of the two shirts to each other and stuffed the two layers with a bunch of stuff from her bag. Lastly, she spread Vicks all over my back, chest, shoulders, and stomach, and pulled the shirt she had made over my body. She wrapped a blanket around me and held me for three straight hours. And she did this every six hours for three days, going back and forth from our home to hers. Finally, the stuff in my lungs started to break. On the third day, I coughed and coughed. I remember opening my eyes, looking outdoors through the window, and seeing a little, black, round face. His hands cupped his wide eyes and a giant grin spread over his face. He screamed to his mom: "She lives! She is alive now, Mama. Rooster lives!"

He was smiling at me as they hurried into the house. I would remember that kind little face for as long as I lived because it was like a vision of an angel. I still like him to this day, though I do not know where his family ended up after his father stopped working for my granddad. One of the most painful things was losing track of him. We hardly left each other's side for four years from that first time I saw him, he was my guardian angel.

I tried to buy Willie for ten dollars from his dad when they started to leave town. I did not understand the concept of slavery, but his dad understood it and he was forgiving despite Willie's great-grandparents having been slaves. I did not mean to hurt their feelings. I did not want him as a slave, only as my best friend and my special playmate. I just did not want Willie to ever go away, and it was the only way I thought I could keep him around. He cried and screamed, and we held on to each other. When I asked my granddad if I could kiss him one more time, they all gasped, and I was asked if I had been kissing him. Willie squeezed my hand and spoke first: "Every day." My mom almost fainted. My granddad and my dad grinned knowingly. They had seen us kissing before and they apparently thought it was all right. It was just on the cheeks—why all the jumble?

"Big Will" slapped the reins at the large, brown mules' asses as the wagon rolled out onto the white, rocky, dusty road. The wagon was loaded with their only belongings. They were carrying canned food that my grandmother had helped Emma make and a large, cured ham my granddad had given them. A big sack of flour, beans, fresh fruit, and vegetables were sent with them as well, so that they could make it until Will got his first salary.

They were headed to Sweetwater, or Fort Worth. Will did not really want to go. He kept telling my granddad that he liked working for him, but Sir, my work for you is done. My granddad said he performed so well and did everything the best possible way, taking a wooded mess of mesquite trees and making the land useable for pastures and farmland. Will produced great terraces in the fields, which were important to control water. My granddad said his work was like that of a painting on a canvas, with his ability to arrange them meticulously for optimal drainage, and for his flawless end results.

Just before the wagon made the left turn out of the gate, Willie jumped out and screamed, "wait!" He pulled up his worn jeans and hit the dirt hard with his bare feet, and began to run toward the black Ford pickup I was having a fit in.

" Young Willie, stop," Emma said to her son.

"No, Mama, I'm not going!" he shouted. "I just am not going to leave my Rooster. Mom, just go on without me!" My whole family watched in dismay. Will pulled the wagon to a stop and shook his head. As young Willie got closer to me, he held out his hand. I reached out the window of the truck and touched his hand for the last time, and he said, "I will miss you Rooster, but I've got to go." And he had tears, as he turned and ran back to the wagon. I covered my teary eyes with my hands and then I jumped out of the truck and watched them as they drove away.

I now had a vacant spot in the corner of my heart that would never quite close. I asked my granddad a few years later what Willie's last name was. He went to his ledger and showed me that it only said, "Will S." No one used last names for such work because they just paid the workers in cash. That was all that was written in his work: laborer. I had such beautiful memories of those four wonderful years we shared together. I will always stand around waiting and wondering if Willie will come back home. My granddad said, "Let it go, Rooster. You will learn that all of our wishes and desires do not come true, and its water under the bridge."

"But Papa, I believe if there stands a bridge, there will always be a connection in this old world to the ones you love even if they are not in sight."

He smiled and we went on home.

Chapter 6

Good times coming

We are now settled in Odessa, and I know it is unsafe to draw drafts on the future, but I really felt like I would have an amazing new life here.

Most of the time, I was no longer dwelling on the past; I was trying to see visions of tomorrow and lay the past down on the echoes of yesterday. But the truth was Carlos was still hanging around in my mind, and I did miss him. Sometimes I could almost feel his gentle kisses and embraces on my eager body and see his soft smile looking down at me. But I knew I needed to come in from those cold thoughts --and walk over to a fire and hold my life down to the warmth of tomorrow. But in a number of ways, it was hard to let go of the tangles in my past. What helped me most was going out to my dad's building job sites very often and I adored watching the subs working. They were building small houses, but there was no difference from the large ones. It took the same procedures. I was drawing house plans for him. So far, he had liked them. We had to have an

Architect's Seal on my plans to get permits from the city, and I had befriended an Architect that would examine my blueprints, make any changes, and seal them. He liked my drawings and had given me things to work on for him.

Our house in Odessa that we moved into needed many things done to make it a nice and comfortable place to live. It was built at the beginning of the oil boom. It was what we called striped. Dad and I were talking about totally refurbishing it, knocking out walls, adding a bath and on and on. Then we would put it on the market. He was building us a new house. One evening, when no one was home, I went downstairs and sat by the beautiful, glowing fire. I soaked my thoughts in the blazing heat with yesterday's dreams. I covered my body with a beautiful fur comforter and sat back and listened to the rain beat down on the windowpanes. But then I turned on the music, it was Nat King Cole *'they tried to tell us we were too young...too young to really be in love.'*

I slipped over to the liquor closet and got the Jack Daniels out and fixed me a strong drink of whiskey and water. I settled back down by the fire and, yes, I was there but a bit lonely, and listened to the music. But yesterday's music will always play on.

I must gaze deeply into the gentle stars as I sweep slowly through this new life, the dew from heaven was falling on my flowers in the stillness of this night, while I was searching for my true wishes and desires.

To find happiness once again, I must remember to climb to the peak of virtue and promises, to find the true height of contented existence.

Chapter 7

Shock to my good life

A year and half later in Odessa: "I might be pregnant," I told Cody, and I waited for her to answer me. She looked over her thick gray glasses and stared at me, and in my mind, we went back to when we were little girls––having our lingering talks in her bedroom. For a long while, Cody said nothing. She was getting married in two weeks and had moved into a fantastic brick home with four bedrooms and three-and-a-half bathrooms, a beautiful backyard with lush green lawns. Her future husband even bought her a beautiful Collie dog named Mimi. The house was so beautiful, and it had a thick red carpet (I really did not like the red carpet), but it was nice. She was placing beautiful white French furniture throughout. It was a little too white for me, but it was pretty and beautiful to her. She looked beautiful too. She had a few things done to herself: eye surgery, straightened her teeth—and a few other secrets—and she looked remarkable.

Her boss was soon to be her husband. He owned the finance company where she worked. He was from an exceptionally wealthy family from Kansas, and he was writing numerous checks like crazy to make her happy. They were not really living together, until after the wedding, because Mom did not think it was nice to let people know they were already sleeping with each other before marriage. So, they snuck in and out. Now what did that prove? Why were people so stuffy, when every one of them did it and would do so repeatedly if they did not get caught? Hello, just enjoy yourself.

"Cody, I had hoped it was not true that I'm pregnant. My prayers failed in so many ways," I said.

"Maybe--Tory, maybe, oh dear God, you're not," she screeched. After my nineteenth birthday, no one called me Rooster much anymore. I missed it, but I liked Tory.

"I--damn it! I never should have gone on that wild trip on the amazing blue ocean." I shook my head with hidden tears in my closed eyes.

"What now?" she asked.

"Well, good question. Now, I am married to Sonny Allen.

"What, how, and who, "she kind of stuttered and then hesitated.

"Well, it's an amazing story and so is the guy who rides bulls in the rodeos. I had been dating him only three months and he talked me into going with him and his friends on a cruise. I was shocked as we boarded this huge, beautiful ship. There were twelve of us, and it was heaven on Earth. After one day and an amazing night we stopped at the port of Guayas, Mexico. The yacht belonged to his friend's father, who was an extraordinarily rich oil man and rancher in Alpine. It was all so beautiful. He and all of his friends love fun times. Nevertheless, I admit that I have had lots of fun with Sonny. We laughed, partied, and danced and yes, sex. I told him "I have not been this happy in a long time. I have missed the good times so much."

She giggled a bit because she knew I was speaking of Carlos. She said, "You must get over him."

"Cody, I know. With Sonny, we had an amazing time, we drank tequila, and more, and more, and so-- yes, we all got married. The captain performed the wedding service for three couples. This was eight weeks ago. Sonny is delightful. He is a student at Sul Ross University in Alpine Texas."

"Whoa," she whispered, "The yacht sounds fun, and does he really ride those bull-- things?"

"Yes, he is a good rider, and he enjoys every bounce of it and yes he's as wild as those bulls. He is an amazing guy," I laughed, "Yes he loves to ride those crazy things and he told me he would ride them until he knew it was time to finish his wild side. I have watched him ride and he does not mind the danger. He scares the devil out of me when he is riding, but when it is over, I can see the feeling of his pleasure in his blue eyes. He is truly a one of kind person."

"Alright, I can understand if that makes him happy or excited. What are you going to do about this whole being married and the-- other? And how do you really feel about him?" Cody asked.

"I like him a lot, yes, he makes this world a *delightful place*, and I love the feeling I have when he is near me. I may have made a shameful mistake. Still, I had so much fun, too damn fast.

Cody, the truth is, it is hard to say how deep this feeling I have for Sonny goes, and does it touch all the corners of love or is it only fascination? I like the thrills and the dares when we are together. But I was happy

111

helping Dad in his building and drawing the plans. Can you imagine how I felt when we built the first house using my plans? Again, it was also in heaven. I like college reasonably well, but I am not the best student around. I passed, but I love the designer courses and I make A's there," I laughed.

"Then suddenly, I am married to someone who does not even know anything about women, except that there is a gold mine in the quarry. We do not even know each other's full names. As I told you we have been dating only three months. Although I know his brother well who is a great person and dear friend. I tried to run away, from all of this, but in vain." I expressed deep sorrow. "I have no place to run. Women have this problem, not men. You know why? It shows, it hurts— women cannot walk away. Men can walk, and often do. It has always made me wonder why females suffer more pain than men."

"That is always true." She nodded her head and closed her eyes. "It is not fair, but to whom do we complain? We were built like this, and therefore I plan no children. My new husband-to-be feels the same as me about children, and you know he is nine years older than me."

We were silent for a few minutes.

"Tory, you are strong and tough. You will get through this, and things will get better in time. We always say, "This too will pass." She poured us some more coffee. "Let us have this happening as right, not wrong," she toasted me, "You can't have wine," she teased, "but go on and have a great life with this strange man, guy. And here's to the good life."

I smiled and nodded yes, with tears running down my sad face. I lightly tossed her back. "I have so many questions without answers."

"You know, more and more, this is when we ask what the hell is this life all about?" she countered. "Tory, I feel like I have many questions every day. I am sure everyone does too. But you will win, Tory—you always do."

I did not think Cody had ever tried to understand me, but now, for the first time, she was trying to understand me--and help me. We had to get marriage papers signed in America to be legally married.

She kept saying, "Dear friend, hold on tight." When I left, we hugged and I had such a deep friendship with her now—it had been lying there, but both of us was too stubborn to pick it up.

Later that night, I told my parents that I was moving to Alpine, Texas with Sonny Allen, my husband, and he had decided to stay in college. "Why?" they asked, "why did you do this?"

My dad said, "Doesn't he ride bulls in the rodeo?"

"Yes," I said, "he does."

I thought, *He is a good-looking guy with beautiful blue eyes and his body, and his sex, is, well, wonderful. He is very smart and clever; he is a straight A student in college, and so why not . . . We have so much fun together—not just in the sensual category. As I said before, women have more fun with men like him, but survival is not always fun or fair.*

My parents did not need to know the part about pregnancy, or anything else, right then. Did they even care? I told them we were married.

"*Au diable* Sonny," Dad growled. He rose from his chair and pressed his fingertips hard against the

114

tabletop. Mom cried, "Why did you do this?" She did not really care. I knew she did not. Why did she put this panic act on?

"Hellfire, Tory," my dad reminded me. "I have enjoyed having you on my jobs. You cannot just run off and marry someone without telling us. This guy may be bad. You may be making a bad mistake"

"I have enjoyed the building and love drawing the plans. Someday I will build many homes. But, Dad, you need to look at your own life. You and Mom both live in misery. I have heard your words to each other and your unhappiness. Work on your own problems."

"Tory," Mom said "you stop that talk this instant! We are happy, most of the time and our life is not any of your business."

"Really, Mom, then is it your business if I am married to Sonny Allen? I will be twenty years old in one week, and today I am happy. "

She just gazed at me. I know this predicament is wrong, but it happened and for once I would like them to help me, not criticize me.

I turned away and my vision began to blur, and I had this strong urge to run, so I did, I left them standing there. Yes again I was not sorry.

We had been living at Sonny's parents' house, they were out of town, and therefore, it made it easier for us to stay there. When I first told Sonny, I might be pregnant and he just stared at me and finally he said, we can make this all work.

One night I told Sonny I felt so strange. He asked, "What do you mean, and what do you want me to do or say?"

"I just don't know," I answered truthfully.

"Do you mean unhappy or what––!"

"Yes, *you* do not have to be pregnant! I wish it were a fifty-fifty thing, but it is allowing me to come in you. It would not be all sweet daisies if it were you who had to carry this baby!" I alleged.

He stood up, and walked over to me and said, "Hey, wait, my darlin,' you never had to be with me or come here, and no I did not have to be with you or bring you here."

I looked at him with tears in my eyes and said, "Well, we did––now what?"

"My darling lady, it's alright and we will make this a great life together."

I knew he was trying to make me feel alright, and I liked his tenderness. But what to do now? He was in college and was going to be a veterinarian in four years, and to top it, he still loved to ride bulls in the rodeo.

"Tory, you know I will take care of you. These last few weeks with you have been the happiest times I have ever known."

He shook his head and held out his hand.

He had never called me Tory, always Rooster.

I scoffed, "Take care of me? How?"

"The best way I can, and yes, I adore you. Why would I not? You have it all, lady. You are the one that came to me the first time and I loved every moment of it," he answered with a smile.

"Thank you, but I am scared," I whispered.

"Don't be," he insisted, "don't be."

We went through a lot of torment those first few days together. We told his mom and dad we were married when they returned home. They did not like it either, but his dad said we can make it all work. His

THE PATH TO WALKERS BLUFF

parents were nice people. I liked them. His dad said he wanted Sonny to stay in school, and he said he would ask my folks if they would help him with the cost.

Of course, my parents declined. I will never forget that nor forgive them. Not one dollar did they gave. Sonny's father was incredibly special, he told us he would pay for everything and keep us in school. I always adored him.

We were packing, getting ready to go to the Alpine, and Sonny was so happy to be going back to the Big Bend area.

I was happy today thinking of the fun times we would have, and I was taking things to the car for the move when my mom came in and told me that she thought I did the right thing by marrying Sonny. I knew she hated to admit that I was pregnant.

"Thank you," she said, "Goodbye. I love you."

I turned slightly toward her and said, "It took you a long time to say that." I walked away, and she went back to her car. I did not turn around.

We drove late into the night to get to his early morning class the next day. That night we moved into the cottages that belonged to the college. They were furnished and were for married students. I loved them, they were perched on the side of this beautiful mountain. There were four rows of this housing area, they had 950 square feet. It was a great floor plan. Well, yes, I knew it was a great plan. He told me when we got there he enjoyed having me near him. I felt the same. We were tired, but happy to be there and finally after finding bath towels, showering, and getting the sheets on the bed, we both flopped down, and he held my hand. I told him I was happy, and he told me he was thrilled. I turned off the lamp and thought that this is a great place to be. Sonny was fair, and we were both trying to make this deal work. Maybe affection kept hiding just around the corner. Soon, we fell asleep.

Sonny had two friends whose families owned ranches in the Big Bend area, and I had been with him to several of their parties before we were married. This group called themselves the BB Gun Gang. There was none other like them. They also called themselves caregivers. We were invited to a party the next weekend, and they dubbed it as the back-to-school-sin party. They were glad he was moving back with me in tow. Indeed, they were wild as sunny rising sin, but that was where the fun began. Nevertheless, down deep these were among several cooler groups who hung close together, but I liked it more all of the time. We were there if anyone needed the other. Sometimes these guys would go hunting late at night and the girls would tag along. There were a few times I was scared as hell that we would not find our way back to the ranch house, but they had great dogs that always led us home. It was so beautiful out there, the moon and stars seemed to touch the great mountains. I felt close to paradise, it was a beautiful feeling. I just relaxed and rested in the wonderful mountain air. These guys also had street dance parties on the highway outside of Alpine. We also had so many amusing times partying in Mexico, it was just a short drive to the border. Yes, they all still got to school every time on time.

Sonny went to his class at seven o'clock the next morning. I did not go until nine. I kept having a fainting feeling and I looked pale and tired. One of my new friends —Audrey Lewis—said there were only three doctors here and she called around and found that Dr. E. D. Greene, would take me today. His office was on the campus, so it was within walking distance of my class. I didn't like the looks of the office when I walked in, but I needed help. The doctor wore little wire-rimmed glasses on the bridge of his wide, ugly nose. He ran a few tests and called me over a few days later. He was nice, but blunt. He looked at his nurse as she came in. She was old and thin, but clean looking. Her uniform was starched as stiff as her face. She had deep lines on her face, but she was not ugly. She told me they were going to do some more tests.

She looked hatefully away from the doctor and then handed me a cup of water and a tablet. I took it and she left.

The doctor looked at me with joy and then frowned, giving me a sense of good and bad news. He sat staring at me for a moment.

"You are not pregnant," he said with a sigh, "but you have a growth."

He patted the table where he had tended to me before. "Hop up here. I would like to have another quick look."

I was already in the backless gown. I crawled up, a little scared, and lay down stiff as a board. He used an exceptionally cold, large metal thing with lots of

Vaseline on it to poke around inside me. He talked to himself under his breath about what he found in there.

He said, "It might dissolve, or we might have to be taken out with DNC," He explained the process to me and helped me sit up.

I closed my eyes and weakly said, "thank you."

He said, "Go ahead and get dressed for now."

He left the room and I started to dress. The nurse came in and told me to go to Dr. Greene's office down the hall. She had some stuff with her and pointed out for me to go on ahead.

"Come in," he said, before I had even made it to the door.

I paused, and he repeated himself. I lifted my face when I stepped into the dimly lit room. I had never been so frightened of anything, but that day I was. The words of the old saying, "Today might be the last day of––" where is my mind? I was afraid but did not want him to know. I was not thinking of anything except following this strange voice. He motioned for me to sit down, never looking up from whatever it was he was writing. His belly was pushed up to his desk and his stubby arms seemed to pop out of him like the dough boy's. A writer's lamp hung over his large hands and a single gold band was lodged onto his left finger. I looked around to see piles of manuscripts all over the floor. Dr. Greene was so old that he probably had come with the building. It had an odor, a smell of sweat, bleach and things left over from the long years.

I know I must have looked frightened because he said, "You are going to be just fine." He continued, "We will start first thing in the morning. I will meet you at the hospital. It will take less than thirty minutes. You will be a little sore, but by tomorrow evening you will not know you had been there."

I did not trust him. I thanked him and cried tears of joy the entire walk home, crossing campus without seeing it. I had suffered for my age, I thought, I had lived enough to be 101. Dr. Greene told me I did not need to worry. I was glad that I was not pregnant, but I still had a lot of apprehensions.

I thought Sonny might untangle himself from this rambling rose, if only he could. I would tell him the truth. That night, I had walked for a long time, and finally I could see the lights of the cottage where we lived.

I took a deep breath. The air was perfectly cool and the whole beautiful sky seemed to tell me everything was mine. I thought I had found the end of the rainbow. Damn, why did I think of a rainbow?

Sonny had been calling me "Sunshine" lately. It was a pet name, and I liked it better than Rooster. I had asked everyone here to call me Tory and slowly they were changing over.

That night, when I opened the kitchen door, Sonny was sitting at the red chrome table, doing his homework. He was a wonderful student and made straight A's with little effort. I walked over to his side, and he looked up for a moment, nodded and then looked back down at his paper.

"Where have you been? You were supposed to stop at the Sub—"

"I've been walking," I said.

"What'd the doc say?" he asked.

I kind of collapsed to my knees in front of him and started to explain. "Sonny, I am not pregnant. I have a growth that is doing some things to my health, which is why I have not had a period." He just sat still with his mouth wide open and shook his head.

"Baby," he sighed, "that's great." He reached for my hand and for a second, I really loved him.

We both held out hands.

Yes, we would try to have faith and believe this was all right, having kids in the middle of growing up, but we both knew we had a hard road ahead.

He was still holding my hand, and said, "We will make this work. I know we are selfish kids."

"What do you want to do?" I asked.

"I am trying to think of where we were when we started all this. I think we should go on with everything as is," he said. He let go of my hand and contemplated for a moment.

"As is?"

"My, Sunshine, you know this has hit me harder than I thought. I was ready to accept fatherhood, hang a few puppets on the hall wall. I have even slowed my drinking down from nine to six a day." He laughed but turned and said, "I really have. However, the force of habit renders many rewards." he laughed and said, "love does the same thing."

"Well good! That gives room for a little bit of true surviving," I whispered. "But temptation hurled from habits, acting upon the elements of passions can knock out truth and virtue."

"Dear, love, I love it, tell me again," he said. "But the truth is here, and things are all cooled down and we can begin again, all new and fresh. I think we ought to stay here for the rest of the year and then go back to Odessa this summer."

He pulled me into his lap and wrapped his arms around me, holding me close for a long time, he whispered, "I would like to know that we are free, but I am not sure I want to be free from you. You have racked my life, and I am a weak son of a bitch. I like your warm body beside mine at night, I miss you during the day when you are not near, I love the smile on your face in the morning--I even like your damn king-sized hot temper."

"You could be a darling friend," I said. "If you want to run."

He fixed his eyes on mine. "I am guilty as sin, I had thoughts, yes, and I know you could. Yes, I could have rushed away. I could have gotten a divorce. I knew what I was doing. Baby, you thrill me, honest, you do."

I had to think about how to respond to that answer—I stood up, and turned towards him, and saw a stranger in those magnificent, unusual blue eyes that did not seem to be as blue as I remembered. Could I trust him?

"But are you happy?" I asked.

"I think so. Look, I am married to a beautiful, exciting woman whom I need in my bed. I do not want to lose you, ever. Do you understand, I am in love with you? "Do you love me," he asked?

I whispered, "Yes?"

But he had lost me.

That evening, we went over to our new friends'—Joe and Wanda's—house and had dinner. We had a wonderful time with them, they were so special. They would be my good friends forever.

Sonny was looking at me every time I looked up. I wondered why. We got home late and were both tired. We had not told anyone at school I was pregnant. I dressed in my nightie and found Sonny completely nude, as always, lying face down across the bed. He dropped his cigarette into the ashtray and turned over.

"Come see me," he said.

127

I closed my eyes.

"Not tonight," I said.

"Fine, let's go to sleep," he mumbled. "I got to hit the books bright and early."

"Do you think I'm selfish?" I asked.

"No, darling, that is not what I meant. Are you in pain?" he questioned.

I admitted: "I do hurt a little, but Dr. Greene said it would pass as soon as the growth is removed. I will be as good as new. I will just go in tomorrow. You do not need to be there. Jean said she would drive me." "Good," he replied. "If it's all right, I need to be in class most of the morning since I have three exams."

"Don't worry about me," I told him.

"Darling do not let them mess up that masterpiece. It is Mother Nature's jewel of the enjoyable and perfect gift to humankinds."

"I've yet to discover a perfect gift." I yawned.

"You will," he insisted, "you will."

We slept on our own sides of the bed, and I rested my tired mind.

Early the next morning, I was at the doctor's office at 8:00. The guy at the admittance desk signed something, and then he turned it around for me to sign. The doctor came out and took me into a small, chilly room with two nurses standing like statues. They were dressed like white snowflakes from head to toe. One had a needle in her hand, and the other had my gown. I looked at the awful table with big silver stirrups, trying to convince myself that everything was okay. I changed my clothes and got up on the table as instructed. One of the nurses gave me a shot in my arm as she continued conversing with the other nurse.

I was cold and wanted to interrupt them to ask for a blanket, but then the doctor knocked and came in. He did not have a mask on, which surprised me, but he did have gloves. I watched as his hands touched my body with the cold metal object. I started to yell out that I had changed my mind, but I began to drift away from myself. Suddenly, something warm touched my hand, and I was convinced it was the hand of my Lord. I could feel myself exhaling when I heard someone ask, "How do you feel?"

I tried to rise and weakly answered, "Pretty good, I think." My arms were heavy, and I had to touch my head to make sure it was still there. I was overcome by sleep, and soon drifted off.

When I came to my senses in a few seconds, I thought Sonny was standing by my bedside. No, it was not him and I was confused? *Am I dreaming—here on Earth am I—going back, going back—*

Now, life is some mysterious wonder, performed by the commands of chance. It takes us on an August journey, a pleasure that angels would envy, and the devil would despise. But within me, in the end the deterioration could lead to punishment, yet I am detached and do not care, I will accept encumbrance.

Long ago I learned: never place anything in the mind that cannot be carried for the rest of our time. Also, remember there is a shadow over us, but a shadow is like dreams, they only shine upon our path. They will never be felt or helped.

Suddenly, a door opened, and I watched helplessly from the examining table where I lay as the shadow of an oleaginous man slowly moved closer to my side. My eyelids were so heavy that I could not keep them open. The sound of footsteps drew nearer, and I suddenly sensed a great, lonely bit of heaviness in my body. Cold dampness passed over my entire body, as if I were on a strange journey, floating over distant places. I sensed something happening to me, but I could not feel anything. The smell of sweat and sperm drifted into my nostrils.

"Who are you?" I croaked, "What do you want with me? Dr. Greene, is that you?"

"Yes, my sweet child," he uttered indistinctly, lazily, with his mouth partially open and his eyes relaxed with the pleasure of release. "Yes, it is I, Dr. Harper S. Green, here."

"Why are you undressed?" I asked shakily. Then, I drifted into lonely, nauseating shadows. I could not tell how much time had passed. I told myself that it was all a dream. No, he was there, walking toward me with a hypodermic needle in his left hand and a shiny object in the other. I could see the whites of his eyes then, what— he is bizarre!

"I beg of you, please let me go. What are you going to do to me?"

I tried to scream, but my voice was too faint and only lonely whimpers were released. I needed to sit up and then I could go. I needed to get up, and finally I struggled upon my elbows and realized my clothes were not on my body. I panicked, wishing the nurse would return.

As I slipped further out of the haze, I realized he was touching me again. My stomach twisted as his wet lips touched my I thin face: "You were not supposed to wake so soon, my dear."

The last thing I saw were flickers of brilliant, sparkling lights behind me and his disgusting smirk.

Time passed....This time I knew that Sonny was there beside me. "I'm glad to see you," he said with a worried frown on his face.

"What happened Sonny?" I asked. I felt strange over the lower part of my body. "Where am I? Where is the ugly, little, green room and the bad man?"

"Tory, the nurse called me, everything is all right now, but you bled a little too much," Sonny answered. "You are in a hospital room. We moved you to St. Andrews and you have a new doctor."

"Oh, thank-goodness," I whispered.

I turned my head to see my friend, Wanda, standing at the other side of my bed. She was pale.

"Hi, Tory, don't worry about a thing, you are going to be alright," she said with little conviction.

I put my hand over my eyes. "Am I dying or something?"

"No, darling," Sonny whispered. "They are about to put you back to sleep. Get some rest. You will be fine, I promise, and I will be back as soon as my class is over, love you."

I told him thank you, love you.

A nurse came in and gave me a shot, and I started all over in my last dreams. I am sure I tumbled all over my bed until late the next morning. When I opened my eyes, I found myself alone. It was like I had been hit by a night train, and I needed to get out of the way before it hit again.

"Help," I said, but no one heard me. I made it to the bathroom, with all the tubes and IVs following me.

Later that morning, my new doctor came by. "I'm Dr. Ames," he said.

I waited.

"You had quite a bit of bleeding during the attempted abortion," he continued, "but everything is fine now, even the baby."

"The abortion?" I squawked.

He looked a little surprised, but only nodded his head, as if he had heard this before.

"Yes. Doctor Greene thought you needed to abort the fetus because you had a growth on your uterus," he informed me.

"Dr. Greene told me I wasn't pregnant."

"Well, you were, and you are. The growth is not dangerous, and you should wait until after you deliver the baby to remove it."

The realization hit me. "You mean to tell me he was going to give me an abortion without me knowing?" I just could not wrap my head around it. "Do they really make people that evil?"

The doctor pursed his lips and said: "I would like to discuss this with your husband present. He told me you do not hear well and said that maybe you did not understand all that Dr. Greene had said."

I started to cry. The nurse came over and bent down, allowing me to put my head on her shoulder.

I looked up at Dr. Ames and explained to him that I thought Dr. Greene was an immoral and corrupt man. I heard what he said, he told me I was not pregnant. The nurse tried to comfort me with a hug.

I sobbed, with big tears running down my hot face. 'Help me,' I thought, 'Sonny will not like this either. I wish everyone would just go, just leave me!' Give me time for all this horror to go away. I could not even stand up to defend myself. I knew Dr. Ames knew something, and he would never tell. He knew Dr. Greene was a monster. Both the nurse and the doctor looked bothered when we talked about him.

"Calm down, Mrs. Allen," Dr. Ames said, "You are okay, and will go home in the morning. I want to keep you overnight to keep an eye on your blood pressure. Do not worry about a thing. You are simply fine," he repeated.

I was all right --but alone--so alone. I was shaking, and I wanted to say, "Please don't make me wonder what happened." I kept mumbling "I was afraid that no one would believe me, and they did not care what happened to me. I was convinced that Dr. Greene had hurt me, and I bled, and the wrinkled-up nurse had called Sonny in the nick of time. I knew that he had been inappropriate and had raped me, I would find out, and that it would never happen to anyone again. He would pay.

One day he did––it is an extended tale. Someday I might tell but at this moment it is not to be told.

A few minutes later, a nurse came in to take my blood pressure. She was so nice, but she looked at me with concern and queried, "What is the matter, my dear?"

"Everything," I lamented, "but really just living in general."

"You are so pretty, and you are carrying a little baby. I am sure of that," she boasted.

I told her. "I just want things back like they were, away from here, and to start again."

"You should be so happy," she insisted. "Children are a gift to you. Dr. Ames said you are simply fine now. You husband has been immensely helpful and concerned about you."

My phone rang, and I looked at the nurse questioningly. She motioned for me to answer, and my sister was on the other end. She had little mercy for me and my condition. I answered the phone.

"I told you so," Cody said.

"So, you did," I sighed.

She pushed, "Just come home. Sonny called me and said you were doing all right. Hang on and I will try to help you take care of all this mess later."

"Alright," I tried to be calm. "I must go, though. The nurse is waiting to give me another pill."

"Mind them, my dear," she said.

I said, "Alright," and I swallowed the pill, drank the water, and handed the glass to the nurse.

The pill made me happy. It was LSD or something happy. The bed was too hard, and I was cold. But in seconds the ugly little green room was not so ugly anymore. Suddenly, I felt joy--then sorrow. I drifted far, far away and could see my grandmother smiling. This was wonderland on the other side of the rainbow. Later the next day we left the hospital, and I was feeling reasonably well.

A week later I got a good report on my health, but to me it was an ill report, still I thought it would all be all right throwing a bit of sunshine at the story and holding on to the moonshine. I could not have a drink, not even wine, end of drinking for now. So, time marched on, we stayed to finish out the term at Sul Ross.

Sonny had decided to stop the bull riding and leave school. He said he was tired of school. I asked him if I had anything to do with him not staying. He said no, "I am happy for the first time in a long time, and I like things like they are with us, but let's go home."

We said goodbye to our friends. I knew we would miss those wonderful people, the school, and the fun at the border of Mexico. I had tears when we pulled away from the cottage. I tried not to look back, but I did and there were some good times hiding back on that beautiful mountainside. We enjoyed our new place in Odessa, and were glad to be back home, but lately I knew Sonny and I were drifting further apart. Sonny took a great position selling oil field equipment with a large manufacturing company in Odessa. He was drinking a lot and partying all the nights away. I stopped going out as I got larger and began to wobble. I paid little attention to him. I had my family and friends here, so I was happy.

When my delightful little girl arrived, I was so surprised at how much I adored her. I named her Lola. She was so beautiful, and perfect. People would stop to compliment her. She had so much beautiful black hair, yes black, and her eyes were soft blue. She was a joy to be around, and everyone loved her. She was so beautiful, she talked well by eighteen months, and our doctor told us she was much smarter than other children her age.

Sonny and I were trying to make the marriage work because we loved our little girl, and we had many happy times with friends and family.

Lola and Sonny were good friends. They loved each other dearly. Our life was a bit better for a while, but then, there was trouble in paradise: our marriage was falling apart.

When Lola was two I started back to work, I got a great position at a bank. My dad was not building anymore, I missed the building very much.

Sonny hated my work, hated my new boss, my new friends, and on and on. He despised everyone who walked by and looked at me. When he was drinking one night he was screaming, and he hit me. That's when I told him to leave me. I told Sonny's father that when he was drunk and we were fussing, he had hit me. His father was furious and talked to him about it, but no one told Sonny what to do. His father also said we should never have left school. He was right in many ways. I was the cause of some of his problems because he wanted to be a veterinarian. However, he told me when we left school that he had changed his mind, too many more years in school and he did not like riding bulls in the rodeos anymore. He said that the last time he was hurt it just didn't make sense.

Sonny would say things like, "I hate myself. I love you dearly, I know I am not giving enough to our marriage, but you are not either. He said; I have many problems with drinking. We both agreed that maybe we should try harder to make it work.

We started going to a neurologist. Sonny called him brain opinionless. He told us we were both depressed, which caused Sonny's anger, and aloofness. He gave us both cooling pills as we called them. Only time proved you have to make it happen yourself, it did not work for us.

Later Sonny said one night, "I know you had coffee at the bank with that coach friend again."

"No, I did not." I lied.

I thought to myself, 'I like him, and he might be a way out of here.

"Sonny, I will try one more time, but truly we need to leave each other. We are a mess, a mistake together, and it will be best to go our own ways."

He turned to walk out, and I asked where he was going. He said, "to the honky-tonk with my sinful fucking friends."

I thought of my old song, *"do we need honky-tonk angels."*

However, God be with us, the good news was, he was making big dollars. The oil field money was there. No one can know but the people who lived it in those days how wonderful it was, along with fun and fun was everyone's middle name. The parties were almost unbelievably great. Truth be told, we all enjoyed every minute of our lives there.

I heard that more liquor was sold in this area than any place on Earth (per size), but my dad said more wine was sold in Paris, France. He would talk about his relatives and how they loved wine. I knew a guy in Odessa that owned many liquor stores. He was really, in fact, very wealthy and powerful all around the West Texas area. He used to say do not let the stars get in your eyes in West Texas unless you are loaded, or you will go blind. Except, this does not mean all the people were wild— most of them were young and had lived poor before coming to the oil- fields. It was a new life that offered money, fun, and much happiness. That was what it was about. It had been a delightful time for so many people and a pleasure to live there. What happened, time changed everything.

Many of Sonny's customers were those fun-loving people and it was the salesman's deal to party with their people–– after work. And so many bought from him, he would party with them. He sold twice as much oil field equipment as other employees. Sonny was cool and highly intelligent. He had more friends than anyone I have ever known. Later, Sonny moved up to be the district manager of his company––at the age of twenty-seven. He had tried to totally stop drinking and had been incredibly happy. He had a heavy workload, his bosses believed in him, and he proved their selection was right. Every day he organized new ways to sell and reach their goals. With his new position, he was away from home a lot. The home office was in Tulsa, Oklahoma. He said the workers were a collection of devoted, smart guys. I went to Tulsa with him a few times and I liked it there, too. The Central Supervisors were talking about moving him to Tulsa, which was the corporate office, and it would be a great raise and opportunity for him. I did not want to go; I did not want to live with him any place on this Earth. I finally decided I had to take a chance and leave him. I knew he would never change, but neither would I. Yes, he admired me in many ways, but soon he was back on his whiskey trails. I thought of the times he rode those mean, dangerous bulls. He loved risky games, like roulette— he liked every moment of the high life, he could not be still––it was his own style.

One night we were having a big argument, but we had been invited to one of my favorite places to go for dinner. We decided to go anyway, and he promised not to over drink and to *behave*. The party was at Jasper Reeves' grand mansion in Midland. The home was beyond beautiful. There was no other to compare in all West Texas. His dinner parties were always impressive, and we always met many interesting people. He had guests from all over the world. He would greet people and toast the presentation by saying "here is a toast to our oil world friends and enjoy all of my friends from all over this delightful world with me and Diana." She was his beautiful wife. I thought there was no place on this Earth like these parties; it was more than a party it was a celebration of life.

His French chef cooked wonderful food and everything he made was magnificent. After we were seated in the large beautifully appointed dining room (which allowed fifty people comfortably), the chef would bring samples of his entrees for the night to the table. We could select what we wanted for our meal. They had several servants, and it was quite a treat all the way.

After dinner Sonny winked at me and left the group, with several guys and they were out of sight for about thirty or forty minutes. I just kept visiting with friends and pretended not to notice. I did not know where he went or what he was doing. When he did show up, he was stumbling around, and he came over where I was and whispered, "I want--to go home." I did not want to go but knew I should take him home. I was so damn tired of this life with him. We thanked Jasper and his wife for a lovely evening and bid all a good night.

I helped Sonny into the car, and I could tell he was just stoned and angry about something.

"Sonny, how are you feeling?" I asked. I was driving.

"Drunk, but fine, and I have kind of a hunger for you, you mean sexy bitch. I want you to pull this car over and then I will take you---," and he kind of passed out.

"Sonny, stop this, wake up."

"Magician, I am, --always know how--to—to get you," He chuckled and then he started cursing and saying. "You don't love me."

"Sonny. Please. We have so many reasons to enjoy our life and you stay too God damn drunk to live in it, with me, or yourself."

He nodded.

"Where did you go when you left the party?"

"I went down to Jaspers' office with some guys, and we had a bit of snuff. I am fine, Sweetheart, you Witchdoctor. Are you all right?" he asked.

I nodded, yes, but I was not. He told me he was buying us another house. A big and beautiful one, maybe in Tulsa. Everything would be good.

"I do not want a big new house Sonny."

He snarled. It was as if he changed in two seconds into someone else.

"Yes, you do,"

I knew down deep in my aching heart it was time to leave him. Each time we fought things would get worse. I was the one being punished.

He said, "I am sorry. I do not know why I scream at you. I love you so much." "Sonny, listen to me, did you take another one of those pills, too? You cannot take the pills and drink," I said.

"I did," he declared. "I am fine."

"You cannot do that. It is dangerous, and you must not keep taking them if you drink. You are out of it right now."

He did not answer.

When we got home, I sent the babysitter home, and then helped him into the house and made him black coffee. As he sobered some, we talked for a while. He had been mixing the nerve pills with liquor, it was dangerous. I told him he had the whole world why, why did he need to be drunk to live in it. He said he would stop tomorrow. I made him go to bed, and he kept talking about his promotion.

I told him I wanted to leave. No, he said Baby, and he begged me not to leave. He said he would change, but how many times had he told me that? He asked me to promise I would not go. I lied. Later that night, I went in to see Lola. I was afraid she would hear us fussing. She was asleep, and I made it back to the bedroom and took a couple of aspirin and crawled into bed. He was asleep. When I woke up early the next morning, he had left at six. I did not go until eight, so I waited for him to kiss my closed eyelids and tell me, 'I love you.' I did not move a muscle until I heard the door close and then I just fell to pieces. I had cried enough tears. It was more than over--as they say, *do not dry these tears another time, on me.* I had to try to live again. This was after several bad spells. It was written on the wrong stars. I would look out at the sky and see my stars twinkling, the same stars I had looked at for many years. It was time to leave this part of my world. In many ways I did love him, but yes, we had many good times together. I still had never known another man more fun when all was well. He had a great mind and collaborated so well with people. Why couldn't he let us work together?

My plans were to leave him that day and I had already made many changes without him knowing. I had been moving slowly over to my sister Cody's, so Lola and I would have a nice place to stay for a few days. I planned to move back into the house as soon as my lawyer got papers signed, getting Sonny to move out and allowing me possession.

A week later Sonny moved out of the house, and I moved back in. He told me he was very unhappy, but for many reasons he liked his freedom. I loved my freedom. When we had talked on the day he moved out, I had promised him I would think things over about living together again. I remembered what my friend had told me many years ago: never promise anyone anything, never believe in a promise, and never promise yourself true happiness. Just leave it all on the steps of chance even if it was make-believe, you are better off with control than risk avoidance.

Chapter 8

New life

I was excited to be back to work. I loved my job at Southland Bank and Trust in Odessa. I respected the people there and my position was so enjoyable. I was called the *floater,* I worked wherever they needed me: teller windows, statements, bookkeeping, or any department where someone was ill or on vacation.

I met new and interesting people almost every day. The oil business was booming, and the money was floating. The sound, and the scent, of oil was in the air, and money was coming in and that is a word that made everyone happy.

One Friday night we had been working late at the bank; the books did not balance. For some reason, I felt sick today but thought it was a stomach virus. So, I really hoped we could balance very soon. Finally, when we secured the problem and most everyone had left, I threw on my coat and slung my purse over my shoulder and headed out the side door of the bank. The night guard wished me a good night. I was walking to my car alone in almost pitch darkness, walking past the bank parking lot it had been full that day and I had to park down the street along the curb. As I drew closer to the streetlight, I could see a figure standing near my car. It kind of frightened me, but then I heard a familiar voice say, "It's dangerous to walk in the dark alone." My heart started to beat again, and my tired head snapped up and there under the dim streetlights stood Carlos Francisco. Yes, my guardian angel. He had this *I got you, baby,* look on his face. I smiled and chuckled; I was delighted to see him. He said he had been waiting for me for an hour. I did not walk, I ran toward him and fell into his open arms, we embraced for a moment. Then he moved me back a bit and we investigated each other, and then he pulled me near, and he kissed me, forever, I thought.

"What are you doing?" I asked.

"Here to see Toy Rooster. Is that all right?"

I said in a happy mumble. "I really think it's great, and I am impressed to have a visitor like you standing under the stars under *my* blue heaven."

He laughed and said, "You still got it baby."

"Hope so," I said.

"Do you want to have coffee, or a drink?" he asked.

"Yes, I--yes," I whispered.

I was speechless. I was back living in the same moment I had lived in the church garden, the first time I laid eyes on him. Once upon a time is not enough.

He stood back again for a second and stared at me and said, "Damn, you look so beautiful. My dear Toy, I had forgotten how wonderful you looked when you were near. Now, I remember why I hated for the men to stare at you. Lady of possessions, it has been too damn long." He hugged me again.

"Thank you and do you want a smoke?" I asked teasingly and chuckled.

He laughed and said, "I'll have a cigar with you one day, but no smoking for me anymore." He flashed that old familiar smile.

I told him, "I still smoke a small cigar now and then, it's kind of my escape from reality, when I needed away from it all."

While we were standing close to each other, I thought, I love to smell him. *'you know people have a scent and it is all of their own.' Yes,* I enjoyed that sensation and smell. I remembered that clean scent from the first time I met him. And the first touch was like no other. What is this old world doing, keeping us away from each other?

We went to this magnificent little restaurant near the bank. I enjoy him so much and I had that old feeling when I sat next to him. We gazed into each other's eyes which had never lost their affection. We talked for about two hours, about our new lives and of course the good times we had spent together. He was so handsome, damn, and I had forgotten how charming he was. I thought, *this is what they mean when they say, "Baby, you got what it takes." His kind is what makes this mess all rock.*

I told him I was happy, which I could tell by the look on his face he knew was a lie. He had checked out my life and found there was a divorce on file. He was working for the CIA and was happy with his position. He told me he had made a deal with the U.S. Government to get out of his troubled past and get all cleaned up. He said his lawyer finally proved he was not driving the night his wife and friend perished. So, after almost three years, he was free. He said he went through pure hell to please the CIA, but it was going to be worth all the work in time. I could tell he was happy.

I cherished those two hours we had together, just loved touching him and talking with him, but I also felt a bit of emptiness---like time had taken so much away. Perhaps, I did not need him anymore; time had changed many things. As we say, time waits for no man. I felt moments of coldness from him, also, like he was not the same guy I had fallen in love with sixty thousand miles south of paradise.

He told me he had business in Midland, so he had a reason for being there and seeing me. Later, he chuckled and said that was a lie, and that he was to be in El Paso and decided to stop at Odessa.

When it was time for him to go, he smiled and said, "It was wonderful to be with you, but all good things must end." We went outside the restaurant and started walking toward my car. He stopped and drew me close, kissing me right in front of the people walking down the sidewalk. One guy nodded. He said that sometimes he wondered where I was and what I was doing. Then, he said he would come back to Earth and live-in emptiness trying to figure out what made all this so damn mystifying and why so many things had kept us apart.

He kissed me again and I never should have allowed it—that one brought back the love from our past. From the moment the heat from his body touched mine, my heart drove off into the south winds. When he looked at me once again, there was that old smile and he said, "Once --this great story began."

He opened my car door. I did not want to get in it, but I did. I put the window down and he put his hand on mine. He shook his head and closed his eyes.

"The cards in our life have been played wrong," he said, "I had to see you if only for a short time -- maybe someday--we will know why and can correct the matter."

I asked, "Who has been holding the cards in this game?"

"That is the problem. As I told you long ago, this time and period is not mine, and we may never know who will win the game in the end."

"Arrange it," I whispered.

He nodded and said, "I am trying and one of these days, don't trim away all of the memories, and I will be back."

Again, he was gone.

When he left, I was extremely lonely. The feeling was like one says--cooling off after a hot and dangerous storm. He said he was kind of married, and it was not working, but he said it was mostly his fault. He did not live with her. He said when he got out of prison he tracked me down and found I was married. He said he came to Odessa and saw me with Sonny and our baby girl. He said I looked happy, but later he found out I was not. He said at that moment when he saw me, he said he wanted to tell me to let go of Sonny's arm and come with him to any place on Earth. But in some ways, he said he was like a man on the run, but he did not know. I was on the run from a bad marriage. However, later, I did not think I should call him when I got the divorce, because his sister told me he was married. So, I closed the book again and thought of my beautiful baby girl and a great position at the bank.

I knew deep down I was hiding passion in this empty heart; I could not go home, not right then. I called my mom since she had picked up Lola from play school. She did not have to do this often, but when I worked late, she would. I told her I was running late. She said that it was fine. She and I had been a bit better friends now,

and she did love my Lola. I decided to meet my friend
Gayle Davis at the Golden Rooster. She was my new
neighbor, and we enjoyed each other's company. The
Rooster not only fit my name but fit my lifestyle. It was
a place that I had always enjoyed. It was across from the
bank––yes--too---easy. Sonny liked it too, and he was
there tonight, and he came by and sat for a while. He
said he was happy and that he had someone keeping his
PJs warm. He said he liked his apartment but missed us.
I wished I had not seen him, it messed up my drive down
memory lane with Carlos––guess I felt guilty. He
seemed happy. I was glad he was content. In some ways,
I missed him, so it was not peaches and cream when he
started to walk away. I went to the restroom, and he
followed me. When I came out, he put his hand up on the
wall to stop me and he said, "I am so sorry. I miss you so
much. We had it all and I messed it up." I told him it took
two, not to keep beating himself up, and to move on. We
had been apart for only seven weeks, but it seemed like
longer. I was so much happier.

Meeting Carlos again was truly what made me
decide that there was something still out there after

struggling on death row. Death row was how, at times, I had felt in that marriage.

Sonny gave me a lot of gifts. He had adored bringing me things when he had been ugly to me, but that did not work. Gifts would not heal heartache, and pain, I remembered two songs, *'don't let your heart see our sins, don't let your dreams break your heart and 'I can't help it if I'm still in love with you.'*

A few days later, during work, I became faint and my friend, Lorie, took me to the doctor.

"No, please, no!" I begged the doctor, "Don't let me be pregnant!" He said, "You are over eight weeks." I remember the night it happened. I thought of Cody and what we talked about a few years ago, all but the problems that women are faced to tolerate. This was all about me, no one else. I had to live with it all alone.

I went home and cried. My maid was there, she helped me clean once a week. She said, "You don't have to go through this mess anymore." She gave me the number of a midwife who had early-term abortions as she had, had one and did fine. I went, but I changed my mind while I was in her waiting room--I still had a Christian heart and I could not do it. Later, I told Sonny.

He uttered, "What do we do now?" I said, "Nothing." He began coming back to the house often, to help me out and see his daughter. He brought us beautiful gifts. After a brief visit one night, he stood up particularly straight and said, "Listen, dear, I know I needed to get help with my drinking, and so I have been going to a great head shrink. So far, so good. Do you think we could make it together now? I am trying so hard to stay sober and do right."

I did not even have to think about it. I told him no and he left, cursing me, mad as hell. I knew he had not changed.

Late one night, Sonny came by, I knew he had been drinking; he had not been over in some time since I denied his request. He wanted me to allow him to move back in with us. I told him no. I was eight months pregnant and heavy, but I was still working and felt good. We walked out to the front steps toward his car. I said, "Please, Sonny, understand we are wrong together. Just let me alone." I started to turn and go back into the house, crying as I said, "Let's be friends and not enemies." He turned toward me and said flatly, "Then live with me."

"No," I repeated firmly. He grabbed at my arm, and I jerked away, screaming at him. He let go of my arm and I lost my balance and fell four steps down onto the pavement. He did not even turn around. I tried to get up, but I went into labor and my contractions were intense. I felt blood gushing down my legs. I half- walked and crawled next door to my friends' house, Wanda and Joe Bryan, and they drove me to the hospital.

My second daughter was delivered via C section one month early, but I was doing well, and she was an absolute doll, *my party doll*. I told my mother she looked like she might be Lola the second, but I named her Ellie. The love you have for your own little ones just beholds no measures.

I wonder how Sonny felt when he looked at her for the first time. I wondered if he felt the pain of what he had caused––but, again, there are two sides to every story, and this was all my side.

At the hospital, Sonny said he was so sorry and that he did not know I fell that night. He said that if he had known, he would never have left me. My dad was really upset with him this time. Sonny tried to talk with him, but he said, "Sonny, I am not anywhere near believing you, so stop. You two need to move on to separate lives."

Sonny shook his head, stood there for a few seconds and said, "Yes," and added, "Ask your daughter if she knew who might have threatened my life if I did not stay away from her?"

My dad said, "Sonny, she said she does not know, but if someone threatened me, I might walk away."

Sonny looked challengingly at me and said, "She knows."

My mother just stood there, never saying a word. Finally, she said, "Why did this happen?"

"Happen? You do not know that people sleep together when they are married and sometimes, they get pregnant. That is what happened." I said hatefully. She looked away.

There were a few ugly words exchanged and Sonny left.

I hated to be there. I was hurting from the surgery and hurting from a disastrous mess. I did not want to hear all of this. I had to think of raising my little girls, alone, without anyone to help. I wanted to be free.

I closed my eyes and went back to the cotton patches and walked with Willie on the trail to the fishing hole.

Chapter 9

My heart is still in San Francisco

Carlos called to ask how I was and left one message after another. His mother had spoken to my mom when she was spending some time in Odessa with her sister. Mother told her there were lots of problems and that I was living alone with my two little girls. So that is why he began to call. After several days, I called him back and told him I was fine. I asked him how he was and where had he been. "Good, and darling I am every place on this tender Earth," he said. I told him I was staying at Cody's for a while until I was stronger but hoped to move back home this week and go back to work in two months.

It had been four weeks and things were much better, but, again, time and rest were still needed. I told him I had some very depressing times, but I was getting as tough as California walnut branches. He chuckled and said he was glad I was doing well and hoped to see me soon. We talked a bit more and he said, "I will see you later. I must go now. I am in DC and need to get off the phone." He hung up. It did surprise me for him to call so many times and it was good to hear from him.

My sister and her husband were getting a little tired of us living with her. I was tired, too, and I wanted to go home. I took great care of Elle, and she was doing well. Cody had helped me with Lola, after all, she was just three, but she was all about love, and she was so beautiful. She was a happy and perfect little girl, and she liked helping me with Ellie. She and Cody had a lot of fun together. Cody carried her with her every time she went out, even dinner at night, with Ross. Elle was my *party doll.* She kept me going. She was chubby and sweet in every way. The next day the girls and I moved back to our house. I was glad to be home and I had help from friends and Mother came at various times when we needed her.

Later, I requested a longer leave from the bank, and my boss granted me one more month. It has been three months now. Thank God, my insurance allowed me four months paid leave. I needed this extra time to rest and enjoy my girls. I was so happy, and things were good with Sonny and me. He came often and helped us numerous times, and he had not disturbed me about our living together. He was doing well, and he said he had met a great lady. I told him I was happy for him.

One morning, the girls and I went over to Cody's for a swim. She told me she had a wonderful surprise for me, but to enjoy the swim for now while she was going shopping and would take Lola with her. She would pick up lunch. I took a quick dip in the pool, then laid back down on the lounge chair, covered my eyes from the sunlight with a towel and rested my thoughts. I heard the door open, and I thought it was Cody. "Cody, is that you back already?" No answer. I took the towel off my eyes, looked up and there stood Carlos Francisco. The truth was--there, *stood* my happiness. My heart started beating again. I was never so happy to see anyone. He touched my arm, and he stood looking at me for a moment, then pulled me close and hugged me, and kissed me on my hot forehead.

He said, "I have missed you so much and it's wonderful to see how well you look."

And there came this delightful smile on his face, and I said, "I have never prayed for anything like

I did for you to come back. I had wished so deeply and now my prayer has been answered."

He said, "Oh, Toy, I am sorry, I tried very hard to come sooner, but this is how things in my wicked life fell."

I spoke quickly, "It's alright. The timing is perfect. I am so much better, and I feel so great. The doctor just gave me a clean bill of health in all means."

"Great," he said.

I had Ellie sitting in the shade behind me. He walked over and when he saw her, he said, "Well, no wonder you call her your happy *party doll*. She is a darling"

He gazed at her for a moment before he looked back at me. "Toy, why don't you and your little ones come stay with me a while? I have a great place. I bought a small ranch a few miles from San Francisco, and I think you will like it there so much. I have some time before my next assignment. Please come."

I had heard he got a divorce—his mom told us. She said he was incredibly happy. He knew I had my divorce.

"Thank you, but no, darling. I cannot go right, now." I said, "I just have too many things--"

"Wait, why?" he questioned. "You need to get out of there, for at least a little while." I sighed and thought that it might be a good idea. "Well, we might come out and stay a few days."

"I would like that," he said. "I will start getting my assignments taken care of, but I might have to leave for work while you are there. But usually only for a few days at a time."

"Alright," I remarked.

"Damn," he said and looked at his watch. "I must run. I must get back on the plane. Do you need anything?" He had a taxi out front waiting for him.

I asked? "Where are you going?"

He started toward the door and said, "Washington, D.C. I have some stuff to do there." He threw me a kiss goodbye. "That's not enough," I teased, and he walked back over and kissed me on the lips. It was like a hello darling but goodbye, but it was still wonderful. "I will miss you every minute I breath," he said.

I nodded and smiled. I took a deep breath and put my fingers on my lips to send him a kiss, but I did not throw it--I will keep it a little longer. He just seemed to always come when I needed his affection.

I was so afraid to love him so much. I had always been afraid to love him, though I did. He looked back at me. "You going to be all right?" he advised. "I will call you in a few days. I will come and pick you guys up. I will work things out with the Choir Boys." The "Choir Boys" were the CIA bosses, who were his real commanders. He called them the Choir Boys because they played the music, and he chanted the song.

I got up as he was walking out "I love you for coming because I know it was hard to get here and stay for only a few moments," I said happily.

"It's okay," he replied. "Take care, of my new sweetheart, and be careful. Remember, you have a friend. Call if you need me sooner." He closed his eyes, smiled, quickly turned and then he was out of sight.

I had asked him many times why he loved me. He said, "That is not a fair question for someone who breaks all the rules to see you for just a few moments–

–and trust me, I do not know the answer. There is no rhyme or reason for this kind of love you and I share, either way. But I think, as you said to me once, let us get this love arranged and get on with actual living." He said, "You are such an original, wonderful, little mean bitch. I still do not know what makes you tick, but no one has or ever will be able to really know you, not even your dear mate or your own kids. I am not sure, but I know you best." Then he said, "Again and again, I am trying to figure out how and when I can come back to you. Each time, it is the beginning of a wonderful and complete passion."

One week later, the girls and I went to his ranch. It was near San Francisco, which was one of my favorite places on Earth. He took us all around that great city; we went shopping for things he thought we needed to make our visit perfect. He worked hard to make it comfortable for us. It was completely wonderful in every way. It was like a dream come true, and I thanked him so many times for the rest that I needed and for his love and help and, yes, pleasures. Sometimes I cried a few tears when we got serious, and I was naïvely trying to understand why we had left so many good years behind. Dwelling on how those wonderful countless years had gotten away and could never be recovered.

"When did we ever have a chance to make this real and to live happy from day to day? Why didn't we try harder?" I asked.

He gazed gently at me and said, "Listen, darling, we did live. We have loved and have lived a thousand years in our hearts, and every damn day I think of you with deep desire that fills my heart with wonderful memories. They go back to the day I saw you on that football field and that night at the church when I first found you. It is *our* past and no one can take it away from us. Never, not even in death."

"You are so right. Nonetheless, some of our time together was only make believe. There are so many unanswered questions." I whispered. For a second, I could hear some of the songs that he would sing to us, *"Make me forget that I am just–– just making these dreams come true, is this real?"*

"Yes, yes, it is real and maybe it is meant to be lived in this manner. Sometimes things cannot be changed or made to happen the way we want them to.

There are no real words to be spoken to answer these questions. We do not know why things fall as they do. There are not always real perceptions, but, darling you know, I respect my position and my work," he said. He stopped and frowned and gazed at me for a moment. "I am afraid you could not or would not care to know why and how I live the way I do. I must have control all the time. I have an almost impossible drive. I know it is not fair––sometimes I do not even like myself. I am in too deep.   I am unqualified to have full-time affection. Previously, when I saw you in Odessa, I wanted to make us happy together some way, but Toy, I cannot make promises anymore. I am up for a long assignment. I am not sure of the details, but––I cannot answer all the questions," he said

To him, answering a question that had no solution was like showing weakness in intent—or seeking a reason or a cause without knowing the ending. I have never known anyone to share what we had, while not knowing what was really going on in each other's Earth, but they say seek and you will find. I did think we were hanging on to a lot of dangerous stars as we grew older.

"Listen to me. I do understand more than you know. Have we been unfair with not just each other, but the ones who live around us?" I answered.

"Yes, we have been, and I am an unfair lover, but so are you. I worship your presence, your smiling, your bitching," he laughed. "You are my eternity and, truly, I do wonder if there is a following behind all this mess, and if you will be there." He stopped, took a long nip of his drink and added, "In my business, they teach us not to ask for existence before death." "I wonder the same thing about the hereafter: Will I have my children? Who is boss up there?" I whispered.

We laughed.

"Baby, you are the damn boss down here," he declared.

He reached over and drew me close. "I love you so *God damn* much," he whispered, while kissing me over my closed eyes.

"No, you are the boss, my darling," I replied,

"It's your work that is the boss."

"I wished sometimes I had lived and worked under more normal conditions, but as one says, I have been riding this fast train too long to turn back. In fact, it cannot turn back. Toy, several times, when things, shall I say, go wrong in my work, or I do not like anything I am doing that day, I think it over and then I hate myself. But truthfully, I am fine, and I am devoted to my work and my people. As one says, sometimes it isn't fair. I have asked many times what this stuff down here is all about. I had planned ever since I met you to fill your heart with love and to be where you were. What happened? Was it my fault?"

"It is all right. "We just do as the cylinder turns on us," I stated.

He nodded and said, "Yes."

He smiled and looked at me and said, "I will check on the girls for you and then let's go to heaven."

I would hear him getting water for Lola and fixing a bottle for Ellie. He would just talk to Ellie about how he wished he could hold her more. He would slip back into bed with me, singing his songs. He loved my babies, and I loved him for loving them, and helping me so much.

And then we went to paradise. It was so beautiful, *this affection and passion we had for each other*. Why didn't we save some of it?

Some nights I would ask him questions about his work, and he would change the subject, except when he was drinking more than usual--which was not very often. He told me truly little about his work. It was dangerous for me to know, and it might have been dangerous to be seeing him. Yes, I may have known more than I should have.

If we were sipping grapes and in the mood to talk, he would say "Gorgeous lady of a hopeful heaven, do you know I'm a wicked man?"

"No, you are not wicked." I would try to express my feelings. You work for our freedom."

"Thank you," he answered. Then, there was a long silence. I did not know what he was thinking, but I had a good idea.

When he felt confident, or safe, and in the dark, he would whisper and hold me close. "I do things I cannot tell anyone about. I work to stop people who should not control this globe. The good guys sent me. They pay me well and I do what they advise me to do repeatedly. After a while it is like going to the market— I gather the necessities and put them in the basket. I have been trained to see no evil, and therefore, do no evil. I like that book you have been writing. Make it up the way you want it to be, not like it really is. Maybe I am not acceptable in this society anymore. But then I say my dear Toy, maybe the best is yet to come. Yes, we might have a perfect future a second time around."

"My d*arling you are* astonishing, you are a good man. You do what must be done to save us from the wicked ones in this old world. I do not want a second future with you. I want this one. I love you now-tonight."

He would nod, but I would see the faraway look in his eyes, as if he were not quite there and he was somewhere all alone. I was silent for a few moments and then I faintly heard the rain. I had forgotten it rained a lot in the Bay Area. The sound was cozy and gave me a satisfied mind. I thought, yes on this good Earth, it will all be done our way. I said a prayer but not aloud. We kissed and went to bed.

While the girls and I were there, every time he left, I was afraid he would not come back. When he did leave, he would stay about two days and come home late during the wee hours--quiet, tired, and depressed at times. I did not ask questions.

Carlos was like no other—I say this over and over from the deepest core of my heart. Who would choose a life with him? Who in this world could understand his life and his work, no one?

Sometimes we would cook together, he liked to cook, and he would always sing. One of his favorites was, *"Are you truthful when you say, 'I love you" Are you just making believe?"* Then I would ask him, "Are you sincere when you say, 'I love you'?"

He would then frown and retort, "Yes, how could you dare ask me again, when I go to hell and back to be with you for just a while? Do not worry about me, I am fine. Trust me, I will see you beneath the rainbow in this spirit of desire. If I am not there, I will be on the right side of the winter stars as they guide my way to you."

It was too good and too great to be true. It was all there and all so real, but can you stay in heaven forever? I wondered again is heaven a place to rest and ride upon the clouds or do you have to stand in line and wait forever more? Life. Amen.

I will always wonder where he was going when he went out on a job and what he was doing when he left us for many hours, but I was not supposed to know. He slept with a gun under his pillow. I had to understand.

He loved to take walks with me and the girls. Even in the cool fall evenings, it was so pleasant and romantic. The girls were so darling and happy. Lola was really enjoying him, but little Ellie wanted him to hold her all the time. He was so happy near them, and he hugged them often, and told me they were so gorgeous and perfect like their mom.

His property was wonderful; it was deep in the heart of the wine area, a few miles north of the Golden Gate Bridge. We visited the city often. To me, I have two places on this Earth that are grand and wonderful: in the streets of Rome and the streets of San Francisco. *"I left my heart, in San Francisco..."* I would not let myself think of staying. He was so happy to have us there with him, but he knew keeping us forever might not happen. Late in the evening, sometimes we would have his sister come over and babysit the girls; she just lived down the road from him. We would go out to one of his chosen restaurants. The Lexington, which I think is still there today, was just wonderful. We talked about my misunderstanding some words and he said he had noticed it when I ordered dinner but told me that I did a great job defending myself and progressing on with the conversation, even not hearing well. He said, "When someone is beautiful and smart like you, it will all work out some way. So do not worry about hearing it all."

But I did worry, and I did not like to cover up hearing problems.

Some nights we would go to the wharf in San Francisco and sit in the little shrimp place he loved and drink and talk for hours. He would try to relax, but even then, he would watch people with a curious eye. Was he slowly turning stone like his directors wanted him to do?

Late one evening, we called his sister, and she came over and watched my girls. He took me to this magnificent dinner place which was kind of hanging on the side of a mountain. The view of the city lights was breathtaking; the moon shining so brilliantly over the ocean waves as they struck the shoreline and moved quickly away—it was a stunning sight. But it scared me, some, it was a bit like my life right now. It was not mine only to look at. We stood for a few moments. He was letting me marvel at this paradise, as he always called

THE PATH TO WALKERS BLUFF

things he adored. He told me he might even like *paradise* or *heaven*. I loved it when Carlos was watching me, smiling, and holding my hand incredibly tight. He kissed me on the cheek. I took a deep breath and let the air hold my life as I observed the most beautiful views I had ever seen. He told me it was a secret place and not everyone could get in there. I asked him why he waited to bring me here. He said because he knew you might be going home soon, and he had kept it 'til last. I did not want to hear the part about going home.

The owner of this beautiful place was from Italy and was a close friend of his. We were taken to a small private dining room with this same perfect view of the ocean. He ordered his favorite Italian dinner for us. When we finished dinner, we stood at the window, looking at the gorgeous ocean. He kissed me gently on the cheek and asked me if I was happy. He told me he loved me more than his life. I told him I loved him, and yes, there was no place on this Earth I would rather be than right here with him. I asked him why he had stared and watched me so closely tonight. He said, "No different, but maybe because I like to see you so happy and I did have this feeling, once again, of seeing this pretty little girl, smoking and drinking beer behind that church in Texas."

"I know sometimes I see you there, too," I said. Then he took my hands in his and said, "Memories, we must use them to make it in this old, wicked world."

We were silent and were just looking at each other for a while. Then he said, "There is no place on Earth that I had rather be than holding you, I wish forever. He waited and looked away, then said, "but you know, and I know it's never going to remain like this. I hate me sometimes, but baby rooster, I chose this life, and I must live it. And you are always asking me to tell you about an enchanting time in my work." He started talking about a Senator he knew.

"Toy, this respectable Senator I knew was an amazing guy, but he had extensive problems, he was fighting drug lords here and overseas. For years, these bad guys had hounded him because he had helped put some of these guys away years ago when he was practicing law in Washington DC. They had films of a visit he had with a dictator in Cuba. They had put sensors on him, viewing him at home, at work, and even caught him with his mistress, yes, but a nice one." He chuckled. "The reason I can tell you this is because there is no evidence anywhere that it ever really happened. Like so many other things in my profession, they are touched in the discard file. Once I was sitting on the dangerous edge of a cliff for him, trying to help him stop the many problems hanging over him, we finally had to ask the government to allow me to help him more."

I asked, "What happened? Did they kill him?"

"No darling. As I said it never happened––but the truth was, if it did happen, it was wrapped and placed in an enclosed storage area and burned with the files covering many lies."

"Did the drug lords get him?" I asked.

The waiter knocked and came in with our after-dinner drinks that were sent by the owner. It was new to me, using strawberries and vanilla with tequila. Indeed, it was good. I liked everything about this romantic place and felt I could do this forevermore. Let there be light, upon my unusual and wonderful feelings.

When the waiter left, Carlos resumed his story.

"One day, these ruthless guys stormed into his office— I mean passed armed guards and the secretary and slapped these pictures on his desk. The Senator laughed, while looking at the pictures for a few seconds, then he gently placed them back down on his desk and said, "Gee thanks. I wondered when you were coming with these. We have watched you take so many of them and we have an album of pictures of you guys living day to day under your nasty life full of lies every day. We know of that mess south of the border you all had been on lately to get loads. We have the amount of the drugs and pictures of you carrying this stuff in and out of Mexico."

"I did nothing about this." the Senator said, "but it is under my pillow of thoughts."

Then one of the guys started screaming and said, it was a set-up. One started to get rough and pushed him back and asked to see the photos. The Senator told him to shut the hell up and back away. First, he said, "If it is not true, you have no problems, no worries, right?" They stood quite still, and one said "Copies?" and I told them, "Yes, seven copies, and if anything, ever happened to me or my family, you will have a nice view from seven different places, even in hell." Then the angry Senator said, "Now get your unlawful bodies out of my sight, I don't want to ever see your faces again, and I'm too busy to study these pictures." The wicked group left quickly with their tails hanging down between their nasty legs. They knew they had no options. They would never bother the Senator again. Moral to the tale: even if you do not trust, you still must obey. He looked at me and asked, "Well?"

"Oh, I like it. Did the Senator really have pictures of these guys?" I asked.

Carlos laughed in that old deep tone.

"No one ever knew. Let us go home darling." And he started singing, '*did you save the last dance for me, do you love me today and will you love me tomorrow. . . then he said baby you send me. . .* '

I had deeply enjoyed these few weeks and I thought, *once upon a time, when this Prince kissed the Princess, did the kiss awaken her—?*

We had stayed with him three and a half weeks, and it was all covered in happiness and amusement, but I knew the whole time I had to go back down to my Earth. He finally told me he had an assignment and had to go away for a good while.

When we left the apartment, Carlos took us to a private airport and when we arrived, the pilot came down and helped us onto the plane. Yes, it belonged to the U.S. I left with a heavy aching heart, but in some ways I needed to go home. Soon I looked down as we flew over the Golden Gate Bridge and I thought of the song, *"I left my heart in San Francisco."* In several hours, we were at Midland/ Odessa airport. The girls slept most of the way. I knew our life together was going over the lost hill,' Carlos said 1 will carry this time with you and those darling girls forever. I love you so much, but I must go on with my weird and wonderful life. He kissed all of us and he had a tear, as I did. He told me several times he was getting too attached to these darling little girls and they loved him too. He said, "It was like a beautiful picnic, but the rains had come in and you had had to go for cover." He added, "I could have lived with you and the girls here forever."

Cody picked us up at the airport. She was so glad to see all of us. She said the little party dolls had grown. She hugged and kissed Lola. Lola was happy to see her, and she told her that Carlos was going to buy the Golden Gate Bridge for her mother because she did not want to leave it down there. Carlos had talked with Cody; she liked him very much.

It was always surprising how he had all these people around him: the pilot, drivers, guards, they were always there and were devoted to him and very polite to me. Some of them stared at me with curious eyes. I knew he needed them, and they were very loyal to him. They whispered things many times that I could not hear. I will always wonder what they said and what he said back to them. I will never know.

Cody stayed with the girls, while I drove him back to the airport. When we arrived, we exited to a special area that belonged to the government. I was not going to the gate, but he took my hand and nodded for me to go with him. He handed the keys to the valet.

"Yes, please come," he said, smiling. "Toy, you must listen, soon I will be out of sight and in reserve for a long period of time."

"What are you going to do, Carlos?" I asked with a soft quiver in my voice. "Why now?"

"It is part of the game I play in my job. I perform the way I am told, and I always as your Bible says, 'until death do us part.' He trembled softly. "My darling all of this will be for many peoples' protection, as well as mine, but for this reason, our life can never be together and you are too young to disappear in the shades of my covered worlds," he hesitated, "I do not know for how long. I put many miles into myself, and I have lived with great purpose and intention. I have done so much in this short time. I am not sure how long it will take, and I won't know until it is over."

He studied me, and my tears began to fall. He rubbed my arms, then pulled me near and kissed me gently on the forehead and then my burning hot lips.

"Toy, I chose this profession, and I put a lot of weight on my back; it is getting heavier. My granddad told me we must control two things to make our life work: the load we carry and how long we can stand to carry it. I try to remember that every year on my birthday. I know it is time for me to drop part of this load. It is painful to do since it is the prettiest part of my existence," he said.

We both stood still.

"I know and yet is not fair," I said. "You knew all this time we were there; I was falling deeper into your tender trap." I covered my face with both hands, bent my head down, and cried.

"I praise your feelings for me, my darling, but nothing currently has been fair. I know it must be this way, for now. but I must leave," he whispered. "I promise you. I did not know this assignment was coming this soon when you came home with me. I thought it would be--much later, it just came too soon."

He took my hands away from my face. "Listen to me, beloved, we cannot have tears today. We need to stay strong and stand firm, this is part of our life of the 'once upon a time'."

He closed his eyes and firmly kissed my lips. It was a kiss that would last eternally.

He whispered to me, "Please, love me forever." He always carried a briefcase with him. He let the strong embrace go and opened the case, and placed a cream-colored envelope scribbled with red ink in my hand. He told me to open it later and then he walked toward his gate but turned and walked back to me. He lifted his fingers to my cheeks and said, "I will always love you. This is not how I had planned it, but it is how it is. Take care of those perfect little girls. I am falling in love with them."

Then he left. He was always leaving. In silence, I stopped my tears. Tears would not help. I was once again alone.

Like a ghost, he drifted in and out, but like a hero, he seemed too always to be there. We both knew it was a strange relationship. He would say our love should go down in history since we were much smarter than Romeo and Juliet. He said we knew there was no need to die for something this good, and the versions of life were here, all tied up with red ribbons in our hearts. I went back to my sentiment that all of this is only a dream.

His plane was rolling toward the takeoff area. In my mind, I could hear these old songs playing that he loved to chant: *"Baby you send me, baby you guide me, honest you do."* Love makes the heartbeat and the soul endure. *"Baby you need me—"* Was it only a song?

It was getting dark. I could see many silver planes sparkling in the last illumination from the setting sun. The plane Carlos was on was unlike the others. It was unglazed, light gray, and free of any markings other than a number that was, b709li US Government, a 747: larger in size, but more so in meaning. I watched with compassion, holding my hand over my rapidly beating heart, as it slowly rolled from the gate. I waved to the man in the curved window. He threw a kiss. I had earned it. I threw one back to him. *God bless, America; you must need this man--but you do not love him like I do.* The plane was in the heavens and now out of sight.

I had a tag on my coat that allowed me to be near the plane gateway, but the guard motioned for me to leave. I nodded *yes*, and turned slowly away from the bright, flashing lights of the runway. No one gives a damn about what happens to these people. I do I love these men who have devote their lives to us. Their journey was far away from our thoughts, which is why one's soul did not ever know what was really going on. I thought of the people who protested the government or were always *bitching*. The foolish wacky people should have a day in the line of his duties and a turn to go to hell.

I walked back toward the covered area and made my way toward the glass doors, which opened into a long hallway. I pushed the large glass door open and stepped back into the entrance of my, now life. I had a long walk to the main area. People passed me with fast-moving steps, and the sounds of the living rumbled around me. I could see happy and sad people. One man with a big shoulder bag flung over him, who had a *New York Times* in one hand and a coffee cup in the other, walked faster than the rest.   He almost knocked everybody down on the escalator trying to force a spot for himself. I wanted to say, "Slow down, fellow, it will be there when you're gone." *When we are gone, are we really gone?*

I walked quickly toward the area where we left my car. I held the package close to my heart. I would open it later. *Dear heart,* I thought, *promise or not, I need to look at what was inside this package.*

I changed my mind about leaving right now and found a little food bar, ordered a coffee, and sat down. It was quiet since there were few people around this area. I wanted to open the envelope, I fell in the box and took it out. It had a ring in it that he had given me years ago. How did he get this back? Suddenly, I remembered he was hiding it, some place at my house when he came for me and the girls. Damn, he was quick and clever—he found it. He had had the opal removed and remounted it with a beautiful, single marquise diamond into the pink, green, and gold setting. He had given this ring to me a thousand years ago. Inside was a note, sealed in another envelope. Written on top, in deep red felt pen, were the words, "Please do not open until tomorrow. PROMISE" It was written in big letters.

"But" I mumbled to myself, "I have to open all of this." I must open it or die, so I did open it.

The first line: "How dare you––I told you it was for tomorrow, tomorrow!"

He wrote:

It is all right, baby I know you.

Dear Toy Rooster,

This is the last of the passing rain. The burning sun is too near. I believe there will always be a rainbow under this crowed sky for us to rest under. Hand in hand, we found the pot of gold so long ago. I will have to take part of mine back for now, but I promise to bring it back to you someday.

Our time together was the greatest thing a person could share. It healed us, covered our paths, and yet it dashed through our lives, then it went away. It is like a section of life that ends, but we are not ready to have an ending, resting our memories of the ones we left behind. Do not let our dreams disappear.

To my dear sweetheart, I will forever remember these words, but most of all how you said those words: "This is the first day of the rest of our life to love and obey."

Once you told me that, I told you I would always have faith. I will send several poems and quotes. I do not know the names of the authors and was unable to find their names.

"Let me live in a house beside the road where the races of men go by…"

"With you, with me, until one dies, down in my heart I live for you. You will never live there alone."

"Theo, the flowers are made sweeter by the sunshine and dew and this old world is made brighter by the lives of folks like you."

I remember how I loved that rhyme, and I said that I had hoped these folks were somewhat like you and me. I said, "Who else could be in the same fairytale with a stranger that is your lover?"

I still have the same copy you gave to me of this text you wrote:

"The patriot who fights the last battle may never have tangled with the truth of winning. He has won the wars, and never admits that a sinner may have claimed all victories. Now, he has called his enemy's friend. Perhaps his heart remained unafraid if the earth was not won." But is there comfort in the truth of winning, if he did not win love, will he know if he lost all in the last breath of life?

Possibly he left a grand example of courage with the strong and powerful way he had lived. Yet did he know there is no end to winning? And he will lose himself in the darkness of eternity as soon as this Earth is over for him.

Darling, please do not cry. I cannot be back to you before the last teardrop falls.

You once whispered to me that you no longer felt the kisses I gave. They were only mine; it was no longer me you kissed. Like a falcon or a hawk, you said my soul has flown away. But love is innate, my darling you cannot see but with our last kiss you left me with satisfied mind that one can carry in their heart always.

All my love is yours forever and ever, see you in your heaven.

Carlos

I put the letter back in the folder. I needed to get up and get to my car. I was out of my senseless mind. I got up and started walking, but first I put the ring on my finger and held it out to the glowing light. This was more than a gift; it was an apology and a note of thanks for love and memories. He knew I treasured this ring. For me, diamonds were better than a best friend, they were enthusiastic material, dipped in a cup of thankfulness.

Instantly, my memories kind of stumbled back, way back to the white stone church where all this started, and all along the way through our time together, our own Milky Way. I thought of how *quickly time slips away*. There would be no tears, not even tomorrow. I would hold them here in my heart forever, and they shall wait until I perish.

Finally, I was back to the parking area, and I handed the Valet my ticket. I felt unusual and stood straight like an unfinished marble statue. No one would know the cold stone feeling I had in my heart at that moment. I rubbed my hands together; they were cold as ice. Stop! I told myself, there will always be another day and another time even if it is not tomorrow, with Carlos. I knew someday he would return, he always had. The attendant tapped me on the shoulder to bring me out of my daze. I thanked him and gave him a nice tip. He was very handsome. So, you see, there are still nice folks out there. I felt a moment of support as I slid into my Jag. This car was so beautiful. I needed something to take this trouble off my mind, so I would drive this nice midnight leather-filled car and let the other feelings slip off in misery lane. I started to drive on, but there was a delay in front of me: someone with a problem who did not know how to move forward so that others could. I was still unyielding, and I started to back up to get over to the other lane, but it was crowded with people walking around me. I did not see the good-looking Black man walking behind my car as I slowly moved into reverse. He tapped the car to let me know he was there. I hit my brakes, my heart beating fast. He nodded. I mouthed to him, "I'm sorry." He looked back at me. I had seen him in the airport before and we had made eye contact then. For just a moment, we both had questions. He walked toward the window of my car, moved his head to one side, yet decided to walk slowly away. I wanted to say, "Wait, are you Willie?" This is the reason we make it in this wicked old world: *hope.* My radio was on when I cranked the engine. I turned the volume up and Patsy Cline was singing, *"Making believe, just making believe..."*

I drove around for a while; I was not ready to face this depraved crumbling of defeat in my stressed-out mind. How long was this hurt to last? Only God might know, will my soul allow forgiveness and overrule my misery. Yes, as I have often said, it is not the end of my world, only the end of this lost part of a vanishing world. All right let me rest, I will go to the Sands Club and have a drink. It was a great private club and I felt safe there, alone. I walked up to the bar and ordered a beer. I never drank beer. I took my beer over to a table in a lonely hearts' corner and sat quietly down to listen to the *lonely love story music.* Why is so much music so lonely? Some guy asked me if I wanted company. I told him I already had company. He left me alone. Now I knew how people felt when they said, *'there is no place on Earth for you when you are alone.' In some periods of our lives, maybe the drama of our entrance will be perceived, and the joy of knowing the truth of the everlasting promise of paradise will be found deeply in the darkness of eternity. The glow and the beauty of our strange existence will be found in the end. Or will it be like an empty seashell where the pearl has been removed? Is living only a dream?*

Chapter 10

Why cry for yesterday

With Carlos gone, I did not lose everything. I still had my perfect little girls, and when I finally got them in bed that night, I stopped, took a deep breath, and had a glass of wine. Because I did not want to mix anything, and it was easy, but I really wanted a strong drink of tequila. Later, I could still deeply feel his presence. I missed his body by mine. I needed him, just his touch gave me a secure and spirited feeling. I missed the sound of his steps coming near me. I missed him saying, "I need and must have you in my arms tonight. I missed the smell of his perfect body." I closed my eyes, and I could feel his hand touch my face, but when I opened my eyes, his smiling brown eyes were gone. I was lost again—but I was lost from the first time I fell in love with him. Tonight, I could have only the memories of how the delightful fascination we had for each other allowed these wonderful times together. Silently, a part of me had been left behind, and in many ways, I was alone without him. I had to understand this was not all his fault, yet he had chosen this life of secrets living without mercy.

Troubler le repos ou Mon ame était mise, in my French, meaning how the soul feels when mistreated. Again, this too will pass.

Later at my job I saw this remarkable guy that I had meet at my sister's Christmas party. He was very handsome, built perfectly, and was a football coach at Odessa High School, where my sister worked as the assistant to the principal. Ben Reynolds was the guy most ladies would fall for at first sight. He came to the bank to see his loan officer. When he started to leave the bank, he saw me and walked over to my desk, and asked if I could go up to the lounge and have coffee. I told him I would love it too, and we had a great visit. He said he heard that I got a divorce. I told him yes, and I was incredibly happy, accepting my new life. He told me he had been offered a new contract as head football coach and would stay in Odessa for three more years. He asked me for a date. I knew he was engaged, so I did not accept. Anyway, I had decided I did not care to date and was happy going out alone or with my two new friends, Sarah Kennedy, and Marcie Long. They worked at the bank with me, and we had fun together. They saved me, they both had divorces and needed a fun friend. I was happily busy with my sweet little girls, and I was living one day at a time, and yes, deep in my heart I missed Carlos so much. Only once had I heard from him, he sent me a message on my phone

'I missed you so much, all my love to you remains. Please feel these hugs and kisses I sent today, All my love, Carlos.' But I could not tell where it was from, nor answer. Like so much of his life it was top-secret and private.

At the bank, I was always dressed, as one says, to kill, and I was learning to live by the man-made rules of banking. It was surprising how our lives were created under the customs of culture. Even our method or beliefs, our thoughts and even our opinions were molded and shaped by what had been the prevailing ways of thinking and achievements. So, at times I began to feel like a robot, but guess that was all right. I did like my position. If I did not go out in the evening, because of the need to be at home with my girls, I worked on house plans and hoping to start building soon. My dad had promised to help me.

My little girls were my main ovation. I loved them so much. When I got home from the bank at three, I cleaned the house and did chores. The girls and I had a lot of fun. Lola was four and Ellie was one. Every evening at six, I made dinner, then we all bathed. Most nights I put them to bed at eight and when they were asleep, I dressed to go out. I had a wonderful neighbor, Helena, who adored my girls, loved to come over and babysit. She had no children and her husband worked nights. She was one of the best things that had ever happened to me. This allowed me freedom, I trusted her, she told me she would guard my babies with her life, and this gave me time to enjoy my life.

The oil fields of West Texas were a planet of its own. Life here was like an endless celebration, again, there was no place on this Earth like it. There will never be a place to compare the oil fields in west Texas. however, we all knew someday it would be over. At this time, I had the whole agreement of life within my grasp and maybe I did not know that I should keep it: as in no lovers, no husbands, and no problems.

However, things changed a bit, a few weeks later. Ben Reynolds came by the bank again, and he asked me out again, and this time I accepted. He was wonderful to be with. We were together every moment that was allowed from work and responsibility. Ben was busy before and after games, but, in the evening, when the coaching was done, he was with me and the girls. He was a winner and, whoa, our physical affair was wonderful. One night he kept smiling and finally he asked me if this great sexual role came with the same deal if we were married. I said with a chuckle, "It's a done deal, my dear, and comes with the whole contract."

"Then I will accept and take it, forever," he said.

We were talking about getting married in late spring. Times were grand and uncomplicated, without very many hints of the past. But yes, they were still up there. I did care for Ben in many ways, but I wondered if I was making this love happen to cover my lost heart.

I knew deep down that I was still slightly shaken from my previous marriage with Sonny, and I still missed Carlos, too much, and I hated myself for loving him. I heard from him several times, but it was short and sweet, he said he would be free in two years. I thought what does he want me to do, wait like always? I chose not to wait.

One-night Ben and I were at the Sands, and they were playing my song, '*Crazy because I am still in love with you.*' "Have a drink I silently whispered, forget the past." I had another drink, but I could not forget the past. Say it Carlos.

I had retained my maiden name after my divorce: I was back to Tory Walker. I talked to Sonny often because we had two darling little girls, so I did have something great from that marriage. I hated to admit that sometimes when I saw him, I missed him. On my birthday Sonny brought me a beautiful bouquet of yellow roses to the bank and we went up to the lounge for coffee and talked a while. When he started to leave, he kissed me on the cheek and told me I looked beautiful. I told him he looked great. He was dressed very impressively and as he walked away, I asked myself if memories from our life together were creating tangles in this web, I was still in. It help cool my dislike for him and there are two sides to every story.

For m*any years after that, I got a yellow rose on my birthday from a secret admirer. I knew who sent them, but I hid the card.*

Later, one cold winter night, as the beautiful white snowflakes fell on our wonderful city, Ben and I were leaving a great party with coaching friends, and I was driving. Ben kissed me on the cheek and said, "Stop the car. I want to kiss and talk." I pulled over and stopped.

"Tory, things are good with us, and we are happy. Let us get serious. I am so in love with you. Let us not wait to get married."

"I love you, too. We will talk later, you are righteous now from all the golden liquids," I said with a chuckle.

"Let's go by the Sands our private club for parting," said Ben. It was mine and Bens' favorite place and a lot of the coaches and teachers spent time together there for nightcaps.

That night, we had so much fun. We danced and danced. When the song "Misty" by Johnny Mathis was playing, he said, "This is about me and you. I want to hear it over and over--with you," We started making plans to get married next month and he took me to Kentucky to meet his parents. We went to the Kentucky Derby; I loved that race. His family was wonderful, and we had a great time. They were beautiful people and happy he was getting married. He said he had found a beautiful home for us. I was happy now, but, deep down, things were still a bit complicated. I had a lonely feeling, but maybe it was from the life I had left with Sonny. Later, I had a conscientious talk with my dear friend Wanda, and she said, "You need to wake up. This is all good—" Wanda was still my best friend and I was so happy when they moved back here after they graduated from Sul Ross. She said, "Listen to me, we have both been around the mulberry bush and it is time to stop running. Ben is so great for you–– and the girls, and you do care for him." She was so right.

There were countless times of fun with Ben, and we had been together a year now. Football season was over, we packed his new white Thunderbird one weekend and the four of us checked out this wide, wild country. One thing that bothered me: Ben was very jealous, and I had to watch my step. He did not like for someone else to watch me too closely.

About a week later, we stopped at the Sands with friends after a great dinner party at Gerald Shelton's home. Ben had so many wonderful friends. Gerald was a football fan all the way and was a number one fan of Ben's. He was a very wealthy oil man. He gave grand parties at his beautiful mansion and the parties were amazing. He reminded me of one of Sonny's oil friends. Gerald showed me different areas of the house. He knew I was devoted to building. I loved the design of the house, and it was just beautiful inside and out. Ben thought he was a little too nice to me and he always gave a few too many hugs and cheek kisses. But I liked him and the attention. Anyway, that night at the Sands, along came trouble messing around in my perfect new pleasures. We started to leave the club when Ben saw a guy he wanted to speak with. I told him it was fine, and he excused himself, but I was tired and wanted to go home. Most of our group had already left. I moved over to the bar and was talking to Dorothy Rivera, owner of the club. She was kind of the necromancer of the town. Everyone came to her about their problems, and she always listened. She excused herself to go over and speak to this very handsome guy who had walked in from the cold winter night and ordered a drink. He turned toward me and smiled and stared a second. Normal flirt, I thought, no not really. This look and stare almost knocked me out of my socks. He was so attractive: the blue eyes, the sun darkened skin, and the whole sweet deal. I did not speak to him, but we nodded at each other and then he said a few things to Dorothy as he walked slowly away.

He turned back to look at me. I had this strange feeling. I had never had that feeling, ever—well, not in a long, long time, yes, once, long ago. I wanted to say, "Wait don't go, don't walk away." *Let me meet you.* This guy knew Ben and walked over and started talking to the other coaches.

Dorothy was watching me and said, pointing at Ben, "Hold it, lady, you've got the whole thing right over there."

"What?" I asked.

"I was watching you and Damon, and your eyes met all too well. He is engaged and he is getting married soon to Anna someone. Yes, he is beautiful, but walk away," Dorothy said. "He has a strange feeling about women. Let it go."

"I will," I said and laughed. "What was his name?" She smiled and said, "Damon Granger, and he asked me your name."

That night, on the way home, Ben asked me, "What is the matter?" I lied and said, "Nothing." I thought of Damon. I could not help but wonder. I told myself to walk away. *You must not think like this— what are you doing? You are to be married soon. Let this*

*man go, walk away. What happened in just seconds is
not always the truth?*

However, I did not walk away––and he did not
either.

A few days later Damon came to the bank. We
went up for coffee and had a great visit. He said, "When
I saw you at the Sands the other night, I asked Dorothy
who you were. Then I found out where you worked
from one of the other coaches. So, that was where I
banked, and today I needed to come in and check my
account. Here you were in the statement window," he
chuckled. He asked me out and I said that I could not
and heard that he should not. He started to walk away.
And I said, "Wait. Maybe I can accept a lunch date this
weekend." I was wrong and unfair about this, but Ben
was out of town and damn I could not help myself.
Bitch, I said, to myself. Go away, what is the matter
with you?

The lunch date came soon, and we felt happy
just talking, and we had only known each other for a
few hours when we both knew there was an
extraordinary connection that neither of us could
refuse. I sat for a moment looking at him and thinking

THE PATH TO WALKERS BLUFF   CHARLOTTE WHALEY

I must go. I said, "Damon, I intend to marry Ben, very soon." He told me he understood, and he was planning to marry Anna Swell this summer. But we stared at each other while we were talking about marrying someone else. Nonetheless, the admiration between me and Ben reduced in comparison to this guy, why I did not know. Damon followed me home after lunch; he wanted to see my girls. When we walked into the house, I introduced him to Helena, my babysitter. He told me later he felt uncomfortable with her staring at him, and he should have quickly gone home. I told him it was fine; she was very shy and used to seeing only Ben. My little Ellie jumped into Damon's lap; she instantly loved him, and she did not want him to leave. Lola was not sure. We talked for hours. It just happened; we did not want to leave each other. But finally, he said he needed to go, and I walked to the door with him. He hugged me then started to kiss me; then he stepped back, said he was sorry. I told him it was all right, we kissed anyway, and that was it. A week later I talked with Ben and told him I needed some time to think things over and to let me go for a while. He did not understand but said he would give me some time to think things over.

Two weeks later, I left Ben and Damon left Anna. It was not easy leaving Ben. We had some wonderful times together; he was a wonderful person, and he was great with my girls. Lola cried when he said his goodbye. Ellie did not care much. She told Ben we had a new friend and that we were moving over to his new house. I almost died, but Ben had heard the news already. He knew and he had some doubts if our life would have worked, he said bluntly, Damon. He was right. Ben had many lady friends waiting for him, so he was not going to be alone. He said, "I really think someday you will wake up and find Damon is not right for you, but for now I only wish the best for you and these perfect little girls. And if you change your mind, I might still be here." I still did not wonder if I was doing the right thing. Damon was my rock, from the moment I laid my head on his pillow, and the moment he said will you marry me, I was there, and happy. I did not miss Carlos so much for the first time in many years.

However, many people, even my mom told me it was a mistake. Damon and I did not feel like it was any kind of mistake. He was different. He owned his own life; he was thirty years old and as one says had 'been there and done that.' However, so had I. We were so in love—all the way—and felt there was a sincere romance at the beginning of this grand affair. Damon said, "You know, we fell in love at first sight and maybe we were compelled to be together. We were fascinated with each other from that moment on. I live that memory; it will last always."

When he asked me to marry him, he held both my hands and then let go and stepped back in great control and said, "I will care for you in loving kindness and in all mercy, forever. Amen."

Damon and I were married three months after we met. We were a perfect match. We had the same ideas and values. We had both had had great affairs before, but both agreed this was different. *This was love, forever love, found, and bound.*

But, yes, we had many problems with the past and on and on and we talked about moving out of harm's way, for a while.

Damon accepted a high school football-coaching job in the Cupertino, California area. He felt a year or so away from our previous lives would ease some of the pressure. I was not happy there, but our blessing was our son, Raymond, who was born in San Jose. I just could not get well after the birth; I was having many medical problems. I was in the hospital three times in two months. We needed help with the girls and the baby, so we decided at the end of the school year we would return to Odessa Texas. Damon understood my many problems and I needed help with three children, and he promised we would be happy wherever we lived. He said he had everything he had ever dreamed of––his wife, his darling girls, and his little boy—he loved us with all his heart.

Nevertheless, Cupertino was a great place—it was new and striving in every direction and we liked being only a few miles from San Francisco. We spent our first anniversary at this magnificent restaurant that the great baseball player Joe DiMaggio owned. We had wonderful times and great memories. I left my heart, yes, in San Francisco. I owned the Golden Gate Bridge, Lola told everyone that Carlos got it for me. She asked about him several times and I told her he had to move for away. Yes, I did think of him; no, I should not.

We left many new friends, it was a great place for the young people to live, but it was time to go home. When we returned to Texas, we moved to San Angelo and Damon was principal of a junior high school. Our new home that dad helped me build was just down the street from a beautiful little creek, Sulfa Draw, and my children played there almost every day. Their school was across the street from our house. They had a great childhood there. We lived there for seven wonderful years, but we decided it was time to try something new. We both thought I could do better in building in another area. I had tried building some in San Angelo, but it was not working out. There were too many builders there for the size of the community. Damon took the principal position at a high school in Denton, Texas. The area was booming, so to speak. He was very compassionate in his work and did an extraordinary part in helping get the school back in good order. They had many problems, but from the day he arrived he started getting things under control.

Gradually I stared building. I had drawn many house plans and I had found two wooded lots in a great neighborhood. I took the plans to a loan officer in one of the banks in Denton and he told me I needed to talk with the president of the bank, W.C. Hughes. When I walked into his office, he greeted me well. He met me at the door, extending his hand. I quickly shook it. He spoke kindly and asked me to be seated. He took my blueprints and studied them for a few moments before asking me who drew them. I told him that I drew them and had many more. He smiled and picked them up again and took them over to a table and spread them out. I followed him. He said he liked them and asked me questions about plumbing and framing. We talked for about an hour. I told him that I had learned the building world when my dad was building homes in Odessa. He helped me understand what I wanted and needed to do, to be a great home builder. Dad called the subs they.

When I was telling the banker about the subs, I said you learn who they' are and how to make it happen. My banker asked me who *they* were. I told him confidently that *they* are those who do not know or care what you are talking about or but trust you and obey you. You learn from them, and they learn from you. Amused, he told me this was so true. He asked me for take-off from the building and how much I needed to build this house. I showed him the take-off was and the cost of building. He read it over and called his assistant who fixed the papers, and they deposited the money into my account that day. He told me later two things: he liked my house plans, and it was the first time anyone had ever given him the real meaning of *'they.'* It helped me get the loan. That day when I left the bank, the loan officer nodded, and I smiled. I found out later that the loan officer did not think he could give me a loan, so he sent me to the boss man. Again, you must know what *'they'* want, and do it and *'they'* will do the same. From then on it was easy, perhaps not actually easy, but wonderful to have a banker that believed in me. It was a winning game now, with a great new future. In many ways, it was hard to become a women builder, they were rare and barely respected. Although, later, I was awarded a special certificate form the Architectural group for unlimited work. I was also the first woman to be elected president of a HAB Builders Association Division. HAB was one of the greatest parts of a builder's life.

Chapter 11

When the music stops;

Let us go down the path of an architect home designer's amassing path: Denton, Texas. "There are more men with a dollar than men with many dollars"—Abe said this, and it was so true. Nonetheless, I still enjoyed building huge, beautiful houses. Of course, they did not sell as fast as the small homes because, again, there are less men with big dollars and more men with fewer dollars.

The joy of watching these homes come into view from the wicked, rocky ground into a beautiful real piece of magnificent work of art was always worth any problems. No one could believe the excitement and adventure I have known from building—this went much deeper than even I could visualize. It was like the Angel of Mercy had kissed my heart. With this love was how I sealed the serious degrees of my talent in my real life. I could see the house the way it would look before it was built. Perhaps that might have helped me to want to build on and on. "You have a gift," my banker had said. Use it forever. I did.

My daughter once said my life was a "chocolate box," sweet and wonderful, but almost forbidden. However, it was signed, sealed, certified, and delivered to me on a silver platter. Every day was wonderful in my building. Except, there were always some oversights—there was a missing plan that had fallen deep down into a small hollow chamber of my hearing spirit. There, it was drawn in scarlet letters: *the sounds of living had begun to stop, and my music had stopped.* I could not and would not let my lenders know this.

I was going deaf. But my heart was made of stone, and my houses like me were made of stones and I planted them with pleasures and drank my wine every day as I looked at them. I folded my happy arms around them and gave my soul back to the Lord. Amen.

I went from one doctor after another, trying to get help. Hearing aids would not help me. I needed what they called a precarious surgery: a Cochlear implant. I watched a film of the implant surgery, and it scared the hell out of me. They cut into the skull and place a cochlear to the brain area and implanted a big piece of metal to hold the aid on ...long story... Now, I was such a coward about the implant.

When I did not like to think of the hearing and other problems, I would call my new friend Delores Dean, who was a lawyer, and she was in my office building that I had gutted and rebuilt. After hours we would go for drinks. She was so amazing, smart, and great to visit with. Her husband, Sam, who would sometimes join us, built race cars, so I had things to talk about with him. I loved racing so much. Bad, I think some of the teachers and people at Damon's' school whispered about me being, as they said, wild but amazing. But I lived my life the way I wanted to. Damon did too, but he would not go to bars, but only the private clubs because of his school kids. We could go to dinner and have a drink, but he was careful. He wanted to set a good example and he did.

Sometimes, I would go shopping and simply adorn myself with lavish gifts, promising that there would always be a bright rose garden at the end of every path taken. I was an admirer of expensive and beautiful things. I knew that an abundance of valuables was something that did not need the gift of sound to be recognized. If I tumbled too low, I would just start another project. Yes, I had too many things going: developments, subdivisions and too many strategies.

But I was doing great, I had very few problems with my subs, but like life, there are always some. They were usually people who wanted attention and I called them *sub-zeros*. I had a great P.I. guy, Big Dog Dublin, and if I needed him on the job, I would call him, and he would take care of

217

things. Yes, he watched over my problem people. But, I had very few bad problems.

Many times, when the work was done for the day, I would rest my mind on a pillow of faith and try to be thankful for the blessings that I did have. Sometimes, at night when I was alone in the darkness, I would place my hands cross my breasts and my cold feet dangling out from under the fine, white, down cover. I would close my eyes and listen for the sounds. The sound of the cars on the road were becoming fain. I could not even hear the winds, but I saw shadows on the walls from the trees fighting each other for the cool caress of the breeze. I sometimes cried out, "Give me back my damn noise! It is mine! I need it to live. I wanted to hear the cars passing beside my road. Sometimes, I rose quietly, late in the night and stepped out into my beautiful courtyard. I would sniff the scent of my roses. It was all mine out there--none of this requiring sound. When the moon was shining upon my troubled head, I would stand alone with the soundless blowing winds and speak to the twisting dusts as it seemed to hit me harder on my face, swirling dust into my open eyes. Here, I stood lonely, knowing there was a strong barrier between the sweet silent thrill and the sounds of life.

Nevertheless, the next day I would be back at work. Currently, now I was drafting plans to build condominiums in Ruidoso, New Mexico. I knew I was working too many hours a day and needed more rest and support from somewhere. I was leaving out my reason for living. I had to remember that the good life was not poured into one's mind. Also, I could not drink the sound. Yes, my hearing did make me gloomy. I needed to rest; and to admit the sound of truth did not show the depth of a tired mind.

■■■

Chapter 12

The good times

Anatole Hotel. Dallas, TX. The ballroom was packed with homebuilders who had come from all over the United States for the National Association of Home Builders convention.

Bryan Jones tapped the microphone and gripped the sides of the podium. He looked out over the well-attired congregation and spoke: "Ladies and gentlemen, we are here to introduce the new officers for the National Association of Home Builders. Let me begin." There was a wave of polite applause.

"I will ask you to hold your applause until I have named all the elected officials. First, I will give their appointment designated by the members of the National Association of Home Builders Committee, followed by the name of the elected individual."

The disembodied voice boomed over the crowd: "Your new President Skip Bedford from the Dallas HAB; President Raymond Wallace President with the Plano

HAB; Mrs. Tory Walker President of Denton County HAB.

He held up his hand. "This lady is an original," he said with a proud smile on his face.

When he called my name, I was not sure if I was there. I stepped across the stage as the crowd erupted into loud applause. My heart was beating like crazy. I wondered if I looked appropriate. I had on an expensive green Chanel suit. My hair was fine; I had looked at myself in a mirror in the ladies' lounge and nodded. Wake up, I whispered to myself, I was back.   Bryan continued with the ceremony. I wondered what Phil and Bob were mumbling. The two Denton guys at one of the front tables had been the cause of most of the cheering.

My friend, Jana, was seated at their table with some associates of mine, and later in the evening she told me what they had said. I enjoyed every word.

"That's our girl," whispered Phil Turner, one of my bankers. I have three good bankers now and two finance companies. It takes lots of money to make money. I still had my love Mr. W.C.; he was a great friend.

"She's got that prominent look," said Bob Starkest, who was a good friend and my lawyer for five years. "Wonder what Damon, *the good husband*, is thinking of all this. He was seated near the front with a group of Denton people and our family." They nodded at him, and he smiled back and bowed.

"He looked great too" said Phil. Jana said they were so cool. She had told them she would not tell what they had said, and they all laughed.

As I walked on stage, I slowed and looked out over the crowd and slightly bowed.

Bob clucked, "All that money she is making now shows all over the place. She has it baby, all the way. Phil, I admire women who can get it done."

"Yes," said Bob.

"Phil —how much is in her bank by now?" Bob pried.

"None of your damn business." Phil lowered his head to whisper, "I should not say, but I am happy and drinking," he said, "Many big M's from just me, and some more over at other banks."

"Phil, Jesus Christ, surely she can't manage that kind of money."

"She can, and she does. Her financial statement can oversee it, too. She has a new subdivision, office buildings, condominiums in New Mexico, a good chunk of Ruidoso Downs Racetrack, a country home, gas and oil wells, racehorses, and then some."

Bob leaned over and raised his eyebrows. "Has she *repaid* you?"

Phil laughed. "Hell no, not yet, and I do not look for it, either. She is cold as an ice clip, and she lives and breathes her building business, and her family, baby. Now, I am a handsome fella," he laughed. "I throw her every opportunity to come at me. She smiles and beats those long, black lashes, drawing me in with those big, strange green eyes. Then she takes my money, hugs me with her sweet handshake, and walks away." He laughed. And said, "Once upon our time."

An hour later, Bryan Hughes stood up with his champagne glass held high and said, "Ladies and gentlemen, celebrate."

I shall always remember those wonderful times with the HAB group. It was so much of my life for many years. The fun, and pleasures, will last eternally.

Three weeks after the gathering in Dallas: 5:45 PM at Dr. David Drake's office. "Tory, I have known you and Damon for a long time, and we have become the best of friends. This is hard to tell a friend."

I was seated in front of Dr. David Drake's desk. I had cold chills running down my spine. I knew what he was going to say. I had been living with this fear for many years.

I wanted to change the subject.

Damon smiled and said, "David, you and I are getting fat." He had said it unthinking, almost as a defense mechanism for me, because we did not want to hear what David was going to say.

He cocked an eyebrow at us and replied, "Yes, I know. I love sugar and spice, Tory just like you like hammers and nails. It is called addiction." He laughed, "But, I am only exaggerated with good food."

I grinned and declared, "To each his own. I am addicted to saw dust." We laughed but he sounded apologetic as he uttered these next words that would stick with me forever.

My chest tightened as he continued.

"You have a great deal of sound loss. The last tests were not good, but you have known this for many years. I would say you have less than thirty percent of your hearing. I know how hard you have fought, and I would call this a win. I know this is wicked news, but it could be a lot worse. It is not over until it is over. Time will find ways to beat this and there are some things you can do, like the *cochlear implant*."

"Yes, I know," I said, "I am so afraid of the surgery."

"It is not that bad," declared David.

I turned my head away and closed my eyes. "I'm scared."

"No, you're not," he said. "Not true. You should only be scared if you are giving up."

"David, yes, it is hard. I am very emotional. I want to run away, but which way can I run? There is a bad display here at the end of my wonderful, brilliant powers. It is raining hard and there is no rainbow, no shelters. Look, I run an extensive home building business, not to mention all the other things in which I am involved. These sounds I have, have worked for me so far. Living with no high pitch, nor low-pitched tones,

225

I have had to invent and use my imagination to make my deaf life work. It has taken a lot of work and time, and yet there have been so many rewards. Now you are telling me I will not even have that, soon?" I panicked. "Now you say I have thirty percent?"

Damon had gotten a call and left the room. He came back in and said he was sorry, but he had to go back to the school. I told him fine, and he left.

David frowned. "It is less than thirty percent now. Tory, it is not the end of your accomplishments. You have Damon to help you. What if he left the education business and joined you?"

"No," I shook my head. "We have too many problems working together."

"I know it is hard to collaborate with your spouse, but you could keep the building business. It is a call you must make," he observed. "Maybe just give it a try."

"No, David, he is *a school people*, not businesspeople. Building is way too different from his job. I was born in this profession. I am mean as hell. You must be able to weather the storms that pass you every day in building and management. He is too cool. It would not work. He is too easy."

"That is true. Are you *that* mean?" he asked "Yes, you would never believe what I must do to keep it all going, or what I say to my subs if they disobey. I must carry a big stick and I do," I answered. In exasperation, I began to ramble.

"David, my business is starting to decline. I own Forrest Ridge Two. I have seventy-two lots left out there, and the builders are afraid to build homes in that price range because of the interest rates and the lack of market in Denton. I have five houses and they are going to cost me in the long run." I inhaled and continued, "It is just bad timing, but when I started out it was great. I have twelve duplexes and they are not rented. I have a partnership in my office building, and he is wicked. He has lied and cheated me out of a lot of money. The roof fell in on the third floor after he said it had a new roof, so, obviously, it did not. We are in the middle of a lawsuit now. Yes, I sued him, and it was a mistake. I cannot hear what they are saying to fight them. I was on the stand, and I had to ask someone to come closer. I read lips, as you know, and people cannot believe I cannot hear them. You must hear the spoken word, or you are out of business. He is going to win because he has hired a group of Dallas lawyers. He is a monster."

"Yes, I have heard of your partner in the office building. He is after everyone. He is in a lawsuit with another guy I know," said David and he shook his head. "And it's hard for you to talk on the phone, to answer questions, and to manage the subs."

I frowned and my body kind of died.

"I own much land, racehorses, and a percentage of a racetrack in Ruidoso, New Mexico. Racing is way down. I cannot sell my part of the track or the horses because the oil business in West Texas is way down. They are not drilling much, and those people are the ones who were bringing in the money to the hills of Ruidoso. I own twelve condominiums there. They are not selling. It must get better, but it may be too late. David, I am sorry. You are not my head shrink. I should not have dropped all that on you," I apologized.

He shook his head. "It is all right; I am here for you. Go ahead and talk. It helps take stress off the mind."

"Thank you. I have known this for a long time. This year I have missed so many phone calls and made messes of answering questions. People stare at me in stores when I do not answer correctly. I cannot even order a damn hamburger without trouble! My subs are wondering how many times they need to ask me the same questions until I blow up. Sometimes we end up having to draw pictures, so I can understand. I have such good subs, they believe in me and me them, but it took years to get those people and a long time to weed out the bad ones. I am afraid to lose any of them now. I could not make it without my farmer. He has been with me for almost twenty years, but I cannot depend fully on him. It is my responsibility––mine."

We both sat in silence, for a while.

David cleared his throat. I could tell he thought I was about to cry.

I looked up at him and said, "I can't cover this up much longer."

"Do not, Tory. Stop trying to cover the problems up and just tell people. They will understand."

"No, they will not. People do not want to know your problems because they have their own problems.

It is like the bartender who must listen to your problems, he is damn glad they are yours. People stare and wonder what is wrong with me. It is not normal to not hear. Eighty-two percent of people in America can hear."

"But you've got a wonderful husband," he persisted. "When you built my house, I did not care for him at first, but then I understood he was on my side, and I liked him. He is a strange one, but he is devoted to you."

"He is an unusual fellow, but he is good, and I try to accept him as he is. He has fits sometimes, but it is all right. He does overlook my fits and my endless changes. Yes, I am always changing things. To me most things need to be changed, even people." I laughed. "He often says, if it can't be changed, Tory will find a way to change it."

"Tory, I like that version—it is inspiring. Yes, if you do not like it, change it." He laughed. "And I have noticed Damon—the tan-faced, French-Irishman look in his keen, blue eyes—has a quick temper, but with cool coordination. I watched him at a party one night. He watched you some, but mostly every woman that passed." He laughed, "It's natural with us men, I know."

"True, very true," I said. I knew he was always watching all the ladies.

"You have got to start living today--," said David.

"David, I will forget what Scarlett O'Hara said: 'Tomorrow will be another day.' Tomorrow is dangerous for me; it is close to over. Yesterday was mine, but tomorrow may never come."

"I know," David said. "You have a way with words, Tory. Why don't you start writing again? You did very well with the first book you wrote."

"Thank you. I have thought of it—another book," I contended.

"Do one on your building," David suggested. "It would be quite original and quite unusual."

"Maybe," I said. "How long do I have?"

He looked at me with a great deal of sympathy and responded: "There is no way to know for sure. It is going fast now, though I am so sorry."

My thoughts wandered back over the good past. I thought, *perhaps it was unusual, maybe even beautiful.*

I must not allow myself to forget the past. I will start another lifespan.

I could still see the truth from his lips slip out slowly and it took a few moments for me to accept what I read and heard. Maybe I did not hear him correctly. Did he say soon?

I frowned and whispered, "What has happened to me; why on this bitter Earth did the devil choose me? What can I do to accept this mean, unfair thing?" I lowered my head and continued, "It's shadowing the good times and taking me into the dark halls of hell."

Silence.

"Do I have possibly a year before?" I questioned hopefully.

My eyes were pacing the room.

"My dear, I don't know for sure," David answered.

I did not cry anymore. I had stopped that many years ago when I decided to kick tears in the ass—they are only a waste of water. I always felt that tears should stay in there and hide, out of sight.

THE PATH TO WALKERS BLUFF

"I will bluff my way through this, David. I have for years. Promise me you will not tell a soul, not even Damon."

He swore, "I won't tell a soul."

We shared a bit of silence. Then his private phone rang. He looked at it and motioned that he needed to answer this call. He walked over to the window and began to talk.

I sighed and waited, I felt like I had been there too long already. I looked at my watch; it was 6:15 and I drifted--drifted. I hated my thoughts. There were too many questions left unanswered. I did not know where to hide. I felt alone, again, despite having Damon and my dear kids. The truth was —yes, they already knew this was happening to me. Deaf, I am damn fucking deaf.

David put his hand over the phone and looked at me apologetically.

I nodded, and whispered," I need to go and thanks."

He smiled and nodded his head yes. "Say hello to Damon for me." I smiled and nodded back okay.

The result of my reflections on deafness would be a feeling of being caught in melodies of a song long ago. A song that told a lie because there was an ending of the words, only the music would stay on. The next day, after I had visited with Dr. Drake, I decided to write the story of a lady builder who rose to the height of her greatest desires––and later, morally tarnished by misfortune, dropped back down to the imaginary base of the modest Earth.

Let me explain why I cared to stay in a building and live inquisitively. First, because of my disagreement with the truth of what someone could accomplish. Second, the desire to touch the things that I was not supposed to touch. Third, I loved to go near the dangerous thing.

My version of this book would not be a perfect work of art, or equally composed, nor would it surpass the high blazing moon of sensation. I had lived with more joy and honor than anyone could ask. I intended to be living proof that anyone could fulfill his or her wildest dreams and still live inside their own imaginations. If one can contribute to a comprehensive degree of will, they will find ultimate success. However, it was not meant for us to live like the good Earth stories are told. Throughout our lives, there are many misfortunes, but this is when we show our own strength.

But in *this story, I will not tell all my secrets or all the truth. Go with me as I walk near the silent waters; the winds are calm. My bare feet touch the cold damp grass. Here, I shall lie down by the still waters and wait for the rising sun. I will weep no more, the Angel of Mercy is near, I am not alone.*

Chapter 13

Until death we do part

I lost my beloved sister, Cody, to lung cancer. She was only sixty when she was called away. It had only been six months since the time she found out she was in stage four. This put me in another stage of silence. I had lost my parents years before. After her surgery, Damon and I sat with her and her husband, waiting for the doctor to come in. When he came in his head was slightly bowed and he said that the left lung was virtually missing, the other was in danger. She held my hand and said, "Sister, we will beat this." "Of course," I said, "we will." Again, I held back my tears. Thank God, her doctor was a friend of Damon's, and he took us to his private office, and sadly he told us she had only a few months, but they did not know how she had lasted this long. She must have been in a lot of pain and could not breathe without oxygen. She had covered it extremely well and never complained. I thought, this is the final period of her living on this Earth. I hated to think of-- her not living here ever again. I asked myself, where do we go after we are here? Why did I keep asking this? Right to the end I had prayed for a miracle that she might beat it, but down deep I knew it would not happen. It was too late by the time it was discovered. My sister and I had become close over the years and awfully close in the last few months of her life. I felt deeply lonely when I thought she was the last member of my immediate family. I fell into another objectionable mood, hit with a seemingly irrevocable wave of despair. I just wanted my sister back. Why, why, did He take her?

At her funeral, I walked to her white, rose-covered coffin, but I could not look at her. I pretended we were little girls holding hands, going to the Easter Sunday Sunrise Service at the Church of Christ. I would always have an imprint of this in my mind, as we walked along our old, unpaved road in thin green dresses with pink satin trim. It was cool, at that time, and the dresses did not protect us from the spring winds. Our mom made the dresses and mine was too long, and I had grass stains on my white socks—I hoped they were not noticeable. I could see Brother Bob Christian, my beloved Sunday school teacher and a very pure person and friend, who was there to meet us at the door. *Heaven must wait, but it did not: she was gone.*

Finally, I had to look at her. I felt her hand, and it was cold as ice. I bent down and whispered to her that I loved her and that someday we would have a delightful Sunday school party together, once again. I promised her and she knew where it would be.

I looked into the crowd as we started to leave the church and there at the back was Carlos. He looked at me for a moment, then he closed his eyes and shook his head. I almost died again; I did not know he was coming. He called me later and told me he was so sorry.

His sister had told him Cody had passed away, and he had flown in and was only there for two hours. He talked with Rosie for a second and then he left. I love that he was there, but it was strange in so many ways. It was like once again this man's strength controlled me, but, baby, it was cold outside, and it was still all right. Yes, as I always say, he gave me that sweet silent thrill in just a moment, and it was what it took to help fill this empty space in my aching heart and it gave me a reason to rest in peace. I wished that I could have hugged him and investigated his amazing, wonderful eyes. They would have said, 'what is this all about?' In just a few more moments it would be the end of this story, again, which would be of no part to him. It was surprising and astonishing, but I had to accept that I had no control of them.

Cody was cremated and I picked up her ashes with Damon and we took her to Odessa to scatter them over my parent's graves. I barely cried that day as I took her home. As the overreaching West Texas winds blew against my tired face. I told her I was going to leave her here, but I would take all our sentimental thoughts that were now embedded deeply within my cold, cold heart.

I mourned her for so many days. Many years later, I continue to feel Cody's presence. I could still see her sitting in that window box reading. I could see her on her beautiful wedding day. Once was not enough.

Death is a mystifying word we cannot understand. It is part of our existence, but we have got to stay until our time is taken. I kind of kneel to her *death*—the eternal sound of the word lives silently and lonely within my soul, forever. We like to think we will be the last man standing.

The next day we left Odessa and my dear friend, Rosie Hinson, came home with me and stayed a week. We had been friends for many years. We met in grade school in Winters, Texas. She was the kind of friend it takes to make it in this wicked old world. Damon went with us to Dallas; we hit the nightclubs and danced the night away. We knocked the hell out of misery for a while. She loved Damon too and she told me that I had the whole damn world. I knew but days I wondered.

After she left, I was very lonely. Damon had work to do, and he had to get back to school. My children and grandkids visited me sometimes, but they all had things to do, and I needed much more than they should have to give. My spirit grew darker and fell into the shadows of doubt. I would never see a smile on her face, nor hear her laughter. It was over—the sweet silent thrills always end this way. She was gone forever. Why, dear God did you take my best friend? Why did I not see how important she was to me sooner? Is this supposed to be? Forgive me, my dear God, but I do not understand. I would think of the things Cody, and I had done together. Occasionally, we would slip off to this Mexican bar, on the Southside of Odessa for a drink or two. We would puff a bit of the weed, not much. I was afraid of it, which was at that time very wrong to be doing. They also had what they called shop-made tequila, and it was strong as blazing hell. We would drink, laugh, talk, and dance with the guys. It was a great way to rest the mind and there was none other like the wonderful fun in Odessa, Texas.

On the way home, we would open the windows to let the air out and try to get straightened up before we walked into our houses. She would say now, Tory, do not get close to Damon, he can smell that weed on you. I would tell her, "Heavens, dear sister, you can see it in the eyes, in the walk."

We would giggle and go home smiling.

There were many beautiful memories. At times, I whispered to her, "Where in the blue heavens are you? Do you want me to stay here or come on, I heard her say you stay there?" I had a dream one night and thought she said you do not know what you are missing. Amen

Chapter 14

My work never stopped on the drawings of my blueprints and getting ready to build. It was my salvation to cover or run from things that had gone wrong recently in this so-called wonderful life. I would work on them late into the night, laboring over the sketches—changing, adding, and switching them around. Of course, technology has changed every part of homebuilding—it is so much easier now to draw plans on the computer.   After I finished the plans, I would arrange them in order that the slabs would be poured and figure the date they should be finished. I used a takeoff sheet to work up the cost, and my cost estimates were unusually close to the initial launch. The profit can never be figured to the penny, too many things can change the amounts, but I was close to the expected figure at the closing of the sale. My banker wanted me to bring the whole package in for him to see. He would smile and say let's get going. When we poured a foundation, I always loved to be there and watch as the big concrete truck backed slowly up to the prepared forms and over the rough ins as we called it and plumbing and electric. When they dropped the first load of the beautiful gray stuff onto the ground, a soft white light of dust seemed to float all the way into the towering sky. It was a pleasure to see every drop of wet concrete emptied. I took beer out many times when they were finished with the last smoothing on the slab. I loved to be there and visit. Many times, I lived and watched the last nails hammered into my beautiful studs. When the house was finished, it was like a gift I had created and made into a real and beautiful object.

Countless times, when all the workmen had left the job and the setting sun spread across my unfinished houses, I liked to check things with no one near.

Sometimes when the raw concrete had almost dried, I would gently step upon it around the edge. I felt remarkably powerful, smiling in every careful step I took. I dared anyone else to do this.

But like all the good things in life, there were always some problems in every house: an electric line lost in the rough, when they were pouring the concrete, and at times we had to kill all the lines underground and move all the lines to the outside walls. The thing I hated most was when a plumbing line was lost in the slab. We had to drill a deep trench, find it, and mess up the beautiful foundation, but we always found them and reinforced and covered the hole. I found that anything could be fixed, one way or the other. I was so devoted to building; I was addicted to concrete and sawdust.

I put a lot of hard work into this addiction, but I got it back tenfold. I enjoyed every single moment and part of those great times.

Chapter 15

The simple things

When I got tired of everything I would race. Yes, car racing. I knew a few guys and we would go out to this country road and drag race. Or we had an area near the railroad tracks, long story. My Mercedes would be slightly hot, sometimes, but it did not hurt it. My dad had taught me how much a car could stand in drag hits. The pumping and grinding on the gas were what hurts them the most. You must hit it hard and go. This car was so powerful and had a bliss-proof engine. I preferred moving too fast, zooming along on dusty old roads. I liked to go fast at whatever I did but driving fast amazed the hell out of me—it still does.

One day I was stopped for speeding on a deserted country road right after we had been racing. I had just cut it down to eighty-nine. I did not hear the sirens. Where did he come from? I finally saw him in the mirror and stopped. I could certainly hear the policeman shouting as he took my driver's license.

"Did you hear my siren?" he asked.

"No, sir. I did not," I said.

Our eyes met. He turned his head back to his squad car and in a low mumble he said, "Tory Walker, you built my house." I nodded in recognition, though I had no idea who he was. I have built over a hundred houses. He continued, "Now, I shouldn't do this, but I'm going to let this go and give you a warning slip." He scribbled the ticket and said hold it down. He tipped his hat. I took the warning ticket from him and smiled. He was still sitting in his car as I drove away. My mind drifted way out––damn––I knew I needed to wake up. I was getting too old to drive like this. That last race was just ridiculous. Do not cry for me tomorrow I whispered, 'you are a devoted bluffing bitch.' What saved me were all three of my beautiful perfect kids. They helped me and obeyed.

That day I had delivered a contract to purchase a portion of commercial land on the freeway out near the Oklahoma border. It was a perfect location, easy on and off. My plan was to build a huge, high-quality hotel with an enclosed atrium. It was a great plan. I knew this could be my ticket to live in luxury and get out of work forever. This was the security I needed to retire. Then came an unexpected call from my banker, W.C. Hughes.

He said that the Board had not reached an agreement on my hotel plan, and I needed to meet with him in his office as soon as possible. I did not like his tone, not to mention his assistant usually made the appointments. I left my office at once. The bank was just two blocks from my office building. My heartbeat so fast I felt like it might be a warning.

When I arrived at Hughes's office, he had a disappointing air about him. He said he had met with the Board, and it did not go well.

I was not totally surprised. I had been restless at the beginning of the meeting with the Board. When I spoke with them, I had trouble understanding their questions. I think I had given incorrect answers— my hearing was absolutely getting worse.

"Tory, I am sorry to tell you that the Board did not approve your loan."

I sat very still.

"Tory, when you met with the Board last week, had you been taking something or were you ill?" he asked.

"No, sir, I am losing my hearing, and I was beyond anxious from not being able to understand their questions."

He bent his head down and asked me, "Why didn't you tell the Board members at the beginning that you might have difficulty understanding their questions?" He got up from his desk chair and walked over and sat down beside me. "On two occasions, I had wondered why you were having trouble with simple questions. You always answered me so quickly. So, the truth is you do reasonably well one on one. Is this right?"

"Yes, I read lips, and minds, if I can perceive part of the question or conversation, I can put it together, but my hearing sounds are vanishing."

"That is interesting. I knew you had great intelligence from the moment I met you. I do not think the hearing had much to do with the Board's decision not to allow this loan. I hope you will understand they had to walk away with too many complications on their mind. You are close to being over- extended."

I sat very unresolved in distressed shock. My mind understood what he said, but my emotion did not.

"I am sorry you did not approve the loan. I think it will be a very—" I stopped and waited a second struggling to get my concerned thoughts together. "I have always made my payments, lived up to obligations, and kept my promises to this bank."

"I know that Tory, but five million is a lot of money. Things are slow, even in banking. Hotel business is a dangerous business to start without any experience. You do not know if it would be successful out there. The property is good, but I am not sure about the hotel. However, I do believe you may be ahead of the times on this, and it is a daring project."

He stood up and walked over to the window. He turned back around toward me and said, "I'm sorry, but I cannot help you this time." But I will return the blueprints. I thought they were just flawless, but this is not.

For the first time, I could not think of a reason to challenge or oppose his decision. Maybe something else was wrong, but deep down I knew it was a risky project.

He continued: "Tory, the Board was divided, and I could not change them. I know you need the money fast, so my best advice is to find financing somewhere else," he said with a sigh. "I am deeply sorry, Tory. I was on the fence, already, and we were also concerned about your many other projects."

We were silent for a moment. A few drops of rain hit the glass on the large window and we both looked at them, and I thought, *why did those raindrops fall today?*

He turned back toward me, and said, "I recall when I made your first loan. It was fascinating and a pleasure the way you approached me, with your great designs and your talent, and the overwhelming research you had done on all the issues of designing, cost, and building. I thought not one builder had brought me their own drawings or plans or covered every inch of their building methods as you did. Also, you are an extremely attractive lady. I always wondered why you wanted to work so hard. I learned you valued your life as a builder, and when you walked out of my office the first time, I assumed it would be a reliable loan, but I had a bit of wonder if there would be another. There are always concerns when you make your first loan to someone," he said, "Yes, I wanted to say to this lady."

He sat back down in his big brown leather chair and moved a few things around on his desk, picking up a black pen and tapping it a few times. I remember he always used black ink to sign things.

"I wish only the best for you, my dear friend," he declared, dropping his head a bit. He looked much older. I had heard he was having some health problems.

"Thank you for the compliments. I needed them today. I will be all right." I spoke, but almost had a tear. But I thought, no, there is always another place and time to get money.

"You are so welcome. Let me know if I can help you." he rose and walked with me to the door and gave me a warm handshake. He had never hugged me.

We had developed a great friendship through the years, and I was sincerely grateful to him. He was one of the most well thought of people in this entire city. I knew he considered this loan for me, but the Board had the last voice.

I walked toward the door of the bank, with my head slightly down, for the first time. I could see the carpet was dark green with spots of ugly orange and brown. I had never looked down on leaving this office. I was offended, but not angry or defeated. As I moved on into the lobby, I floundered slowly past people in the bank. They looked at me questioningly. Maybe it was only out of concern, or it could be my imagination. I had on a beautiful, new, purple suit. I do not like purple clothes anymore. I mumbled to myself and thought, *I will toss this ugly suit.* I only like violet-colored flowers, not clothes. There was a slight mist dropping a dab of rain as I headed toward my office building, and I walked slowly to let myself be mad and wet.

It was not the end of living––or building. Conceivably, there were still some ways of survival out there. But that afternoon as I reached my beautiful new green Jag, I just kind of dropped into it. I loved this new car--it helped my moods some, but I still felt lost or trapped. For a few moments I just sat there. I could not move. Finally, I said, "You crashed, but you did not burn." I started going over things in my head that I needed to do the rest of the evening. I still believed in this hotel project very strongly. I must not allow total defeat. I will be out early tomorrow to shop for money. Why did I feel a tad strange this time? Because, down deep, I knew there could be trouble on cloud nine.

I knew money was getting hard to find and interest rates way too high and sales were low. Some of my horses had been on the market too long. However, I believed that the economy would improve soon. Even so, I needed money fast. As one says, it takes money to make money, and to be able to stay afloat. I went to one of my wicked friend's office and had a shot of tequila and a smoke. I haven't smoked much in years, but today I needed to knock something down in hell to even the tide. I laughed at myself, this was not fair but so, what is?

I could not find a bank or loan company that wanted to make a loan for the hotel. I had too many things going on-- too many irons in the fire; apartments, subdivisions, condominiums, office buildings--and they were right. I was over-extended, but that is how you make big bucks. I sold the commercial land near Oklahoma and lost money on the resale. I spent too much time running around and hunting money--and way too many hours on the blueprints table for the hotel. I had a great Architect partner on the hotel deal, and we were both regretful of our defeat. But that is part of this game, but always before I had found money. I remember. . . now I needed to walk away.

Two years later, two vast hotels were built on that land, but they were franchises. I wanted to go to the bank and say, "I told you so," but why waste my time or theirs'? Mr. Hughes had retired, and I heard he was in bad health. I missed talking with him. I still had some business accounts at that bank. His son had taken his position, but I was never able to collaborate well with him, although he was a great guy. I knew times were bad and the bank did collapse later.

Before my depraved bank deal failed, Fox and Joyner, one of the largest homebuilders in the country, offered me a position as a troubleshooter of sorts––to find issues in the blueprint drawing and building process. I went on a tour of the Parade of Homes in Dallas for the Home Builders Association. I was seated on the bus beside Dalvin Fox, one of the owners of the company. We toured many homes together. As we walked through the houses, we talked about problems that we could see, and he told me that he was amazed at how quickly I could detect a problem and come back with a solution. Dalvin and I conversed for a lengthy time, and that evening, with the group of builders, we all attended a dinner meeting at the Adolphus Hotel. After the meeting, he told me he was getting out of the home building business and that the company could use someone like me. He asked if I would be interested in collaborating with them. I told him I respected the offer, but I was set on doing things my way and did not want to answer to anyone else. I liked my independence. However, years later, I wondered if I should have taken the offer. But deep down I was now spending more time with my beloved kids and adorable husband. He was busy but he would laugh and say if you've got the money I've got the time. Yes, we spent a lot of money traveling the world over. And the truth was, we saved each other.

Chapter 16

The elegant side

I walked barefoot from the entry hall to the living room skipping and hopping into the den. I tried to jump over the big white shag rug in front of the fireplace. I missed and landed right on my butt on the hard cold floor. *I never liked that rug and would change it. I smiled to myself, remembering that Damon, laughed and said, 'if something did not, please you, you would change it, as we have heard many times, you would try to change the stripes on a tiger.' I told him, yes let me find my scalpel.*

I may live to betray the elegant side of my troubled mind, which at this point fooled many with charming grace.

Damon and I were fighting—a bit. *That man!* He was grouchy, but so was I. We were struggling too much with life problems. What was happening? A lot of it was because of me, but not all. One night Damon packed some stuff, said he was going to Houston on business and a rest from everything, but just for the weekend. I did not know who lived in Houston, but I guess someone did. Why do people who love each other make such hateful attacks against each other and try to get even?

That night I felt free, but alone. To whom would I run? Did I need to run? So, to whom would the bell toll if I punched it?

My beautiful kids saved me again. We played cards and laughed and talked about the good times. They all knew Damon had run away for a while. But we all knew he would come back.

Early, the next morning the sun came out shining bright, like a contribution from above. I looked up and I asked the question I had asked *Him*, so many times: *How far is it from here to heaven? He would say to me it is just a short walk from the rain, yes it may be, I hope so. Amen*

I drove through my subdivision and turned on my radio to listen to the song "Wild." It fit my mood. I flipped to a CD: "Misty." No, I could not hear it well, I cannot hear high pitch sounds, anymore, but I turned it way the hell up. I played it again and then changed it to "Any Place on Earth." I called Carlos and he quickly answered his cell phone. I was not supposed to call him on this line unless it was an extreme emergency.

"I knew it was you, Toy, few people call me on this line, but you and them."

He could laugh like no one else. Most people laugh, and you forget it, but Carlos' laugh stayed on your mind. I knew he was smiling just by how he said *hello*, and it sounded as if he was in a full bloom of happiness. That is how he had smiled the first time I showed him my French lilac bush in Winters, Texas, and where I would lay under it for hours when I was a mean, little kid. Whoa, that was many years ago.

His strong voice asked me, "What is going on, dear Toy? I know there is trouble in paradise, or you would not have called me."

"Not much going on, but, yes, a little trouble. What about you?" I replied.

"You were out when I called you a few days ago. Someone answered the phone. He said you were out on the jobs."

I was confused. I thought of Damon. He must have answered. That was what made him go to Houston and meet his girlfriend. Yes, I know he may have one.

"Liar," he said and laughed.

"Sorry I missed you," I relented. "Will that do?"

"Guess it has to," he said, "I have been out of the country lately and, oh yes, I got the divorce. End of that section," he chuckled. "I will go to Mexico City Friday night and then back to Juarez early Saturday evening. Do you want to meet me?" I can have one of our planes pick you up and fly you to El Paso.

"Yes, I do," I replied, "I will see you in El Paso Saturday afternoon and let you know my travel time," I said.

"Good, I will email you and I might be late. So, if I am not there to meet you, go with Claudius, he will take you over to Juarez. I will be there about eight or so. I will not be too late. I must move off this line. See you. Shake 'it all off before you get here, babe. I am sure you have trouble, or you would not have called. Thanks. I need to see you." He laughed and started to hang up, and said, "This trip will save me and you, love me, if you can."

"I always shake 'em off," I said and snickered. "I cannot love you," I laughed. He chuckled, and said, "Bitch and see you then." He was gone.

What in heavens did other people do without a friend? Maybe they had one and just kept it in the closet.

Carlos Francisco could be dangerous to be nearby. He was under his own spell, under his own control. Who was he? A devout Sunday school boy without faith. He was never really mine, not all the way, but from the moment I met him until now, and maybe for as long as we would live, I would care for him. Ours was a convalescing kind of admiration. The thought of him and it heated my tongue.

I got on the plane to El Paso; it was owned by the US government. Was I legal, yes, I am on a mission. Start the story, I laughed. I was nervous finally when we landed, Claudius was there and took me over to Juarez and to the hotel. He was a nice guy. He didn't talk much so I told him "Thanks" and he said, "My pleasure."

Carlos was late and seemed to have problems. I felt I might be one of them, but he kept telling me I was saving his life.

We had a great dinner and, yes, we went to our room. Wonderful night, end of telling the story. The next morning, he took me back to El Paso and helped me on the plane. He had several calls.

I said, "Carlos, you have problems?"

"Yes my dear sweet Toy but I have loved every moment of our time, please love me forever. He had to go, and he was getting on a different plane.

He told me to never let go of our memories and tonight, in his dreams, he would chase me around the mulberry bush. Call me someday, when you need me, and he is gone.

This was part of the collection of loving someone, you were not supposed to. It was like we passed a plate around to see who could get the most from the offering. He told me once to let things that are wrong go. Do not hang on to anything for too long. It will grow on your heart, and that isn't good. It is too hard to shake it off. Yes, we all have memories, let them be felt only at times. I remember Carlos chasing me all around the mulberry bush before I finally let him take my heart. And he had gotten down on his knees on my birthday and asked me to marry him, giving me a beautiful ring that he had worked for all summer for. I asked him where we would live, and he said we would live under the mulberry tree or maybe you could build us a house under the lilac bush.

Chapter 17

How to win, using self-confidence

Triumph is when we have won all our demands. Things obtained by hard work, using confidence, and physical and mental programming, formed by devotion that has been planned and arranged by cautiously going down the right path. We all love winning; it takes us to the magnificent pleasures of life. Even when one struggles, and falls under the game of thorns, we know we can still rise above again and again. We can hold the rewards of success in our left hand.

Today, I had to check with a guy named Will March. I built his home a few years back and he wanted to sell it but had some questions. In this area I had built several larger houses and, as I drove through the area, I saw Will Fairburn working in his yard. I had built a custom home for him. I stopped building custom homes after I had built his; it had been a nightmare to build. He had made too many changes. I did not like other peoples' changes, but in the end, he was incredibly happy. People did not know what a mess it was to keep making changes after the house was almost finished. It was hard to explain to them why it caused confusion and cost me and them. My banker was worried when I stopped building custom, but he soon accepted that I did best with spec housing. I liked to build them my way, under my terms. I could build two spec houses for the same time it took me to build one custom. Finally, I met Will, and he showed me throughout the house how he had decorated and furnished it. I thought it was perfect. He said he wanted my opinion because he knew I had built it and had sold many properties. I told him the house was impeccable. And it was a remarkable feeling to see something you had built to be so perfect and outstanding. He called me a few days later and said he sold it for a super profit.

When I got home that evening, I stopped under the portico and looked at the color of my new home. I moved from house to house too much. Anytime someone wanted my house more than I did, I sold it to them. But, darling, they paid damn well. Why? Money, Darling. If they had the money, they would get the house, and we would move to another house or one of our apartments. I had done this more times than I wanted to tell or remember. When someone asked me how many times we had moved, I would not tell them the truth because I was afraid others would call it *greedy and silly*. And it was.

This house I just built was extremely Mediterranean. Beautiful stucco painted a sheer, light creamy white/yellow. I had drawn this house plan long ago and finally built it. I liked it and it was one of my best. Everyone thought it looked like it belonged somewhere by the sea. I did care, though. I knew that it did not quite fit in with this same old cloudy neighborhood, but to me it helped the others and made a more beautiful setting among the simple designs. I sat for a few minutes looking at the nice grounds, the big fountain dropping sheets of clear water into a large circular bowl.

I made myself a 'tequila sunrise' and walked out back to look at the pretty enclosed pool. Sitting beside it was my perfect pup, Chippy, a glossy, white American Eskimo. He fit beautifully into this picture. When he saw me, he ran over and quickly licked my leg. Then, he went back to his mat in the shade. We had a pooch door, so he could go in and out of the house as he pleased. People spoil their dogs, but they are such a gift and are a great part of our lives. They can help relieve pressure and give us happiness without a price. I adored this one, he was mine.

No one was home. The kids all had things to do. Yes, I was back trying to live with Damon after he had a little deal with one of my used-to-be friends, but it's ok. It is called get even to match Steven. I felt better and I thought this time, somehow, we would make our life work better together and not drift apart. We needed each other. I was ridiculous not to admit how much I cared for him. Our feelings were like a traffic light: red, yellow, and green. Tonight, he was at meetings in Dallas and would not get home until late tonight. I looked over the mail and tossed it on my desk. I thought not tonight; I will rest my tired mind until tomorrow.

Lois, my beloved housekeeper, had left for the day. I hated to think of ever losing her. She helped raise my last child, my son, Ramon. She was my friend also.

I walked through the house in great admiration—it was perfectly beautiful. The walls were an exceptionally light yellow and the moldings on the ceilings were deep white. From the entry was a large living room windows and twelve-foot windows across the back. There were specially made French doors that had cost way too much, but that was what made a house so beautiful and, yes, one day I would sell. Again, I smiled at the sixteen-foot ceilings throughout the house and all interior doors were ten-foot. That is hard to find in any house, even the top of the line. Most of my furnishings were French. But I had a lot of Chinese pieces, too. I was very fond of Chinese culture, and I had brought back a lot from our trips to China. China was so special, in many ways, but it was changing and was over-crowded. But many cities are nowadays, and it will get worse.

My living room flowed softly into the large dining room, which had four large columns at the entrance area and a deep cone-shaped ceiling that held a huge chandelier in the center. I had moved this beautiful fixture from one house to another, determined to find a home to keep it in one day. I bought it in Venice, Italy. These fixtures are true treasures of Italy. Italy was my very favorite place on this Earth to visit. I hoped, someday, to spend more time there.

I thought this house was a *great way to live, but again, have I truly been living?* I alleged that sometimes lately I realized I had been working many hours and not enjoying my family enough. However, when I didn't work as hard, I felt like a hawk that had been caged and then later found out I was free but needed to fly away.

The grand kitchen had top-of-the-line, stainless steel appliances, granite counter tops, and fine birch cabinetry. I loathed cooking, so if I cooked, I liked a very appealing kitchen. My dear husband and daughter loved to cook; I would clean up. The kitchen extended into a large family room, with a huge white stone fireplace that started the entire north wall. The furnishings were beautiful, but still comfortable. The master bedroom had a beautiful view of the garden, with a special covered patio that served as a place for me to hide out. Today I took my food that Lois had left for me out there and had a mind rest. I had too many questions on my tired mind. I tried to pray. Did I truthfully believe? Once again, I wondered if I could take my secrets and sins up to heaven and sort them out.

One cannot leave them down here. Who in the hell would want them? We live on these paths on this strange Earth together, share all things, but baby, we walk out of here alone. But if we really look, we are a small weed on this Earth that will soon fade and blow away.

Chapter 18

Foundations of enthusiasm

I was driving through one of my subdivisions. I loved to own this stuff. It's hard to know how great things are for me, although my hearing is causing me to be a little troubled, but I keep making it happen. It was a good development, and I was proud of it. The truth was that houses and lots were not selling well, but I kept thinking it would get better. I was working twelve and fourteen hours a day to keep up. My husband saved our lives by helping with the kids and so many other things. Sometimes my kids would come to the job and watch me and the subs then we had helpful talks. They loved giving me their opinions.

Today, I was watching them pour one of the foundations, lately I had been too busy to stay during a pouring, I missed it. Now I only came back when they were smoothing the slab. This slab could have many problems, it was on split level. I hated split level, but the lot was like a damn mountain side, so I had to do a split level. Later when I checked on it, it was looking good and tomorrow we would start framing. My farmer was like my supervisor, helped me in so many ways. He often told me I worked too hard and that I was too demanding. I know some of my subs called me an over-worked magician, but most of them liked and respected my views. If it took profanity to get it done, I used it. Damon did not like for me to curse, but sometimes it was the only way to get a sub's attention. So, I cursed in my dad's French language. Damon heard me get after an electrician who had punched too many holes in the wall to find an outlet. I had given him a rather good French cursing, told him to straighten his ass and run while he still had two legs. He did not know I was behind him at that moment. He was cursing me, saying that god-damn-bitch should be home mopping. When I got in front of him, he looked a bit sheepish, and I told him how my mop flopped and how he needed to get the hell out of my house. I fired him on the spot. But there is more to that story. I had to file on him to keep from paying him workman's comp. That is just a part of the treatment I received for being a builder. Still, I loved my work, and did not mind the time and effort it took to make it product. But still some nights I would plead: *Dear Lord, do not ever take this away from me. Let me stay. Dear*

Lord, let it be-- but I knew my patience was growing weak and I was afraid. I had a light stroke the week before. When the doctor checked me, he said, "You need to slow down. He said when we did the EKG after so many hours, we cannot always tell if it was a mild stroke. But you must take better care of yourself. I did not.

Today had been dangerous, as we had poured my sixth foundation this week, which some consider too many for one lady boss.

As I walked around the wet slab, I could hear my devoted concrete man, Conner Buren, bellow, "Ray, pick up the slack! Damn it, this stuff is drying too fast."

It was blazing hot today. On a hot day, they had to work fast, or the concrete would dry to fast. They had to keep spraying water on it to keep it cool, and the crew had to work so hard and fast. I stood still watching them. They did not know I was behind them.

"Get your ass over here, Walt! Do you think you are at a birthday party here? Work faster, ladies." He liked to call them ladies when they slacked-off. Conner Buren was barking orders before he looked up quickly, and grumbled to his right-hand-man, Ray Collins.

"Damn, here comes Miss Tory. I do not need her to see this mess. She probably heard us."

He was the owner of a large concrete company in North Texas. He ran seven crews and worked for four builders, who all kept him just as busy.

They did not know I could barely hear them as I walked up. I had to park down the way because of the concrete trucks.

"She's going to eat my ass up," he lamented.

"You hope," said Ray. He mumbled something I missed.

I told him to cool down and that it would all work out. I did not stay long. I felt they could move better without my company. I loved to be here even for a few moments. It was heaven on this wicked Earth.

The next day, just as I cradled my phone and crawled out of my new Mercedes SL500, I looked back at it. It was glossy, black, and beautiful. The shine on this thing was as bright as a new Texas moon. I could always appreciate a beautiful ride while going through heaven. It was a reward I had given myself for my hard work.

At the job, Ray told me some of the guys said my car looked like what someone in the Mafia would drive, and they would say things like, "Look at that lady sway." Another worker, named J. W, asked him, "Why does she always come out here looking like a queen?" Ray told them, "It is all part of the deal, man, and it is working for her. And never wonder who she is or what she might belong to, but, yes, I have wondered, many times. There must be some strange ties."

No one answered him.

Tommy and Ray were black and my favorites of Conner's concrete crew.

Tommy was good-looking. He had handsome features, and he was built like a Greek God. *Do not be* senseless, I think, *we are all human, and can see.*

Conner told me that when he told them we were starting another foundation on Monday that they had a shit fit.

Tommy quickly encouraged them: "Saying we can do it because she will take care of us, let's do it her way."

Conner had also told me to be careful about Tommy. "They all think he is in love with you," he said. I had just nodded and moved on, talking about the weather.

Sometimes I worried about what my subs really thought of me when they stared or whispered. However, I would feel better about myself by thinking, *who is paying their damn bills? Who is making the money? I am, and I am devoted to what I do, and doing it under my system. I shall not let gossip bother me.*

"Boy, I like that car," Ray Collins said.

"Thanks," I replied.

I evaluated my new car a week ago and did a little bit of drag racing. I had gotten a hefty warning from a nice highway patrolman that I outran. I was afraid they would get me at my house if he had seen my plates, so I went up to the Police station to explain myself. I made up a big lie about going to see my dying grandmother and they bought it. I waltzed out of there without any trouble.

Later that night, when the kids were in bed, I jumped into the pool and went deep underwater. I felt the heaviness of the smooth liquid gracefully steeling its way to my brain. When I came up for air, I could hear Damon's car pull up in the driveway. I said aloud, "Go away." I did not want to see you or hear you say a word. Damon was yelling. I could not make out what he was saying, but he sounded strange, and it looked like he was walking in a bewildered fog and his voice was mean. The dog had gotten out and he had to chase him. He had been out tonight for his "poker night" and the boys all went out to the club for drinks, afterwards. Guess they drank the whole time they were playing cards too. Yes, he was drunk.

I was still in the water, floating around topless. I liked it that way, *ho, ho.* It made me happy to halfway--skinny-dip by myself. I felt like this magical influence roamed around my body, setting me free. The moon sparkled brightly upon the movement of the waves I made on the water; it was beautiful, and I was happy for a mere instant.

Then, Damon quickly opened the large French door, frowning, and snapped me back to reality. I climbed out of the pool and grabbed my towel. I could tell that he had caught word of my encounter at the police station. "So, yes, my dear assistant, I raced today," I said. I waited for a moment for his answer. I picked up my half-empty glass and shook it at him. "What the hell is wrong?" I asked.

I was drinking margaritas. I took a long drink and set my glass down and turned away from him. I could tell what he was thinking.

He stood straight, looking hard at me.

"I think I might jump back in," I said.

"Do," Damon replied. He was skilled at giving morality lessons. But he was a great Principal.

"If you are mad about my racing, I only got a warning ticket. So, do not cry for me, my sweet dear heart," I said coldly.

"Tory, will you just shut up."

"Alright, I will and what do you want?"

I could tell that he was mad, in more ways than one, not just my speeding, although it did not matter one way or the other.

The margaritas had made me bold, and life had made me happy. "Shut up and I will sit my pretty ass down," I said.

"I am in the school business; in case you have forgotten! I do not want things like that to get out to my faculty, and surely not to the students. Tory! Look at me. What about your own kids? What are you thinking when you do wild-ass crazy driving like an anguished fool? And a police officer chasing you?" he shouted.

"Nothing, Sweetheart. Thinking of nothing, but freedom," I answered.

"Freedom from what, Tory. Now, come on."

"I just like to have fun. It is on the top line of my study list, baby."

"Did you take *me* off your study list?" screamed Damon.

"Yeah, darling, and you are drunk, and you are in the school business," I laughed, "Yes I took you off my hope chest list, too, and now I will use all the good stuff while it is here." "Really," he said. He just kept staring.

"I felt like I was getting old. I wanted to use up some of this good stuff before it falls off," I said as I shook my butt around a bit. "I just want to be able to say I've been there and done that—twice and live happy ever after. Yes, hope in heaven."

"My darling wife, you're drunk, also, and you have already used your stuff up sevenfold," he laughed.

"Go away, Damon. You are just sorry I did not give it all to you," I frowned. I jumped back into the pool.

277

"Tory, get out of that damn pool and go to bed. You are too damn drunk, and you are going to drown."

"No, I will not. Look at my fingers. They are covered with fine trinkets that make me float––I made! I made! I made them, but who gives a sweet–– shit? Do you care?" I asked worriedly.

"No, honestly my dear, I don't give a damn, and you're as damn wild as the dissatisfied angry winds. You own the world." He shook his head.

The he smiled and said, "you don't know it and don't care."

"So, you would rather be poor and for me to knit you a shirt. Or maybe some fancy under shorts to show the girls." I shouted. "Go in the house you are messing up my night take my rings in for me."

"The lady who wears jewels within her heart needs none upon her fingers," he teased.

"Now what was that my darling man? However, I have no heart, so I need to put them. . . on my fingers and neck," I said and laughed.

"I don't want to be any part of this discussion," he said.

"You're not," I said. "You're not. It is I who is drunk. Right now, it looks fucking good up on my wicked soul," I laughed.

Damon watched me. "I do care what you do, Tory," he said.

"You never did care. You do not care about anything, do you? Right, Mr. Instructor? You do not care that I am losing my hearing. I am losing it all, Damon, as in suffering—defeated by my hearing." I grasped my ears and shook my head. "I am having it all taken away, but was it ever really mine?"

"You are a beautiful grown woman with everything. Why are you looking for more, in this preposterous world of yours? You can still hear rather well," he reminded me.

"Rather has no meaning and I do not think I am looking for a thing, dear heart. I found it years ago. Ha!"

"Really? Where is it, Tory?"

"What—who. What do you want? Do you ever say 'Thanks, lady? It has been a good time and you have done it all remarkably well?' Has it ever occurred to you that I have made us rich?"

"You'd think you get enough praise from your doctors, lawyers, and bankers," he snapped. "But you need to stop that damn racing."

"Why are you scolding me, Damon, about my driving or drinking? You have had so many damn tickets, and you drink all the time. It is kind of ridiculous for someone to tell someone else how to solve their problems. I treasure cars and racing. Yes, yes, I know that I should cool it and that I have too much going on, a lot going to hell too—"

"Your pockets are too full," he answered. "They are sure to split open, and it is all going to fall out one of these days. I am not going to give a damn when it does. I am tired of this kind of stuff: this fast lane, dancing in the great rat race."

I thought for a sober moment: Damon lives in another resolution under another promise from mine, yet he wanted to be admired, and he was. The ladies adored him, and he knew and loved it.

I drifted back and remembered how he found me and my two darling little girls.

"Did you hear me, Tory?" Damon was screaming. "Just because you are a big homebuilder who has all the banks by the balls does not mean you are entitled to wipe your feet on the good-girl accompaniments. I know you are making money—big money—but it takes every penny to live the way we do. Damn it, Tory, what happened to us? Where is the harmony?"

"I don't want to talk harmony or about it," I screamed. "Damon, the melody you are humming will stop and the money will, also, stop." He shook his head.

"As I have said before, racing makes me happy, I will cut way back tomorrow or the next day. Indeed, I will. I could have been killed when I almost turned the Jag over a few months ago. No one knew how I came out barely scathed, but I did. The daredevil in me was on the run, running away from reality. I felt like a big 747 that could not get off the ground. So, I crashed, yes, and almost burned."

Damon brought me back to life, "Maybe everything wasn't enough," he said, "I do love you with all of my wicked heart."

"Damon, I love you too, but have you valued our time together? Truly, no, and you never allowed anyone to love you all the way. Why?" I asked. "What is this stuff you carry around in your heart worth? Was once enough?"

He turned and looked at me deeply.

"Oh, yes do you want to go to Vegas this weekend and meet Joe and Wanda, and three other couples we enjoyed years ago."

"You know I can't go this weekend its homecoming." "Is that a––no!"

No answer. He walked into *my* house, that I built, that I loved so dearly.

Cold night. I thought and crawled out of the pool.

Chapter 19

Changing the clouds

Under an autumn mist, many dark clouds drifted over my beautiful life, and it was changing my common values extremely quickly. These changes were alarming, and I felt like something heavy had been fastened to my heart to hold down my soul, slowly eliminating my once joyful and perfect life. Yes, my hearing was fading away; I had lost most *sounds*. Deaf is the only silent handicap.

When I was young, I was delighted witnessing the aural rules and loved snooping around to hear things I should not. Truth was, I was born a curious creature, marveling at the idea that I could live a wonderful and beautiful life *forever, Amdn but nine oif.* Except to live you must hear.

As the summer sun came out one more time, it dried the dew on the dripping flowers, another new day ready with what was left from yesterday's dream. Would this sun rise again? I realized quickly that neither the dew nor the flowers life would last forever. I knew that I was not always receiving life and accepting my existence. I must accept deafness, but I kept asking and praying for other rewards. I must think of the things I loved and, my gift of three wonderful children, and all the wonderful times with Damon and the places we had been: China, Italy, England, Ireland, Switzerland, and many more amazing countries. And my great love for Rome, I loved it there; the people there were happy. In many other countries most people could not speak my language nor me theirs, so it was not always interesting. Deafness was not a problem there, you had to smile and enjoy what you were doing. A friend had laughed and said, darling those guys you loved so are from France. Maybe I felt it in my blood. Yes, we are French. Speaking of Rome, I thought of Mickey Melia, my best friend's uncle. I was writing a book on his life story. He also had been selling diamonds he bought at an auction. He was so amazing to know. But deep down I knew there were questions and dangerous answers about him. I had not heard from him in a while, but I had reasons to believe Mickey was in Rome. I needed my money from the sale of the diamonds I bought from him. I tried to find him but could not. I had another thought; I might call Carlos to see if he knew of him.

Mickey had left Texas fast for many reasons and problems; I do not even want to know them. He was the man with the iron heart and soft fingers of magic—a large portion of his mind was past genius. He robbed the rich and gave to the poor. When I started drafting the book, I had to promise him I would not print the book until his death. I like to think of him as the other side of the double 00's. Some things he told me were shocking.

As I got to know him better, he was on the other side of midnight. He told me that he thought there were two kinds of people inside us: one good, the other mendacious. I believed him. He told me if I ever needed anything he had great helpers, on the honest and dishonest side. I laughed, but it was true. I know because I assessed him. I had him look up Dr. R.D. Green in Alpine, Texas.

Weeks later, he called and told me Dr. Green had killed himself. He had many lawsuits against him, and he had jumped from a bridge and died. I felt relief after all these years, and I thanked Mickey for the information. During many talks, he told me he had found a way to knock out lasers. I wondered if he would tell me a code. *Wicked* thought. Could I even imagine how much that code would be worth? He said it had to do with crystal, batteries, and water, but he could not tell me because it was too dangerous to know.

Chapter 20

Money is the route to all happy endings

Two days after many depraved thoughts, I was back working. I drove over to Dallas to meet with a new group of lenders at the Central National Bank on Midway Road.

As I stepped into the main lobby, my feeling of win was not with me. My skills for getting money had deserted me, along with the hearing problems. I was afraid I would fail. *What is wrong,* I whispered, *be a big kid. You have done this many times.* Finally, after a long wait, I was taken into Sam Richmond's office, the vice president of the bank.

"Hi, I'm Tory Walker." "I know who you are. I met you at the HAB meeting," he said. He had a friendly smile and strong handshake.

"Yes, of course," I said, beaming, but I did not remember though I pretended to.

I told him that I had found a subdivision owner with hot hands who needed to scrap it. It was a great deal.

We talked for about an hour before he said, "I like it. I will take it to the Board." He asked me questions that I could not understand very well, so I bluffed my way through. I told him I had a sinus infection. He said he had it bad sometimes, too. Still, I threw him a rather good pitch. We shook hands and he said he would call me tomorrow.

I had to think fast because I knew I would have trouble understanding him on the phone. I asked him if I did not answer my assistant, Sara Stevens, would speak with him. I wanted to cry out and say I cannot hear well on the phone. I did read his lips and mind— that was good enough for today, but what about tomorrow? I had Sara relay for me; she was good and covered things well. But I still knew this was not always going to work, but what was I to do? *It was not over.* But like life sometimes, *it was cold as ice out there.* I remembered telling myself, *come in out of the cold and warm your icy emotions.* Yes, I needed to finish some more of the houses before it got any colder.

He called a few days later and gave me money, but not enough. But I had decided I did not need to buy that subdivision. Maybe I needed to back off for a while and get out of this damn hard-hearted business, but it was stuck to me like glue, Tato.

Chapter 21

Never say never

It was getting late, and the black rain clouds were gathering fast above.

"Looks like we are going to have a shower," I said to Conner.

"Shower? Looks more like it is going to rain cats and dogs on my foundation," he replied.

"Damn, I told Conner this was too much to pour for one day. We should have done everything but the garage. If it rains hard, we could lose this one," I said and was mad as hell.

"No, we won't lose it," he promised. "I'll see to it."

Tommy walked by us and said, "Evening."

"Tommy, do you agree with Conner," I asked?

"Yes, ma'am," he declared. "He's the boss."

Everyone was Laughing, but Conner. Tommy said, "Yes I do, and we'll cover it."

Tommy pulled on his rubber boots and stepped onto the wet concrete. He smiled to himself, slowly turning towards me so that Conner could not see him and shook his head, no. He picked up his rake and started working the loose mixture. Several of the guys started helping him.

That night, as the storms approached, I left the house to run over and check the concrete. It was about 10:30 and I pulled up and Tommy was there. He had been worried about the winds blowing the plastic off the wet stuff. I was glad to see him, Tommy was the best. He always took care of the rough edges, and he worked for Conner for many years. He was black and beautiful. The other crew boys called him "pretty boy." Everyone knew he had a fantastic crush on me. I knew it, too.

"Hi, Tommy, you think we're, okay?" I asked. He swiftly turned when he heard me.

"You scared me," he said. "We might be all right, but if we get more rain it is going to be a hell of a mess. We started pouring much too late."

"I know. I tried to tell Conner, but he did not listen."

"He never does," said Tommy. "Never does anything any way but his way."

Suddenly the rain dropped from the broken, dark sky. At the same time, a gust of wind blew through, and parts of the wet concrete was exposed. We worked fast and furiously to get the problem areas covered, and soon we were both shaking and soaking wet.

He turned his head away and said, "Miss Tory, you can see through your shirt." I looked down.

I whispered, "Don't call me Miss."

He walked over and covered me with his jacket.

It was wet, too, but better to be covered.

As he approached me, our eyes met. His hands were trembling as he covered me with the coat.

The radio on Tommy's motorcycle was on, and as he looked over at it, he said, "Well, the song's not wet. You want to dance with me, Tory?"

I hesitated, and he quickly shook his head. "I've got to get out of here," he said. "I know better."

I stood, shaking in the cool rain, unable to move. Maybe my heart came back alive. I said," yes I will dance."

I moved toward him, and we started dancing atop the damp ground. The rain was not so cold anymore.

My wits returned to me, and I stepped back after a bit. "Tommy, I have to go," I said.

"I know," he answered.

Sheets of rain were bearing down upon us. The moon had been covered by someone else's clouds and suddenly it appeared, casting a large shadow from under the trees.

The earth was not dark anymore, but I felt as if it was giving me a message. "I just kind of forgot what I was doing," I said. "We are all just people, all the same, you know?"

"I don't know," he said, and put on his huge, smile. "Tory, you will never know how many times I have backed off. You are out of my league, and I must get out of your way. I now know why everyone says to me, 'Don't even try it.' I have the whole damn-deal reminding me of this black face, but my heart is the same pink as yours. I have to say this, Tory. I am so damn in love with you. I hate to be a black man when I am around you and tonight especially."

"Do not say that. It is wrong," I said. "Tommy, this has nothing to do with 'color,' believe me. There are many colors of people in this world. People do not look at people of color like it was a shame anymore. We are equal, no one thinks that at all."

"What and why should it matter so much? I see people looking at me, looking at you. You should not even be in this business. Yes, you are a builder, but you are too much for all of us. You do not even know you are a beautiful lady in the wrong kind of work. I am sorry to say I wish you were not near me; it hurts."

I was still standing there like a wet, half-finished statue, moon or rain drops not covering my emotion.   I did not mean for this to ever happen. He shook his head.

"Tommy, For God's sake, I identify my life as a builder. My greatest desire is to build. I live and breathe it. Why do I have to choose something else because I am a woman? And as for our visit tonight, it was fine, but do not mess up your life over me. You would not even like me if you knew me. I am bad, bad 'Leroy Brown'."

He was studying me, and I saw a gentleness in his manner.

"It's just not fair, Tory," he protested.

"Nothing is fair. It is life and if it falls to hell over and over, you pick it up and nail it back together. It will only hurt you, no one else, when you allow the nails to punch you too deeply inside. Leave the things you cannot control and walk away. I do it every day,"

I spoke. "Every day. I need to go."

I cursed a bit, in French knowing he would not know. Then thought no--do not. But to all my subs I knew I cursed like a magician sometimes. I would be fair, but they all know, it was to place things as near to me as possible.

He looked at me and nodded and said, "I'll be seeing you," and he turned quickly, leapt on his motorcycle, and sped away before I could even blink my eyes. I screamed at him don't go you are to drunk Tommy. I could still hear the music on his radio as he reached the corner, going too fast. His presence had slipped away in the wind and the rain. I got my stuff together and pulled it into my car and went home to forget. But I was sorry he liked me so well. It would all pass in time.

At 5:15 the next morning, my doorbell rang. It was Conner, and I could tell by the rawness of his eyes and the look on his face that it was something bad-- something bad.

"What's happened?" I pushed.

"It's Tommy," he said, as he looked me straight in the eyes. He glanced away, and when he looked back at me with wonder and blame, I felt a heaviness in the pit of my stomach. "Tommy was killed on his cycle last night. He had this note on him for you." He held out a bloodstained piece of paper.

I reached out with trembling hands and took the note, not taking my eyes off Conner. He stared back at me with dark, half-closed eyes. He had not shed a tear and I could feel the coldness coming off his face.

"What happened? He adored you," Conner said.

"Do not do this. We talked and covered the whole damn slab. No one else was there to help us, were you?" I asked.

He just stared and then looked down.

"Well, I knew he would be there, and I am not the boss of this shit. You are." he snapped. He turned and started to walk briskly away.

"This has nothing to do with who the boss is," I said. "I cannot control the World, give me a chance to tell you what happened."

He did not turn around, just went out and got into his truck and sat for a moment.

I walked out to the curb where he was parked and said, "Conner, he was drunk, and I tried to keep him from riding off in the rain and the storm. He could barely see."

"Wait," I said. He drove off.

Damon came to the door to see what was going on. I told him about the accident, and he shook his head and said, "I'm sorry." Then he said he had to run, and he walked away. He was always walking away from me. This was not his responsibility.

I held the note close to me but did not read it until later. When I did, I cried, and put it away forever. Conner was never the same to me. I hated this as it was not my fault. I will take the blame for things that are mine, but this was not fair.

Soon I had to hire a new concrete contractor, one problem after the other and I fired Conner. I missed the old crew. They were a joy to work with and the new guys were never as much a part of my building life.

Then one thing after another started to happen. I lost my devoted framer; he had worked for me for twenty-two years. He had problems after an automobile accident, and he could not climb the ladders anymore and soon he completely retired. He was an ace at my hand for twenty-two years; he helped me with my building business and my life. Then my lead plumber retired. Things started to fall to hell all the way away, tearing my system apart. My hearing was going away too damn fast. I tried to combine the good with the bad, but that is like mixing cold oil with leftover rainwater; you can see the pile of the good life and bad do not mix. Once more, I was falling and rambling on the wrong side of my path. Weeds and sticks kept hitting me in the face. I had fallen off the main path of *Walker's Bluff*.

Chapter 22

The stars in my heaven were taken away.

As time passed, I stopped building but a few houses and started buying older houses that needed improvement to flip them. I just had trouble successively running the jobs without hearing. I was almost totally deaf. But there was danger in the house flipping business because so many guys stepped in and thought they would make big bucks, but that is not how it worked. There were too many problems that most eyes could not see.

Thank goodness, I had the experience of repairing them. I bought a house that had beautiful bones, almost a mansion. No one wanted it, so I bought it at a good price. It had a huge island in the center of the kitchen that held the sink and dishwasher, which were leaking badly. I killed the water lines to the island, which was not easy. I had to have a lot of concrete beat the hell out to get to the line. That is a big mess, but you must find the leaks and cap them, so you cover your nose and close your heart. Smile with your helpers and step on it. Then we moved the sink and dishwasher to

THE PATH TO WALKERS BLUFF

an outside wall, which was not hard to get to lines. I had to take out all the bad–bad– black marbled floors and put wood throughout the house. I knocked out a few walls here and there. But it was easy or quickly done.

I made big money on this one but lived in it for a year and half.

But stepping out of my previous life and going into a new development was dirty dancing. The dirty repairing was hard as hell. I did not hate remodeling, but I liked building new houses best. I missed the papers on my desk, and I missed the feel of the wind blowing over my wet concrete. I wanted to have that old feeling that I had gotten when the sun polished the newly finished rooftops. And the entries of a new home took your emotion. I kept thinking that there was another way back to where I once was, but the truth is, you should never go back.

Chapter 23

Try to forgive

When my ex-husband Sonny was terribly ill, he called me and said he wanted to meet me and would bring a peace pipe and let us smoke it one more time. I heard him laugh and I remembered that gentle laugh. I met him at the Sands Club in Odessa. He was on oxygen, and he was extremely weak. I never thought that my heart would see pain for him, because, truthfully, I hated this man. I told him so. But in the last few years, I had realized there were two sides to everyone's life and that I was wrong about some of our problems. He was awfully jealous, and it caused a lot of our problems. But because he needed mercy now, I felt like I needed to forgive him for certain things and give him some kindness. So, I told him let the devil take yesterday and let's live in gladness today which meant there may be an easy out of this wicked Earth, but I didn't want to go anytime soon. But I knew he was going very soon; may God bless him.

He chuckled and said, "Thank you. I needed this visit. Let us call it my arrival to a resting place of accused, so I can bury some of my problems with you forever more and lead this path to the doorstep near my heaven or hell." He smiled. He had tears.

I agreed and I had tears, but I did not own them; they were what I was giving to him for no fee.

"I know that innocent look on your naughty face," he said. "You always weigh your words and are in damn deep control, but I am aware there was always a purpose for it, and, at times, I miss it."

I had forgotten that he was very cool and unusual; I knew he was a very intelligent person.

He told me that he was happy with his wife and their beautiful children. He said that he adored his and my beautiful girls, as well. He heard that Damon was a great guy and he loved them dearly, which gave me some peace in my wicked mind.

"I hope you will get well soon," I said, but I knew that he could not.

"No, I will not recover. It is like, in youth, I learned long ago, to sip from the cup of the good life only when you owned it. I do not own this life now. And the cup is weighed down with wonder, wondering how long after you see the lightning of heaven, or will I hear the crash of thunder from hell.

"Oh, I am sorry," I said.

"Well, but later you look down and your cup has run over and is now empty. I'll know it is over," he said. "When someone tells me that the best is yet to come, I tell them to fuck off and that I never was going to have it. I will always remember the good times we had together, and I think of it more than I should."

These were my tears I used, and I whispered, "Me too."

He thanked me for coming and I thanked him for our little girls. It was a load off our hearts.

Within two months, he died at the young age of forty-eight. I went to the funeral service, and I had forgotten how many friends he had. They came from all over this country. It was a large church, and it was filled to the brim. There was standing room only. They valued his friendship, and they were there for him.

After the funeral, I took my daughter, Lola, to the airport. She lived in Farmington, New Mexico. On the way we talked about her father. She was glad I had a moment of forgiveness in my heart for him. I told her it was hard to do, but I was glad I did. I walked into the airport with her, and we visited for a while because her plane was late. She was sad, but she talked about old times when she and Ellie were growing up and there was just the three of us. We had lived alone with no husband or father for almost two years, and we had what I call: "freedom of fun and a new promised life."

Lola was truly a beautiful girl—big blue eyes, warm blond hair—and her smile was always nearby. The best part was that I do not think she knew it. We had two of my favorite drinks of tequila. Finally, she got on the plane. And we said good-by, she said, "Thanks, Mom for everything and I will miss you." I had tears, yes, I will miss her too. I remembered the good times we had with her dad.

Lola's husband worked with a large hotel-building company because his father ran the business.

On my way to my car, I saw a black man who turned toward me. Our eyes met, and he straightened his body and smiled widely. I imagined him saying, "I knew someday, someway, I would find you, Rooster. Shall we go near the river and dig up some big, gray worms? Cause maybe we will go fishing today. Are the mulberries still in bloom?"

"Yes," I would say, "and you know, Willie, there is going to be a little rain today. What good fun this day will be."

This was all about wishes. I just miss Willie but guess I will never know him again.

Early the next morning, I remembered Willie again and I hated it because the guy I saw was not him. I knew it was only my imagination, or maybe just a nice bit of daydreaming. I leaned back against the soft pillows and looked out through the tall glass windows that my subs had placed there for me. I gazed out at the beautiful sunrise through a mist of fine raindrops. I could not describe how beautiful the rain's amber colors were, shining so brightly. I whispered, 'Go there, enjoy them.' Now that I had seen them, I knew they were mine; I surrendered my helpless passion and thought how nice it was to live in a beautiful house beside the road.

Now, my thoughts reached deeply into the hidden treasures of my heart: my beloved children— and my husband. My life with them had been wonderful, and they were the amazing subjects that made me survive, succeed, and understand why this old world existed. Most of that part of my life I control. What worried me most was the time when men and houses would no longer thrill me. That was when I would know it was truly over. Was this once-upon-a-time the part nearing to the end? Yes, there would always be another crowd of living people. One group would end, and another group would begin.

I walked out the terrace door barefoot with my thin pink gown clinging to my damp body. My heart felt no pain. I watched the motionless sunlight setting atop the world, burning the clouds and covering the last rain drops. I must try to understand life as it is and the evening breeze began to blow, tossing the silken threads of my hair. I bowed my tired head and placed my feet upon the glorious, damp path of Walker's Bluff. Do we live again? We do. I think our resting place may be just a short walk from the rain. Hope we can all be there.

Chapter 24

This is along ago spell

I closed my eyes and lowered my tired head as I moved slowly into a haze of countless blazing lights toward the path of my life. Now, I was drifting down the first pathway of my beginning life. This was as I went slowly under the anesthetic for the surgery of my cochlear implant. I feared death—but I must do this, I must hear again, and I must trust my doctors.

Down the path I can see my faithful adorable husband and my three darling children. I am not sure if this is all mine. I shall look very carefully again. Yes, it is mine and I made it all happen. It is so beautiful and extremely astonishing. We are all together and I see we are standing in my beautiful gray, marbled entry hall of my Hollyhill Street. Above my head is the sparkling wall of mirrors. On the high ceiling in the den is a beautiful chandelier that I had made in Venice. Now, suddenly I can see my condominiums, and the office building I reconstructed. I can see many beautiful houses, and oh my dear horses. My favorite was Mail Call. He was perfect and beautiful and down the path is the grand life of which I am sitting. It is so perfect. Will it last forever? The lilac bushes beside the dining room windows are still in full bloom.

Then, my memory is embedded deeply in the meeting of my behalf. It was a beautiful and magical night in early September, and even the stars seemed to be carefully arranged around a brilliant full moon. We were passionately brought together by chance. In time, faith touched us, but anxiety added boundaries––or was it intended to be taken away and fade slowly out of sight? Yes, again, there is Carlos Francisco. Yes, I found him standing beneath a huge, rose-covered archway on the west side of the white stone Catholic Church in Rowena, Texas. I felt a fire burning inside my emotions that I had never felt before. Something beneath the shadows of the church trees had caused me to say, "I love you." It took a few moments for him to smile and examine my strange, quick remark, but soon he said, "I'll love and care for you, forever."

I could not define the remarkable meaning of or control this content feeling of such a grand passion. I whispered that I must not close my eyes so tight, or it might go away—but I did close them very tightly, and suddenly I felt like I was sitting in a huge, remarkable sailboat in the middle of the beautiful ocean. Everything was splendid. I was drifting slowly beside the green groves, looking over the brilliant slopes of the mountains, and it was absolutely beautiful. Even the air I breathed was flawless. Then, suddenly, the gusting winds hit me like an explosion and blew into the mighty sails of the beautiful boat, which quickly drifted dangerously toward the deepness of the roaring sea. What happened next was only evidently feasible by how the human heart wishes for vastness of triumph over every single dream that comes in their life. Can we make it happen? Is it the beginning of lies and defeat? What are lies? They are thoughts buried from the human eyes causing defeat.

I realized nothing was made to last forever, not even true devotion—not even purpose. Yes, even purpose fades in time and there is no known method to delay time. I never used regrets they are useless. I shall live with a desire to gather only the "jewels of this grand life," and this is how I will move forward.

Now I am at a Rodeo in San Angelo, Texas. It is raining. Sonny, my husband, is thrown from the bull he is riding, and he falls to the muddy ground. The bull is running toward him, and it hits him--knocking him into the air. I cannot breathe, I need air. I am not sure if Sonny is alive.

Later, I perceived another great moment as I softly walked down a delightful path toward an incredibly handsome man. Damon's eyes were so blue and filled with feeling that I wondered if they were real. He smiled and opened his strong arms to me. I sprang forward and collapsed into those open arms. I always remembered that fascination is the other word for desire, and passion is the hunger we have in our heart. Passion happened when I met Damon Granger. A new kind of fire burned—a new kind of strange and wonderful manner. I adored this wonderful man from the first time I laid eyes on him. Would this sensation last forever? Did he promise he would care for me until the end of our time?

Down another path, I whispered, is *this still my life– – why is it not in grand order?* I recognized my long-ago black friend Willie. We were so young and happy. He was smiling and tossing stones at the gray-tailed ducks that were swimming on my papa's enchanting creek. He told me he was going away. He cried and I held his hand until someone pulled him away.

Down the next path there was an extreme haze. I am smoking my third Lucky Strike cig, which I took from my mom's café. I am moving some long, heavy boards toward my friend Ken. We were laughing and talking about building the bridge over the dry creek behind my house on Magnolia Street. I told him I would build many things--even bridges someday. He said he knew I could and that he hoped someday to see them.

Down a strange and lonely path, I saw my sister. She stood near me and reached out to touch my face. She looked so beautiful. She was telling me to listen, trust, and follow; everything was going to be all right. She said she was happy and not alone.

The next path was maybe the most perfect. It was covered with a gray mist and a bit of dampness. Oh, yes! We were pouring a beautiful concrete slab; the seventh of the month. Conner, my devoted concrete man, was nearby. He thought we were moving too fast. I convinced him it was all right and that we must pour

311

four more this month. Tommy, where are you? Did you smile and agree?

Slowly, I awoke up to perhaps the final path in the dream of dreams; my doctors had implanted a cochlear with a magnet deep in my skull. On the outside of the head was a device that would be clamped that also had a magnet. At the back of the ear, an implant would connect the sound straight into my brain. Lots of cutting and pain. It is strange, but the mechanism is magic. I met one of the doctors who invented this device: Dr. William F. House of Los Angeles. The other doctor was Dr. Hough in Oklahoma City. They were both, of course, geniuses. It is a medical wonder. After the surgery, I suffered pain, headaches, and loss of balance for over three weeks. For many reasons, I had only one cochlear implant, but it takes two to balance you. With one, I have a loss of my total balance, because the inner ear must have the same weight on each side.

Nevertheless, it was all worth it. Seven days after the surgery, they placed the hearing device on my head. Yes, it clips on the magnet on my skull. When I first heard the sound again, I smiled, with tears dropping upon my cheeks. Now, when the sound of the dusty winds blowing on my face or raindrops falling on the ground, I rejoice. Only the deaf can know how it is to be devoid of sound. Not any-more! I pledge harmony with life, because before this I almost lost my life.

Today, I could hear the true spoken words; but wait, it was not perfect. I gained only 54 %, but that helps to understand what people are saying. Again, there is a bit of a guess, but it can be done. I could hear music playing in the background. Dear God, thank you for my music. It had been playing all those years without me. I could hear people laughing, not just see a smile. Even the movement of a foot on a sidewalk made noise. Absolutely everything made sound. I had forgotten how there was nothing in this world like sound. I could go outdoors and listen to the birds, and the sounds of everyday life, and thanks to someone up there. Again, the kiss of the Angel from her smile was placed upon my soul. But do the Angels look down on our Earth and see the pleasures we have and almost envy us? No, but it is still a wonderful world full of many blessings.

But I was back on this Earth in many ways. I got back the loss and trust in my life on this Earth.

Do not cry for me, my successes were mine it all happened in my own charming and demanding ways. I have had a hell of a wonderful life. I never permitted *loss* and I never gave up. Once was never enough. I did it all over and over until it was mine. The doctor had said, "Tory, all people have problems." Most people can close their eyes and listen. But they may still not know the answers, but you did, by watching them and reading their mind.

Nowadays, I can hear and see the beautiful sky as the raindrops sound their way upon my smiling face. "And today and tomorrow shall be among the greatest days of the rest of my life," I whispered to myself, "I love this amazing world of noise." *Thank you, Dear Lord, thank you I have the whole world, again. Yes, it is mine again. I shall never forget this blessing.*

■■■

Chapter 25

Dallas, Texas

The Twinberry was on Welch, a side street between Commerce and Main. The building was an outstanding antique and one of Dallas' most magnificent works. Crowned with a great elevation, the beautiful building had existed, from its origin hull. I had a feeling of connection here, long ago in this era. My great-great uncle, Frank Glover was Sheriff of this wonderful city. There were many stories to be heard, my granddad had told me. In front, the main focal point of the building, there were four huge, beveled, leaded glass windows that were made in England by Robert Twinberry in the 1820s. The gables above the windows were large and turned towards the front of the structure with large black cornices lining the front of the building. When Robert Twinberry came to America, he prearranged for the windows to be finished and brought to Dallas. In his pocket, he held two thousand dollars, which was quite a nice sum in those days. He bought the land where the hotel stood, and five acres around it. History stated that it took him five years to build the fine hotel. In time, he made a fortune on the land he sold that surrounded it, which slowly became a part of downtown Dallas. The Twinberry family still owned the hotel and restaurant. I adored the hotel and restaurant and had met the owners many years ago at a Builders Convention when we rented space for some great parties. The restaurant was always booked, but I could always obtain reservations. Damon and my family were regular patrons. Today I turned and drove north towards the front door of the restaurant. A fast storm, of rain and wind suddenly caused a metaphorical downpour. I had been feeling sluggish, and dreary so I was glad to be here. I had been doing a lot of soul searching lately, and this meeting I was going to was all about now, nothing to do with yesterday. I arrived at the front of the restaurant and stepped out of my car. Jennings, the doorman, greeted me warmly, "Ms. Walker, how pleasant to see you. Have a terrific evening with us." "Thank you. I shall," I answered. He held a large umbrella over my head, but he lost control, and the winds whipped the rain across my face and tumbled my hair out of place. The silk material of my new green dress was slightly covered in dampened circles. It would

THE PATH TO WALKERS BLUFF   CHARLOTTE WHALEY

dry soon I hoped. I made my way into the Grand
entrance of the restaurant where I was greeted warmly
by the maître d', and he quickly seated me at my favorite
table.

Now that I was out of the rainstorm, seated, and
ordered wine, I still had many reasons to feel a storm in
my heart, blowing the chilly dampness over my mind
and giving a bit of wonder, should I be here. However,
I had convinced myself that it was all right to ask my
long-ago beloved lover Carlos to join me for dinner.
Many years had elapsed since our last encounter when
he had called to wish me a happy birthday. I did not
respond to the message he left; I knew he had been
living overseas for several years. He had been living
under protection for the previous deeds he had done for
America long ago. Nonetheless, before all of this is over,
the deep dismay of sins and love might overshadow the
real secrets of why or the actual truth might be brought
forward. Ok, I wanted to see him, for help. But the
matter in my case were illegal in nature, maybe, but I
think I can send a grand purpose for Carlos to view. It
had nothing to do with the long-ago lover part. It was
simply to inquire about where Mickey Melia might be. e

had vanished from the face of this Earth with some of my money from the sale of diamonds. So, I needed to find him. I felt like I was living alone, from my world when I stopped building. At the end of my building, I lost over five million, yes, big bucks. I hurt every day thinking of that fucking number. There was a continuing parade of depression, but I was slowly coming back to a new world. But do people really come back? I do not believe one comes all the way back after losing their devotion and money.

A friend had told me to have your fortune ready, so you could carry it in your hands. I can carry diamonds, but it was hard to carry a big house, or hide it. I laughed to myself. So, I moved quickly and quietly into the wonderful business world of diamonds. Although it was risky, in some ways, it was amusing, and precisely rewarding.

∎∎

I smoothed my hand against the navy velvet chair and my eyes flickered towards the soft glowing lights. I needed to adjust my hair, I took a deep breath and a long drink of my wine, then another one. I do not like wine, but it is better right now than tequila would be for me. I do not know why a little wine makes me feel dizzy.

I was seated a good distance from the front entrance. What made this area so charming was the glows drifting lighting from the candles on the tables, although it was slightly dark, but darkness made it very romantic. I could see the front entrance as people walked up to the maître d'.

Suddenly, there he was. He paused for a moment and then he saw me. He smiled and moved compassionately toward my table. I could see him in the complex lighting, and I studied him carefully. As he came closer, I dropped my napkin to the floor. Like a bird trapped in a glass cage, my heart felt as if it had sprouted wings and was trying to find its way out. This picture was yet to be well-framed, but I would simply allow it to fall to my feet beside my linen napkin, and whatever else was down there.

Carlos was watching everything in the place all at once, from the floor to the walls, and out of habit his eyes absorbed and filled the entire room. His facial expression was calm and pleasurable, as if he knew he could rearrange this whole damn Earth, and then, my heart skipped deeper into memory lane. The candlelight did not help much to keep me out of trouble. It just made his skin even more olive, his smile easier, and his thin lips smoother. It defined him as a beautiful physical hunk, not offered to all girls, just me. Damn, he was so handsome and remarkably dangerous. What is this life all about?

Go home, I thought. *You need to run away from here as fast as you can. You are falling into agony of defeat, let me go. This feeling is against the rules--but they were man-made rules only.*

I remembered Carlos telling me the last time we parted that there were many paths we could have taken, and when you looked back you wondered if you had taken the right ones. As the years went by, maybe there were no regrets, but you might never stop wondering just where the other paths would have taken you.

Yes, you will always wonder what happened while getting so damn close to old age. Did you leave the gems of life behind you, and then wonder if you could untangle the webs of life hanging on you? No, you cannot, and regrets are useless. Shut up and go back to the path of life and gather only the precious stones.

His steps came closer. This could cost the hell out of me. My hands trembled, and my fingers rubbed my dress down softly on my nude feeling body. Yes, the sex deceives; yes this shark was near. Those were the things that came with being of so-called conjuror, but no, I was not a magician nut––though I could read people like an open book, absolutely and quite naturally, from the inside right out to the smile they would give me. Many people have tried to trick me, but I see through it, ninety-five percent of the time. Honor me, baby, I am a true illusionist.

Those footsteps were near now and commanding attention. They were heavy and he seemed to carry the weight of time on his shoulders, or could he control the weight of time.

"My dear, Miss Toy Walker!" He stood slightly slanted toward me and said, "Damn, I have missed you so damn much. I know our lives are quite different now, but many pages of the old book are still fanning around us. Whoa, my Toy, you look wonderful."

"Thank you," I said. "And you look charming."

He pulled me from my chair, and embraced me, kissing me on both cheeks, and then gave me a light dab

THE PATH TO WALKERS BLUFF   CHARLOTTE WHALEY

on the lips. I could smell perfume, but I did not know if it was mine or his. Would my heart allow this request? I must not trust or obey this feeling. I remember the old stories that if you touch it and its still burning, that is all it takes, and touching is what makes it happen.

I sighed, and he smiled for a short second. I backed up a bit. The eyes and the lips were the same.

He helped me into my chair, and we sat slowly down. "Let the game begin," I thought.

"I am delighted that you are here, my dear," I said. but kind of mumbled.

"I am glad to be here," he said, "How are things? What is all this B.S. about Mickey Melia?"

I gasped. I remembered this guy as being way above most of the boys his age, very street smart and kind of a rebel without a cause, which only thrilled people like me and made his chances of winning my fragile emotions so easy. Years ago, when I told my sister about him, she said, "Goodness, you are going to get in trouble. She told me, "Tory, he is bad news––but interesting, and handsome."

"Whoa! Wait for the motive," I said.

He laughed. "Sorry," with a well-guarded voice. "I am delighted to be here with you once again, whatever the reason." He said and chuckled, as his eyes searched deeply into mine.

"Thank you," I said.

"Okay, the fact that I came tonight might be evidence of how time heals all things." said Carlos.

"Yes, so it does," I said with a deep smile on my face.

Once again, he bent closer to me, and I wondered if he remembered carrying me home one night over his shoulder from our first drunken bash. I wondered if he remembered the last nude swim we took at Seven Mile Crossing, during a deep, hot summer night under one of the most beautiful moons I could ever remember seeing. That night, he was singing, *"They tried to tell us we were too young."* But even now, it was fascinating to see him in a different setting after so many years. I felt like a runaway kid once again, and the hell with our wandering thoughts that makes sins. I remembered when he said, "If a sinner may be so bold as to enjoy his sins, let the devil take tomorrow." Therefore, I was going to be extremely careful where I left mine lying around tonight, so nothing could find them.

"How are your people?" he asked.

"My mom died at an incredibly young age. She was never happy after she sold her café and the life she lived there after. Dad lived forever, but sadly lost his memory the last years of his life,"

"Carlos I loved you for coming to Cody's funeral."

He shifted, "I heard from my mom, and she told me about Cody. I went through a little hell to get there for just a few moments. I wanted to walk down to you, but too many people and your dear love was holding your hand. Toy, I liked her dearly and I know she was an import part of your life. I am so sorry."

"Yes, thank you," I said, "She was too young, and my life has never been the same without her. Carlos, your sister called me one day out of the blue, and I had not heard from her in years, and she told me you lost both parents and a bit of history of things about your life."

"Well, I was not always there for them. I hated that part of my work; I just could not be there for them.

I did not even get to my dad's funeral." He looked down and shook his head and spoke. "I am sorry this profession has taken so much of my life again and again, but I chose it," he said.

We were silent for a few seconds.

"May I ask about your true love?" he asked.

"I am happy with him. He is a devoted and dear person. We are sincerely contented with our family life and our love life together. We like to travel; we have traveled all over this beautiful earth. We have a great group of friends to enjoy. We are remarkably busy working together. Nevertheless, no-one's life is perfect. But Damon is an incredibly happy person. We love our kids, and they love us. In many ways, he knew what he wanted, and he found it and took it. Carlos I am delighted that you are here."

"Good, thank you and congratulations that you have a great life." he answered. "I must confess to you that my coolness is appropriately masked, but yes I am delighted to see you," he said and grinned.

"I remember that line so well. "You still like Shakespeare," I said.

"Yes, I do, however I have forgotten or misplaced most of my collection of words." Another pause.

He chuckled. Then came that faraway smile he had always carried, and he waited for a moment, as if searching for more words and for the reason for his being here.

Things were silent, but then we heard the music from the live band that had grown louder sometime between mine and Carlos' conversation.

We waited a moment and listened to the grand music.

"One thing, I have been in France for some time now. This is my first trip back to the U.S. in a while. Things feel as backwards as they are. South is not south, and the North is too far to the South, everything is reverse to me. I need to work that out," he said, laughing. I searched my face; My thoughts rushed around in my mind with hopeless wonder, yet it was filled with endless bounds of its possibility.

"Your daughter told me you were in France. "

"Yes, I know, my Toy, in just a few seconds of time, you can make a man want to tell his life story, and while talking to you. This caused him to expose his bare body to you without ever taking off a thread, but it leaves one naked; and then you will find a way to take his heart out."

"God, thanks. That makes me feel so worthy for something. Now, let us start with why you are still wearing your clothes. I chuckled.

He laughed and said, "You still got it, baby. And I do not think I need to explain the truth as to why I came."

"Do tell. And don't you forget, I'm just another fellow citizen, and it should be no trouble for me to ask a favor of my dear friend."

He smiled and got remarkably close, and said, "Oh I don't like to give out special favors without pay."

That moment in the restaurant things seemed to be getting louder as the band kicked the music up a notch. The sound of the music was good. I could hear some things too well, like that song. It was Tom Powers, *"I'll always need you."*

"I needed that song," I said without thinking before I spoke.

"Yes, I love it, too, and yes it alarms me, my dear," he said.

"Could you be mistaking an alarm for the sound of passion? You know, here we are meeting again, and maybe we both know this meeting could cost the hell out of us," I stated.

He grinned. "Yes, dear one, but no. No desire or passion should be used here tonight. Besides, passion is somewhat like death because it will end. It leaves no claims, no trace, no outline, not even a simple shadow because it holds no truth that it could be the end or possibly the beginning of something. Whether it is delight, love, or arrangement."

"Where on Earth have you been to find out all of that?" I jested, and then calmly agreed, "You are right. This is hardly passion."

"Darling," he explained, "I've been around this globe on both feet, barefoot, forward and backward, twenty times, and bit by bit it's all the same, the same story and the same kind of existence." He continued, "Sooner or later, you just let it all go, and you live like another overlooked bit of nature. Like a vein in a leaf floating around in someone else's pond, waiting for the coolness of life to send it off tomorrow."

"My dear, you are right, I always feel like that, constantly," I said.

"Do you?" he countered. "My dear I wonder to what extent you are involved with this corrupt man you have asked me to help you find."

"I am not that involved with him in his business, if I may say so, but I need to find him and to get my money for the jewelry he is selling for me. Money, I think is a damn good reason to find him." He studied me and asked, "Toy my love, is the jewelry hot?"

"Yes and no; not on my part. I bought them in an estate sale from an old rich lady. I found out that they were a bit hot. I tried to get my money back, but she had left town, so I was left holding someone's problem. I tried to find out from whom she bought them from but could not located anyone who even knew anything about the lady or how she got the diamonds. She did a great job with her cover."

"The diamond business is dangerous," He shook his head incredulously.

"Yes, I am finding that out the hard way. I promise you I thought it was all on the level, but once I had them and could not find a way out and did not know what and how this all happened. You could not just pitch them out. I tried to sell them. But could not even get my money back."

Look, about Melia, do you really know him?" he asked. "Do you know what you have trampled over?" "Yes, I do. As I told you it all started when he wanted me to write his life story. He just wanted the world to know, yes, a noble thief, it is strange but true. Do you know of him?" I asked.

"We all know him, but we do not know his location. If we did know, we would be able to bring his wicked ass in and keep that huge fraud from laundering drug money and scamming banks," he replied irritably.

"Really, I do not believe all of that. I am not precisely involved in anyway."

"I'm sorry it worries you for me to know him, but I do wish I could talk with him about the money he owes me and about the book I am writing about his life is a great seller. You are scaring me."

"Sorry, Carlos you have my sincere apology if I disturbed you, knowing him."

Carlos just shook his head no.

"Carlos, I do not know exactly what you mean about the laundering, but I may know a bit about the scamming. But I need help finding him. Carlos, not all bad people are bad all the way. I know he did not mess with drugs. *That* I do believe. He hates drug dealers—he lost a son to drugs."

He frowned, nodded to the waitress, and pointed at my glass, gesturing for her to bring more wine. His sleeve moved up and I glimpsed his expensive watch. I assessed that his clothes, too, were expensive and well chosen. He lived the same way he dressed: perfectly. After two attempts, the waitress finally poured us wine, and nestled the new bottle back in the ice bucket. I did not hear the scraping of the ice, but I watched the fog on the bucket billow for about a second. I kind of felt like that ice, considering that I would maybe melt down like a flaming candle and just drop off and roll over stiff. I did not need to be too cool here with this man. In many ways, he is still mine. And he has the good grapes of wrath hanging on him. I was getting controlled by the grapes long ago, I chuckled to myself. What did I expect?

"Darling Toy, really, if you are part bad, you are bad all the way and you know that. I do not have a shiny soul to help you with that sorry son of a bitch. I have only got a cosmic nervous system attached to me like a wireless phone," he said. "But this wicked man doesn't have to let people know where he is and what he has done."

He took the bottle of wine out of the ice bucket, again.

"More?" he asked.

"No, thanks. I am fine."

"Do you mind if I keep drinking this stuff? I would rather have Crown Royal, but this will do."

"No, help yourself," I said.

"You can hear better," he mumbled, smiling.

"Yes, I had the cochlear implant." I held up my hair and showed him. "You can see the processor of the device is small and grand. It is a gift, from my God, but I do have a hole in the head."

We both frowned. And he smiled.

"Wonderful." he said, giving that big smile. "Wonderful Life now."

"This small accessory or ornament gives me sound straight to the brain. It is magical, unbelievable, and is one of life's favors. I can live again."

"That's what you should have done years ago," he stated. "That is amazing."

"Yes, it has saved me," I said.

I felt a tear trying to come down, but removed it quickly, along with my thoughts.

Finally, we ordered dinner: a strange salad, veal scaloppini sautéed in Marsala wine. Oh yes, more wine, and delightful green apple pie for dessert. We ate in near silence. *Do I still know this man?* I thought. He was either very hungry or nervous and in need of something to chew on. He studied me and then asked a few questions about my family.

"This food is wonderful, so is the place," he said, as he looked around the room for the thousandth time. "It reminds me of a restaurant we went to in San Francisco. Do you ever think of that?"

"Yes, I do. This place has the same charm, but nothing was like that view," I said with a sigh. We were both incredibly quiet for a second and I wondered what he was thinking, once upon another time.

"I take pleasure in this restaurant," I said. "Though the hotel area has begun to decline some, it's still busy and people appreciate the fine service, and it is always thriving. The restaurant is always booked. Every night they select or reject who they want to serve. You must know them to get a reservation. As we say, it is not what you know, but who you know."

"So true--but to me, the whole of creation seems to be in *decline*. Lately, I have really realized how everything wears out: places, things, and even people ultimately wear down to the bloodless bone," he said.

I agreed, "Very authentic. I never thought it would happen to me so soon. It is a bitch, and I thought it would happen to everyone else, but not me."

"Well, I am three years older than you. I really noticed it was down the hill and across from the bay at sixty," he laughed.

Damn he stares so deeply, I thought, *he always did.*

I cannot let down my guard. He is moving me slowly into a corner, his corner. I had the first doubt of my strength. I thought, *okay, you are here let us play. We are both competing in this risqué competition, and I will prevent you from scoring.* Except that I knew he was going to require many answers to the most unreasonable questions. This was all exceedingly difficult and, apparently, I had no other solution. However, it was my court, and I knew he would play out of sheer curiosity.

"I am getting the impression that it's not good for you to be near me, or be here," I said.

"Toy, I just told you, yes, it is against the system rules. It could cause a lot of trouble and subsequently, it could cause system failure on my part. I could blow the whole Melia assignment," he explained. "No, I am not supposed to be anywhere near Dallas. It is a long way from New York City to *here*, yet it seems I am here, and I have accidentally strolled into a certain restaurant and *gosh*, I saw you, walked over, and hugged you, and said, 'Hello there, Toy! My, it has been a long, long time.'" His face straightened, and he looked tired, "How did you find out I might have any of this info?"

I reached over to stop his hand, as he had been waving it around in the air.

"I was not sure but had a feeling. I hate it when you use the words *system rules*. I do not want to be mixed up with any kind of 'mission impossible BS,'" I said and smiled as I stroked his hand for the third time.

"I just asked a simple question, Toy. How?" he persisted. "Fact is, I do not know how you found me so easily?"

"I just did," I answered.

Wordlessly, we looked intently at each other for some time. Then he spoke: "You are still mean as hell and weigh each word in my gold. He laughed. "I do miss you, but you study me so deeply."

I laughed and said, "Okay, okay, I miss you. Carlos, because I was going deaf that I studied people, and I made-up things, then often it was not true. People are dangerous to themselves and others. I watched people so deeply, it surprised me how I could read their story, given them the answers they wanted to hear. It's in the eyes."

He chuckled, "I love that, and I do believe you."

I steered us back to the point. "I think you don't know where he is and if you did," I looked away, "you would not tell."

He was smiling again, and it swung around my very wicked soul. I waited and looked over toward the people at the next table.

"Please look at me," he requested. "Don't look away." Exasperated, he sucked in a deep breath and questioned, "Do you understand that it's like asking me to protect you from a dangerous man after I told you where to find him?"

"Amen! Pass the bullets, missiles, and the passion," I joked and smiled.

There were several people passing and he smiled, nodded, and one looked back at me. I smiled and waited.

"Game it, spy," he whispered. We both laughed. "I am here."

"Do not consider this a pass, but you look beautiful in that green dress. All the shades of green belong to Toy. All, as in money green, my dear Toy," he said. "You look cool."

"Passes are always accepted. When the passes stop, I will surely die, even if I am wearing my green money belt," I said, beaming. "Give me green and I will have freedom. You know Carlos, I had to change. I had no choice. I had to leave all the things I loved and march in a different band, go down a different path."

"As always, you win," he appeased me. "You mean, amazing lady."

"Thank you," I stated.

I watched him closely out of the corner of my left eye, and the frown that he had on his forehead finally relaxed, permitting the smile that I had known from the beginning of our friendship time was there. I watched him moving his finely shaped hands as he talked, which belonged only to him. I followed the rim of his lips to the dimples in his cheeks.

"Let us start over, and I am sorry for being such a bore. We have so many problems at my work, and a lot of 'crash and burn stuff' happening lately," he revealed.

"You are not a bore." I held my glass close to his hand and nodded for him to stop pouring.

As the waiter took some of our dishes and silverware, he dropped a knife on the floor near Carlos's well-polished shoes. He was very apologetic, and Carlos picked the knife up for him the guy thanked him and moved on.

He shook his head, cleared his throat, and organized his thoughts back to being a loyal warrior for the CIA.

"Toy, some days when things are not good for me, I wonder where you are and what you are doing. Then, I straighten back up, fasten my seatbelt, and ride off into the wild, blistering sunset," he said. "The letters in the old book are stained and starting to fade, but I wonder if they're still readable and true enough to possess." He grinned a sly, saucy smile and continued, "And darling, the truth will not set me free. It will so often only block the things I am trying to uncover."

He reached for my hand, and I moved it as the waiter strode over to see if we needed anything. Carlos told him we were fine. He smiled. I knew what he was thinking about the long-ago story of a soul.

Then I heard his familiar hollow laugh, and he smiled once again.

He held up his empty glass and answered, "This whole fucking drink contained the ingredients satisfactory for most men: no defense against the intruders, just an oblivious high." No, I do not drink, much, but the truth was I had a drink before I got here."

We gazed again at each other. Was he going to help me find Mickey?

"Do you understand, my dear Toy? Do you drink much?" he inquired.

"Yes, I do."

"Really," he expressed amusement and said, He checked his phone again and asked, "Shall we have a nightcap?"

"Yes, why not? We are both drunk," I chortled. We made our way to the front of the hotel area where there was a nice dark lounge to the far left.

A very pretty girl seated us in a private spot in the back of the lounge. Carlos watched her as she twisted her ass on the way there. Then she tipped her boobs at him, and he ordered us a couple of vermouths and thanked her. Then, his eyes came back to me, but they held sadness, and I could see so many questions.

"Are you happy?" I asked.

"No! Yes! In some ways, I am. When we get down, our supervisor lifts us up by telling us to consider how we have helped strengthen and improve the fundamentals of the system. Then, they give us a raise and a short vacation anywhere on Earth we want to go.

I will die for saying this, but many times I wanted to go where you were. I did not because I could not, so I did not try." He sighed once more and said, "Then, we go somewhere to rest for a while and when we return, we are happy to be back home. Home was wherever we were told to go and hang our hat."

"But you accomplished what you wanted to," I said.

"Yes, I presume I did. I do not mean I cannot live normally. It is just that—well, in the real world, I know that I must remember to be what I am: garnished for others. But my darling someone must help save this wicked, old world. It is a screwed-up system that we have in this land, and our group tries to make it a better place to live," he said. "I am not behaving right now to say these things, but I trust you." He stopped and looked around the room, then he looked back at me, as if he were a little boy lost, he held out his hand. I took it but wondered what would or should happen next. He wondered where we were going, too.

I rubbed my forehead to see if it was wet and hot, It was.

"Yes, it's my way with a story so well written," he said.

"I like to hear you tell me every word of this version of your life. You are a hero."

He laughed and there came that old smile again. "You will always make things *your* way. I am not so sure it is not the way to go. Thank you," he chuckled. "Do you want to take me home with you?" I shook my head yes, but I meant no, and I smiled.

"Nevertheless, on an occasion like this, my cup runs over, I keep over-filling this cup and it keeps running over. Does that make sense?" He chuckled.

"It does, but only if the one pouring is talking to the one who understands," I said. "Do you know that verse is in the Bible?"

He nodded, "Yes, and you got it again baby, and do you hear that song?"

We listened for a second.

"Yes, I do hear that song," I replied.

I could hear the music well. It was '*Autumn Leaves.*' How did they know to play that? Then they played, '*Your Chances Are.*'

I still felt right with him, but what is right, in the shades of wrong, --the man I once enjoyed so very much, was gone. It was the end of a true story, the end of our time. I frowned deeply at all these thoughts and decided that tonight there was no bridge to cross, I must stay on my own side.

"You are frowning," he said.

"I'm sorry," I said, "Your life is quite different from most."

He touched my hand and moved closer to me and closed his eyes.

"Some, but I have too. You have a good heart and are mild-mannered, and I find, of course, people like me believe in you," I assured him. "I may go so far as to say you kind of pitched a tranquil cascade over me that ended up being a shield to cover yourself," I said.

He nodded. Did he believe me?

The waitress came, and he requested another drink. I did not.

"Listen to me, Carlos." He turned his head away. "What I am asking you to do for me is so simple. Let us go back to the subject and talk about it," I stated.

343

"No, Toy, it's not so simple," he barked. "One does not mess around with an animal or criminal like him, nor does anyone associate with him. They are bad people. It is like they have an illness, and their main symptom is to steal, to get it all from others, and get away, and they often do. Does it end there? No, I do not think so. Wake up little Toy, my dear sweetheart, there is no such thing as 'halfway' in their business. They are so smart and if you think they are always getting caught and going to jail. No, hell no, these kinds of people live a long and happy life in sins, because they can outsmart the law. He has done so many things that you do not even have the right to know, and I do know. Toy, face it, they are like mafia. They hate that name, but it fits. We call them 'PC's,' which means: *Planned Clique.*"

He smiled and looked deeply into my eyes. After a second, I let go of my thoughts and moved closer. He kissed me.

He smiled and said oh I missed that taste. You control some of the scarlet devil."

I was quiet, silent. I wanted to kiss again, so we did. People around don't care, I hoped.

"People like you write movies, books, and stories about the wicked. The popular media makes it all look like fun and games covered in rosy *sinful* blossoms."

"Gardenias," I said.

"Yeah, what about lilacs?" He shook his head and laughed, "Yes, you allow in these stories for the villains to march down the path of bliss Gods, which should really be death row. What has happened? Where are all the good people that could be helping us make it on this wicked Earth?"

"Carlos, wait, people are not all bad, and Mickey, is only––he is only a thief," I said.

"Only a thief," he promptly retorted. "There is no such thing as *only a thief*, and you just do not want to hear me say the word mafia. We are taught to quickly seize any type of thief and quietly place them away forever, if possible. You know, as I said, we do not always get them like they do in the movies; so many times, they walk away smiling at us."

He took a short, deep breath and shook his head as he ran his fingers through his dark, graying hair. He looked sharply at me and rolled his green-brown eyes.

His lips were on fire. I knew that whatever he said, I would always know his true feelings. I needed to go—I am stumbling on my own path.

I looked at him and thought about how after these long years of living dangerously, underneath what *they* called the vile purple sky, allowing myself no feeling, no heartbeats, truly little air to breathe. He was still so damn beautiful. Could a man be beautiful? This one was. Dear wild pet, yes, he was. I wondered if he knew it.

"We need to go and get the hell out of here, my Toy," he whispered. "Let me go."

"Ok."

He raised an eyebrow and asked, "does anyone but me, call you Toy?"

"No. Just you," I said.

Do you know that 'Tory' means *thief*?"

I playfully shrugged my shoulders and smirked. "I know," I said. "You told me a hundred years ago."

He placed his fingers on his lips and tossed me a kiss. I did not reach out to catch it, but it was there.

"It can't hurt if you just tell me where he is." I waited. He sighed.

He frowned and said, "Maybe I am just anxious, but I might have an idea where he is. And I'll trade you the truth for the bed?" he teased.

"Best offer I've had in years," I joked.

"I can close my eyes and still see you all hunkered down in that cute pink dress, smoking a used Camel cig. You were hiding behind that Catholic Church in Rowena, Texas. You were the cutest little girl I had ever laid my eyes on. Baby, you had what it took."

He signaled the waitress for the bill, reached for my glass, and took the last swig of it.

"Yes, I have framed that picture in my mind, and I will carry it with me every day I live on this bitter earth. It is a picture from a story that has no ending, a story that should never be told."

"Thank you, Carlos. I love the version of your thoughts. You should have been a writer or a great scholar," I said with sincerity.

"No," he laughed, and he left a stack of cash on the table. We walked to the entrance of the hotel, taking cover under the awning.

Carlos sighed and looked out on the street. The rain had slowed to a slight drizzle, but the wind was blowing.

He turned a twinkling eye on me and said, "Let me do one more memory, on your seventeenth birthday in Abilene, when all of us chipped in and bought a motel room and gave each couple two hours."

"Don't go there," I said, "It scares hell out of me, still," We laughed.

"Yes, I remember what you said--every word of it, Toy baby, I lived every moment one thousand times, and then I wonder what the hell this old world was all about" he stated.

I looked at him with a cautious mind and tried to be explained, "I was so afraid, as you say this is a bitter earth, ours has the story that just started."

We both glanced away again for a moment with a slight wonder on our faces.

"One more thing. Several years ago, you asked me to find your dear friend, Willie. You were not sure of his last name. I traced him from Coleman, Texas then to Dallas. I think I may have found him. I will let you know if I did. His last name was Adams."

"Great!" I said hopefully.

His phone was ringing again. He looked down at the message and said, "It's my partner," He said, "I need to take this. I will be right back." He took him a long time, so I moved down to the entrance.

***

I drifted back, way back, to my friend Willie— somewhere in Winters, TX.

Countless years ago, on an extremely hot summer evening, when most ten-year-old kids were home with their families having dinner or in their bathtubs soaking off the excitement of a perfectly pleasurable day. I sat like a knot on a stump on the mud encrusted wooden steps in the back of my mom's café. I had been trying to clean the mud off. I do not know why I did that, it did not look much better, and no one seemed to care. Anyway, I was as dirty as a fat pig that had rolled in the slop pen. I was sweating like a plow horse, and cursing like a sailor, (yes, in French that my dad used) at the whole damn, wide, shitty, world. I was mad because my friend Shirley was treating me so trashy for being so dirty. She had marched on home. But I had my friend Willie.

"Willie, do you feel much love?" I asked.

He nodded and then frowned. "Yes, I do, I think, but my momma said there isn't no love in your house."

"Yes, there is," I protested. "Some, maybe. I will bet it is hidden like my last report card."

Willie was hunched over on the third step with his bare feet flopped onto a used flour can. I thought about this for a second and decided to go inside the café and whip us up a gigantic banana ice cream cone. In my sharp little mind, I could already see how it would look, all stacked up and doubled on a crusty cone.

Because Willie was black, he was not allowed inside the café. My mom asked me what I was stealing, but I just kept on scooping. I came back out with both hands full of stolen ice cream, licking at both cones since the damn heat was already making them melt.

Willie's eyes bugged out when I handed him his ice cream and he fixed a broad, tooth-filled smile on me. He always thanked me kindly, because this was quite a treat for anyone as poor as he and his family were. They did not get free treats very often. I asked him if he wanted to go to the movies with me, maybe tomorrow. I had free tickets. He said no, he did not like make-believe stuff. I thought he was right. I told him the last time I saw one of those silly things, the candy bars were walking and the marshmallows talking. We laughed, and he said he liked "shoot 'ups." I told him that was not real either, but he said it was, so I let it go.

It was not nice back behind the café. The alley was not well paved, and what used to be small scuffs in the earth had become shallow ponds thanks to decades of abuse and rain. There were smelly trashcans scattered up and down the back walls, all the way to the main street. The only thing that mattered was that it was, at that moment, private. We licked our ice cream, and I began to think hard. I frowned and said, "Willie, I have some serious stuff to talk over with you."

Willie groaned. "About what?"

I forgot what it was that I wanted to talk about when my eyes suddenly fixed hard on a wall that had been blackened by grease traps caused by the cafe kitchen exhaust.

"Look at this mess of grease!" I said loudly. Willie whipped around and looked.

"Hmm," he thought aloud, while he gained victory over his last bite of ice cream. "I can clean that up for 'yaw for a whole two nickels."

"No, you cannot. If I thought you could, I would steal a dime, that is two nickels, out of the cash register. I have taken them many times," I answered.

He looked away towards the end of the alley.

"Willie, you're not listening––gee whiz, good grief, ice cream's dripping all over your clean white shirt."

He looked at his shirt and frowned.

"Now listen to me," I said knowingly, as I pulled a piece of old, red-checkered table napkin up from my lap and wiped at Willie's shirt. I licked my ice cream for a few more moments, and I said, "My mom always said time waits for no man. Whatever we are not doing we'd better get on it."

"Waits for who? What does that have to do with us?" asked Willie.

"Go fighting in the army! I bet they make my dad and yours go on over there damn quick," I said, grimacing.

"Sounds mean," he said.

"Never mind," I mumbled, thinking he might be right.

Willie was my best friend, but like everything else, confusing, that I had learned in the last few years, he was black and the son of my granddad's hired hands.

"It's serious talk, I tell 'yak, and the war is going on and men of all kinds and colors are taking their guns and going over to fight Hitler," I continued. I hesitated before I said, "I hope my dad will get told to go on over and leave us alone here."

"Rooster, even I know that is a big sassy thing to say. Why do we need to worry about something when we do not even know what they are talking about?" he demanded while I worked out my answer.

"Willie, alright," I said in a weak tone, "Do you still want us to work on the tree house tomorrow? Are we going to read, too?"

Willie looked over at me and grinned. His teeth were big and very white against his dark skin, and his eyes were so big and brown that they sometimes looked strange to me, but in a beautiful way. "My ma, Tory, is smart and everybody knows that. She can read out of those big leather books that doctors use, to tell people what to do about being sick. Ma says you are not going to hear well one of these days because of that brown bottled-up stuff that your Aunt Ethel had gotten at the Airbase in Abilene, Texas where she worked as a nurse. She said it was made for adults, but they had to give it to me because I was ill, and they were afraid I might die. Being that you had both of your lungs filled with awful green snot. She said that your mind is much better than most folks' and it would be to your liking to not have to hear their nonsense all the time. She said you were very smart with thinking."

"Well," Willie said cautiously, "she said because you do not hear *words* like other folks do, and Ma said you jabber all the time because people are too slow thinking, up their talking and it makes you nervous."

"Ha! Your ma is really something and my mom said she is very smart. I would like to know all that stuff," I said.

I wore a clever smile as I explained, "No, Willie, the word is 'genius' and I heard them say it after all us kids in my room at school took that messed up and mixed-up bunch of questions. I guess it would be nice if I am just too damn smart for them, but what good is a smart stick when you cannot hear who to hit? The teacher says, "Get out your pencils and tablets and I thought, I will just sit until I see what the others are doing. I get so damn tired of wondering. I pray, yes, some, but so far *He* has just told me it was the way it was in this old world."

Willie raised an eyebrow and looked at me like I had gone plum crazy. He pursed his lips together and rolled his eyes. "If you say so, smarty pants. Do not curse in my visit."

Suddenly I was coming back to now.

"Hey! Toy"

"What?" I asked.

I looked up at Carlos, who was shaking my shoulder. "Sorry it took so long, but I had to make a trip out to my car, and it is parked a good way down the street. My darling Toy, I must go now."

Carlos said. "You really drifted back. A few drinks and I wonder if you will do that when I am gone." He laughed.

"Yes, forgive me. I thought of Willie. Yes, I do this when I have had too much of the grape." I laughed.

"Toy, why were you in Italy?"

"For the pleasure of Italy and to get some of my money," I answered. "And Damon and I like to go there. Mickey told us he would try to be in Rome on a certain date. We were there, he was not; he had gone back to London. We finally talked with him, and he told us he was sorry, but he could not leave London. He had many problems, and would we come there. We should have gone, but we chose not to. He told me he would get in touch soon, but he did not. Then I started trying to find him again."

Carlos eyed me suspiciously, "Okay, I do think he is back in Italy. I will do what I am not allowed to help you."

He looked over at me, then down at the wet sidewalk. I moved quickly toward my car as the valet pulled to the curb. I said I need to go, and you need to go."

Carlos grabbed my hand and said, "Wait, I don't want you to go." He stopped for a second. "Oh, I am sorry. You know I am not a good drinker. I do this, maybe once a year," he laughed. "Toy, it was a quick reaction. I was gone for a moment when I realized you were leaving, maybe forever."

"I know," I said.

"You're tougher than the goddamn nails that you had those guys hammer into all of those houses that you built," he said. "How many did you build?"

"One hundred and thirty-one houses, plus an office building, and a dozen mountain condominiums, alone with five duplexes, and I did five retorsions," I laughed, "Carlos I got a high on concrete and sawdust, I loved it," I said.

"Whoa, wonderful, I love that, and you know I am addicted to work," he said, as he stepped close to me, hugged me, and kissed me on the cheek. "That is as close as I'm supposed to get to the lips," he whispered. We gassed for a moment, as I always say eyes tell a hell of a story. "Toy be careful, it is a dangerous business in diamonds. They are not a girl's best friend. Ask yourself if it is worth it. My guys say they are going out of style, this younger crowd could care less about them."

I nodded. "I know," I said, "I know. But in this life, it takes more than money to make it happen."

"You are right," he said.

357

He helped me get into my car as I made the effort not to look at him. We were still under the covered area, but the winds were blowing some drops of rain.

"I need to move my car down a bit, so the valet guys have more room," I told him. He got in the car with me.

He grinned and winked at me. "Is that a tear in those green, green eyes?" he asked.

"No, dear, I do not cry anymore. I have already done that. Although, many times I think I should cry when there is a possibility of no help to be found in the ending."

"I understand, if you saw what I see sometimes, you need the few tears you have to tighten your heart and brace your feelings," he said. "Some days, I think, *'Today might be the last day of the rest of my life.' Be* careful, darling, Toy, we may never know."

"Yes, and Carlos you do the same, be suspicious of life as you told me many years ago. I know you live in a dangerous world," I whispered.

"I do, and I will," he admitted.

He decided he would throw me a curveball and pried, "I hope you will live happily ever after with your current husband forever."

"I love him, Carlos." I stated. "Damon and I are good for each other. He is a wonderful and generous man. I need him every day of my life. But I still view and talk with the *angel of mercy*, which holds this tangled web for us together.   You must make love and life happen and there will be rewards. From here, one can watch the parade as life goes by to the path of heaven."

"Toy, I knew when you canceled that trip with me to Mexico, how you really felt about our life and love. And all these years I thought you missed me more than I did you. But then, tonight, I could see another story and hear another tune playing in those old songs we loved. 'Frankly my dear, you did not give a damn.' Did you?" he whispered.

"Not true, I cared for you. But dear heart I had to accept our love as in the past, and I had a great life and love with Damon. He was a gift to me, and I did love him very much, but yes, the truth to be known, I loved you too. How can you love two hearts? I do not know why or how, but I did. You could not be a part of this life

I live in now, so I had to walk far away, but it was a long lonely and dark way running in many different directions. So, I had to take you out of my, now, life. I had to move your heart over and let this new one come in. I did not ever know how or if could do this. Looking back on yesterday; it was like we were holding out our hands waiting to grab a bit of stolen life. We were living in a make-believe life and but not make-believe love."

"Precious, my Toy, Oh damn, you torture me when you talk to me, like this, or are you lying? Toy, I can see it in your wicked eyes. Those strange eyes that should have belonged only to me. I'm trying to understand, but yes, I will miss you. But you are right, we must stay far away from each other. Then I will not have to hear the words in our old love songs, but I will live it in memories of the melodies we loved." he whispered, "*Making believe*, just *making believe––. I can't help it if I am still in love with you...*"

He had such a pleasing singing voice. I had forgotten how he loved to sing when he wanted to tell me something––he loved his music. He was silent, as he stared deeply at me.

"Toy, there will always be a place in my heart that will make me wonder where you are and what you are doing. I use this in my memory pages to make it in this old, wicked world."

"Yes, Carlos, I have many memories I use, to survive. Some people will tell the truth, others prefer to let memories stay away, forever. I know Damon has them, he is careful not to let me know, but I see it in eyes, his feeling. It is all right. Damon saved me from my wild side. He anchored my crazy soul down and taught me the thrill of real life and love, and how one must follow this thing called love. He really protected me, and I must tell you he is the true love of my life. I learned years ago if you find it, you must work extremely hard to keep it, forever.

Carlos frowned and looked away and finally turned back to me and said, "It is true, but I will carry this love of ours up to *your* heaven and find you." He shook his head, and said, "And I should go now."

I trembled a bit, as cold chills were tangled around in my lost body of webs, and I thought, *Dear Spirituality, do you have my soul to keep, because I am having a heart attack. Or is it just persisting moments of memories? You gave me this life to live and to love and now you will want it back someday. What is this all about?*

He remained silent for a moment and then said, "Why don't you write a love story while you are wasting your time on this thief's wicked book?

"I may write a love story someday," I whispered.

"Baby, this has been a hell of a story; an unusual story of pleasures and sins. A one-of-a-kind story filled with excitement and enchantment, which can never be erased from our thoughts. It is a gift. Except, as we know, this kind of gift can end up wrapped in the wrong kind of paper and lost somewhere in shipping. You and I lived it, my dear heart, now we can dream it. I know you had the most amazing imagination of anyone I have ever known. I liked to think of the things we talked about then and how you would string them up in pearls to make believe. This allowed us to leave the true world. But listen to me, it will *never* set us free, my dear. And where is the end of never? You once told me, 'Never, say never, just drop the *n* off," he expressed with deep feelings, "where is ever?"

"If you do not draft that book about us, I might write it someday, when I am too old to gallop around, when I lose the passion to chase the strangers in this wicked world, and when I am too slow and tried to catch it. I do not think I am going to fit too well into old age."

"You have to—you must like to live," I said, "or die young and never know how it would have been to live a long, wonderful life."

"I am not young. As you know, and I have lived one hundred years," he said.

"I have lived a bunch also, but I like living and I am afraid of dying," I said.

He said, "I remember that old song from *River Boat*," and he very softly sang, "*I'm tired of living but afraid of dying.*"

He turned away for a moment, and then slowly turned toward me. There came that old smile again. He sighed and looked at his watch, frowned and said, "Lady of charm, I must go now."

I sat quite still. My heartbeat told me to rest and obey.

"Goodbye, Toy Rooster. It was wonderful being with you. I will miss you, forever." As he got out of the car, he turned toward me and smiled.

I whispered., "I shall miss you, also." Then, like always, he was leaving.

The valet had just returned to his car and Carlos walked back, thanked him, and gave him a nice tip. The rain had ended, and as he walked toward his car, he suddenly turned, put his hand on his lips and threw me a kiss. I held out my hand and the breath of the Angel of Mercy came near my face and placed the kiss upon my lips. A kiss that was heavy with power, covered with memories, promises, and now a long story of goodbye. I closed my eyes and rolled up my window, a window of life.

I adjusted my rearview mirror and watched him pull away from the curb. In this mirror was my past life, wandering down a long passage of recalls. I must let this go and cover it with many, many drops from the falling rain.

In the deepness of the dark night, under the shadows of the large, old oak trees along the damp, flower-fringed sidewalks, I was allowed only a faint image of the man driving away, the man I once knew. The flames that burned between us had begun to fade slowly away; time had changed so many things. What is in the truth of time, I whispered, *"What is this vis-à-vis?"*

The sounds of a siren in the distance brought me back suddenly to this reality, but the siren paced and sprinted on.

I reached for my phone and realized it had rung several times. Checking the caller ID, I answered the next ring and said, "Hello, Big Dog." He was such a faithful friend and had helped me on several occasions over the years. I had called him recently to help me find Mickey.

Big Dog said, "Hi, I saw you and your friend. He saw us at the restaurant. I will get to work on this now and try to find out who he calls and where he goes. It is hard to race with them; they are so calm and collected." He chuckled.

"So, true," I said.

"These boys are Goliath. If they want you, they can get you. We call them the Highway to Holly Boys because they can reach anything and pull out anything they want, in heaven or hell. They are so damn skilled, big-time trained. Tory, he watches the area like a hostile hawk. He is cool but maybe dangerous, to know."

I had deep thoughts and wondered *was he dangerous to me*. No never. Who are these people?

"How much he will allow us to find remains to be seen," I alleged. "I just cannot tell at this point, but he knows I desperately need to contact Mickey. Perhaps I could not read him as well as I had hoped, but then again, I know he possibly will never outright tell me. His eyes were not readable, not *anymore* like they once were, but, if I still know him, he will show me the way. Perhaps it would not be a clever thing for him to do, crossing his own employer and all, but in the name of loyal friendship, one must deliver a favor from time to time. Besides, you know, these are not real people, all the way. I think he will help me."

He laughed. "You are so right, and you can help, and I know your roar is greater than that of the lioness, but I know you will not bite unless you must."

I laughed.

"Tory, where on Earth did you find this dude?"

"It's a long and an enchanting story, which was laid carefully upon a narrow pathway."   I thought of somewhere along the *previous path of Walker's Bluff,* long ago. It would take too much walking time to get there. "It is a long story. I answered," I muttered, "*Long ago*," as my thoughts drifted in a thousand different directions.

I heard him chuckle, and he said, "Okay, I will hush it up for now. Give me some time to walk under the shadows of this man, and I will be out of town for a while."

"Thanks, Big Dog, and watch your step because he will be expecting you. Call me tomorrow if you have any information," I said and turned off my phone.

I will find him, I said to myself aloud. *I want my coinage.* I thought, *that mean son-of-a-bitch.* Carlos said he was more than a bad man—he was a wicked man of incredible charm. Charm, yes, that is what saves him, con artist. But I do not believe he is wicked. I wondered what Mickey would have been like if he had not been a thief. How could I admit I knew a thief? It was all very strange, even to me. In the version of wonders, one makes many choices of friendship. Except, he was not a friend. I knew he had been in prison for a brief period. He had told me it had been set-up, and at his trial, his lawyer proved that he was not in Chicago at the time the robbery occurred, and that he was in Cancun, Mexico. However, I knew that the crime squad still stayed on his tail, regarding many issues in his present and past. I knew they might even watch me.

Carlos had said, "Darling, you are no better than the company you keep." I thought, he is *my company, only for a good reason—and sometimes it is not what you know, but whom you know, that gets you what you need.* I simply wanted to draft his story, and to get my money for the sale of my diamonds, the diamonds I wish I had never bought.

Carlos admitted that he had a close friendship with a guy that had been stolen from the government, and he had helped put him down. Three years later when the guy got out of prison, they were still friends. "However, each time these things happened, it changed me," he said. I wondered about these stories and how they had changed me. At times, I felt like I was in deep and dangerous waters, getting out to swim past the heavy currents.

Stop thinking of this mess, I thought, and I looked around my beautiful bedroom while taking off my jewels and putting them in the safe. I thought, *"Is this not enough? Is this all there is? What are all of us after?*

At 2:30 AM, I finally went to bed. I was glad Damon went fishing with his friends, so I could worry alone, but my mind was scorching the air. I was breathing too hard and too occupied with the past to sleep. I lay the whole night meditating about my visit with Carlos, wondering if I was making the wrong decision about Mickey. *Now I lay me down to sleep; if I should die before I wake, I beg the Lord my soul to take.* I reached over and turned on some music. But the music whirled too deeply in my weird thoughts. The truth was my hearing aid was a great help to hear but my love for music had been taken away. Can one think how it would be if you had no real music to think of? There were two kinds of music in my mind—one from the past, and the other that might only whisper while floating over troubled waters, but I had to play my music to live. I shall take it with me up *there*. Recently, I have wondered if you need to go past hell to get there. Where is there?

I was awoken by the phone ringing; it was only four thirty. My son was on the phone, He said, "mom come to the hospital. Dad had a stroke. "

I lost my mental judgment for a second and said, "what?" I got up, put my clothes on and was soon on the way to the hospital.

When I got there, Damon's friends had brought him in. I went to his room, and he smiled but was on so many hook ups, it was hard to see him. Suddenly, I saw what a damn stupid fool I had been all of these years. There, dying was my life, my whole soul, yes, my life. I kissed him on the forehead, and he whispered," love me forever and always keep looking beautiful. I'll see you later, then he just kind of choked. The nurse was trying to help him. The doctor came in and called me to the side and said, "Tory, maybe a few days but there is nothing else we can do. He is too old to go through surgery. My daughter and granddaughter came in. They hugged me and whispered let's go down to the lobby. I said, all right. But I turned around to go down on my knees by his bed. I said the first prayer I had said in many years, "please don't take him from me, he is my life, oh please. I know I may have been a bit unlawful in this life, but he was too. I love him more than anything on this bitter Earth. Yes, I love this man more than life.

I just didn't always trust and obey. But he was mine and I his, Amen.

In a few days he was gone. Just before he died, he said, again, to me, "Please love me forever, don't forget me ever..." Our days of life together were now gone. Where was he going? Deep in my wicked heart it was over for me in this old world in many ways.

My children gave him a pleasant funeral and he had so many friends there. So many people stood in the entry; it was true that so many people loved him. That night after the funeral, my best friend stayed with me, and she saw in my eyes I was upset with some of the last days of our life we spent together. She said you can't be concerned about some of the mistakes you or he made in the past. I did at first. Finally, I said, there are two sides to this story and we both did our best to make this life wonderful together. Let him rest in peace.

But I knew down deep my life was mainly gone in so many ways. I still talked to Damon every night. I think I can see him in the clouds. He told me he had my heart and soul up there with him, this opened a closed door to my Christianity. Yes, I felt a Lord or a God in my blue heart.

Aging was bad enough, but now this. What else can happen to me? Well, it's in the next chapter.

Chapter 26

Italy, I will always love this place.

Two months later I decided I needed to move on, but it was hard to do. Today I was at the DFW airport.

When I talked with Mickey, he said come on, no problems. He said you should have come with me long ago for the fun, and to see his new, well-organized living quarters. Tonight, I will have dinner with him and his friend. I will let the kids know how it goes. I called each one of the kids and told them I would be back home in eight days. I was missing them already; they had really helped, as we say, make it through the nights and days. We had not gotten over our loss of Damon.

I started to turn off my phone when my daughter said, "It is me, Ellie. I just ran by and heard you are leaving a message. Mom there is a letter that Lois signed for. It looks important, from Washington D.C. - The Central Intelligence Agency. You want me to read it?"

"Yes," I answered, "yes, please read it to me."

Dear Ms. Walker,

We are sorry to inform you that on Friday, April 12th, 8:58 AM EST, Carlos Francisco's life ended in a plane crash in the south of France. . .

I took a deep breath while she read the entire letter and then she was silent. It took me a moment to answer. Finally, I had to thank her for reading it to me. She asked if I was all right. I told her, "Maybe," but I was not all right, and I said, "Thanks, darling, please put letter in my safe."

I thought love was the most satisfying thing in our life. It's ours forever to keep and it raises our hopes and takes away our fears, but do we take love to heaven? Why did I have to think of this? We hung up. I did not want to know if I were going to die or just hurt and wonder as he would say 'what is it all vis-à-vis. There had always been a missing piece in my life's puzzle, and here today it was in plain sight. The last piece must be placed with tears upon my wicked and lost heart. I had been living as one says, most of my life, my way, I had to, but maybe a bit of an immoral vision could be seen.

I just kind of stumbled around in the airport but soon I was on the plane to Italy. I felt quite strange and isolated even with people all around me. Carlos had told me several days ago where Mickey was. He had not talked much. He said he was going to France and then who knows where, in his voice he sounded troubled, I shall never know why. It was like going up steps and suddenly there were missing steps, how do you get to the top, or is there a top?

Now thoughts of Damon:

I went down memory lane for the last time I saw Damon and hoped he was happy and in heaven. I loved and missed him so much. This was when I had the whole world. Did I know it until now?

I also thought of what Carlos said the last time we were together:

His story. . . You torture, you lie to me, my dear beloved Toy. I can see it in your remarkable cool eyes; those strange eyes that should only belong to me. I will miss you, but I must stay far away. It is the only way I can live my own life. After this visit, I won't have to touch the words in our songs, only hear the melody," he whispered and then he began singing, "This strange love of ours---don't leave me now---don't tell me how your life is treading... I love only you.' I hope someday to see you under the radiances of our beautiful rainbow. If not, I will catch a glimpse of you in my collection of memories. I bend toward Your God, and ask what is this world for, or all about? We, my darling, had every kind of lasting love. I can and will carry this love and memories all the way up to your heaven and someday I will find you there." Carlos had lowered his head and looked away toward the falling rains, finally moving near me and touching my hand. He had said I must go now and say goodbye, but always remember, please love me."

My body had trembled as cold chills tangled in the webs of those memories. I wondered, 'Dear God, do you have my soul to keep? Are there two worlds, are there two loves. You gave me this amazing thing called life, but now it is hard for me to understand why I do not get to keep it, forever more. I had closed my eyes, and then suddenly opened them I watched the sparkling rain and remembered Carlos had said I hate goodbyes. Now he was *gone forever. Your paradise to live in two worlds hangs on the rotation of balance. To live a life of such purpose is a privilege yet the cost may be painful.*

But down deep in my heart it was Damon I was going to miss the most, it is not the end of a struggling story. He Called me after he died. He said he was in heaven, in our beautiful sky. He said I'm thinking of you, and you know I gave my heart and soul to you, but I had to go. Just remember I will love you and one day you can meet me up here. There is no hate, only love and there are no tomorrows. There is forever today. Love me forever, Damon.

Twelve hours later, we landed. I was tired and depressed. I did not know if it was from the tangles in the webs of my past or just the whole damn situation, or because of the death of Damon and Carlos. Yes, I had a few unbreakable dropping tears. A blanket of nausea sweeps over me, watching over my exhausted body. Maybe it was from my many mistakes. I closed my eyes for a few seconds to get the world off and out of my mind. I missed home, I missed Damon. I was extremely confused. Do I have the chains that link the circles now of my lost path?

377

I still had to meet Mickey. I did not know why all of this had to fall on my path today. I shook my head and thought, but with all my problems, I am here, and I love Rome. It is a wonderful place to wander about and leave your troubles behind. There is so much faith in this city, and most of the people are happy. It is kind of a circle united in treasures to give fun in one's astonishing way of life. I do have several enjoyable things planned for today. I must get control, and concentrate on living, not death, not mistakes, not tribulations. I must allow courage, and admit many good memories are still mine, and remember sorrows are part of our existence. I must live this day only, and plan this day only, I remembered an old quote, the richness in the scent of the flower is like the scent of love. It cannot be kept. It drifts away into the winds of time for every more.

I followed the departure signs down the long hall to exit the airport and proceeded toward a taxi. I turned my face away as the sun began to rise upon the living shadows covering the man-made creation of people, who were passing me. Some looked stressed, as they hurried into their new day. Then I silently whispered, there is still splendor in the grass of my earth out there, some *place on this astonishing earth, there is a beautiful rainbow.* Let the golden clouds light the heavenly streams as they gather in the mist of death, giving peace and joy to one's soul. We must remember that human life is only ours in the last breath of air and the last beat of the heart... *I whispered today was the last day of my perfect life. He leadeth me by the still waters... I shall not want....will I need that old song.. Making Believe, just making believe ...*

The driver asked me for the second time in a heavy Italian accent, "where to, lady?"

I whispered," heaven."

He said, "pardon me?"

I said, "The Duca d'Alba."

The cab driver nodded but was still looking at me in his rearview mirror.

THE END IS NOT FOR EVER